Bruce E

Murder Mere Murder

Detective Inspector Skelgill Investigates

LUCiUS

LADY OF THE LAKE

IT IS ALMOST three decades since the body of a young housewife was pulled from Wastwater, England's deepest lake. The corpse had been weighted and sunk twenty years earlier – wrapped and concealed in a carpet, a submerged landmark that was actually known to leisure divers. Such a grisly fact only added to the horror that haunts the neighbouring dales; how long before another picturesque Lakeland mere gives up its dark secret?

BRUCE BECKHAM brings a lifelong love of the outdoors to the contemporary crime novel. He is an award-winning author and copywriter. A resident of Great Britain, he has travelled and worked in over 60 countries. He is published in both fiction and non-fiction, and is a member of the UK Society of Authors.

His series 'Inspector Skelgill Investigates' features the recalcitrant Cumbrian detective Daniel Skelgill, and his loyal lieutenants, long-suffering Londoner DS Leyton and local high-flyer DS Emma Jones.

Set amidst the ancient landscapes of England's Lake District, this expanding series of standalone murder mysteries has won acclaim across five continents, with over 1 million copies downloaded, from Australia to Japan and India, and from Brazil to Canada and the United States of America.

"Great characters. Great atmospheric locale. Great plots. What's not to like?"

Amazon reviewer, 5 stars

TEXT COPYRIGHT 2024 BRUCE BECKHAM

All rights reserved. Bruce Beckham asserts his right always to be identified as the author of this work. No part may be copied or transmitted without written permission from the publisher.

This is a work of fiction. Names, characters, places and incidents either are the product of the author's imagination or are used fictitiously. Any resemblance to actual persons, living or dead, events and locales is entirely coincidental.

Kindle edition first published by Lucius 2024
Paperback edition first published by Lucius 2024
Hardcover edition first published by Lucius 2024

For more details and rights enquiries contact:
Lucius-ebooks@live.com

Cover design by Moira Kay Nicol
Beta reader Kathy Dahm
United States editor Janet Colter

Quotation from *The Talented Mr Ripley* copyright Patricia Highsmith 1955
Quotation from *The Western Fells* copyright Michael Joseph 1992

EDITOR'S NOTE

Murder Mere Murder is a standalone mystery, the twenty-fourth in the series 'Detective Inspector Skelgill Investigates'. It is set in the English Lake District, in particular the area surrounding Buttermere, the name shared by the lake and the hamlet which lie amidst precipitous fells at the upper end of Lorton Vale, Daniel Skelgill's boyhood stamping ground. These locations can be found on Ordnance Survey Outdoor Leisure Map 4, Keswick, Cockermouth & Wigton.

Absolutely no AI (Artificial Intelligence) is used in the writing of the DI Skelgill novels.

THE DI SKELGILL SERIES

Murder in Adland
Murder in School
Murder on the Edge
Murder on the Lake
Murder by Magic
Murder in the Mind
Murder at the Wake
Murder in the Woods
Murder at the Flood
Murder at Dead Crags
Murder Mystery Weekend
Murder on the Run
Murder at Shake Holes
Murder at the Meet
Murder on the Moor
Murder Unseen
Murder in our Midst
Murder Unsolved
Murder in the Fells
Murder at the Bridge
Murder on the Farm
Murder at Home
Murder in the Round
Murder Mere Murder
Murder at Blind Beck

Glossary

SOME of the Cumbrian dialect words, abbreviations, British slang and local usage appearing in *Murder Mere Murder* are as follows:

Adam and Eve – believe (Cockney)
Any road – anyway
Arl – old
Arl fella – father/old man/husband
Arl lass – mother/old lady/wife
Bach – 'my little one' (Welsh)
Barm cake – bread roll
Beck – mountain stream/brook
Bide – live/bear
Blether – chat
Bonkbuster – sexually explicit novel
Boorach – clutter/mess (Scots)
Brass tacks – hard facts (Cockney)
Brew – tea/make tea
Brownie – brown trout
Bubble-and-squeak – fried mashed leftover potato and vegetables
Busies – police officers
Butty – sandwich
Caff – café
CCJ – county court judgement (an enforceable debt)
Chaff – steal
Chicken oriental – mental (Cockney)
Chippy – fish-and-chips takeaway outlet
Chuffing – euphemism in place of an expletive
Clobber – excessive clothing/paraphernalia
Cob – bad mood
Cock – mate/pal (especially Manchester)
Comb – rounded glacial hollow on mountainside (also coomb, corrie)

Crack – gossip
Cuddy wifter – left-hander
Cut – canal
Daft apeth – fool (daft halfpennyworth)
Dale – valley
Deek – look/peep
Doghouse (The) – name of Skelgill's inherited rowing boat
Donnat – idiot/good-for-nothing
Dubs – river pools
DVLA – Driver & Vehicle Licensing Agency
DWP – Department of Work & Pensions
Estate car – station wagon
Estuary accent – from around the Thames estuary
Faff – unproductive effort, inconvenience
Fell – mountain
Ferox – carnivorous trout
First-footing – visiting after midnight on Hogmanay (Scots)
Force – waterfall
Gaff – place/home/base
Gan – go
Garth – small field near farmstead
Gidday – hello (New Zealand)
Girt – great
Gill – ravine or its tumbling stream
Girdle scone – baked on a griddle
GPO – General Post Office
Hank Marvin – starving (Cockney)
Happen – maybe
Heck as like – no way!
Hotpot – stew
Howay – come on
Hoy – throw
Int – isn't
Jill – female pike
Kit and caboodle – entire bunch
La'al – little
Lavvy – lavatory

Manc – Mancunian
Marra – mate (friend)
Mash – tea/brew tea
Mek – make
Met (The) – Metropolitan Police Service (Greater London)
Mind – remember
Mispers – missing persons (police jargon)
Mither – nag/bother
Monkey's – couldn't care less
MOT – certificate of roadworthiness
Nebbing – nosing
No-mark – worthless person, loser
Nowt – nothing
Offcomer – incomer
(Know your) Onions – be knowledgeable on a particular subject
Oor – our
Oppo – sidekick
Ower – over
Owt – anything
Pike – peak
Pillock – idiot
Plonker – idiot
Prop and cop – work as a pair
Reet – right
Rigg – ridge
Ruddy – extremely mild expletive
Savin – juniper
Scotch – item of Scottish origin
Scots – person of Scottish origin (often wrongly 'Scotch')
Skelp – slap/smack
SOCO – scene of crime officer/team
Suet – hard animal fat
Summat – something
T' – the (often silent)
Tack – peculiar taste
Tapped – mad/crazy
Tarn – small mountain lake in a comb

Tek – take
Ten a penny – very common
Tod – fox (Cumbria)
Tod – alone (Cockney, Tod Sloan)
Tup – ram (male sheep)
Tupping time – mating season
Us – often used for me/my/our
Watter – water, lake
While – until
Wyke – bay
Yatter – chatter
YHA – Youth Hostels Association
Yon – that
Yourn – yours
Yowe – ewe

CHARACTERS

Buttermere Hikers' Hostel – Kevin Pope, acting manager; Ann Johnson (née Wilson), assistant.

Ellerbeck Bed & Breakfast – Betty and Ted Hindlewake, owners; Roger Black, regular guest.

Catthwaite Holiday Cottage – Margery and Gordon McLeish, owners; Jean Thackthwaite, cleaner.

Pike Rigg Cottage – Royston Woodcock, owner.

Hassness Cottage – Lena Longstaff and Valentina White, tenants.

Hassness Castle – unoccupied; builders Alfred Lord & Sons, Cockermouth.

Hobby divers – Bob Tapp (plumber), Pooley Bridge; Abel Ketch (boat repairer), Whitehaven.

Missing person – Martina Radu, Manchester.

BUTTERMERE MAP

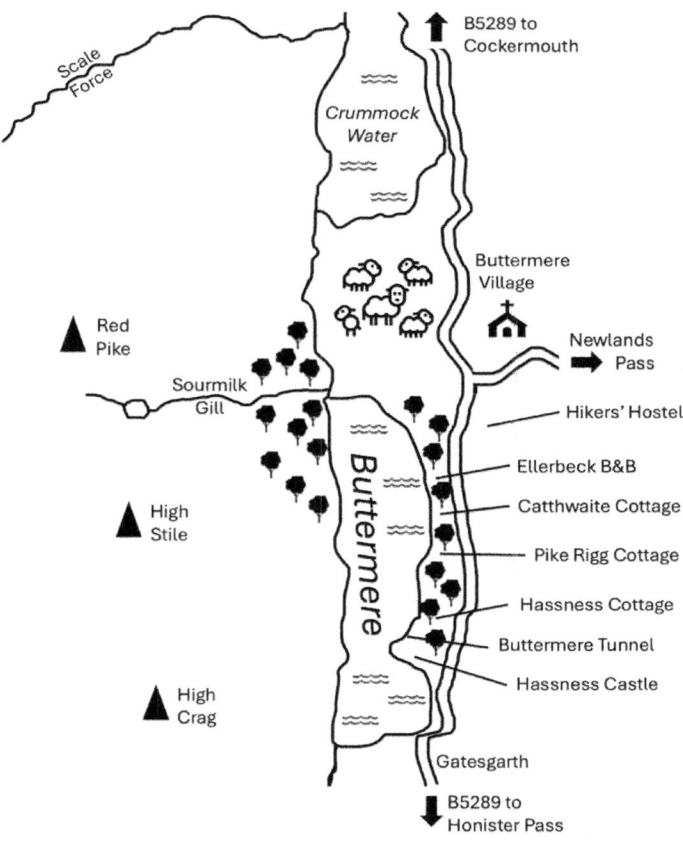

1. UNDER WATER

TO SKELGILL'S MIND, there is something particularly sinister about a female corpse that has been sunk from sight. Tragic accidental drownings, though thankfully uncommon, are not entirely rare – this is a land of sixteen large lakes and hundreds of icy mountain tarns and fast-flowing rivers that receives almost twenty million visitors a year, many expressly to interact with the waters. There is a poignancy surrounding such deaths. Often they are of the young, lambs to the slaughter. Or lowland anglers, naïve to the perils of mountain snow melt and cold shock response.

The same species of lament can attach to suicide by immersion. If there were no easy means, no wherewithal, perhaps catastrophe could be averted. But – what? Prevent access to the water? Wouldn't they just climb the nearest cliff instead?

Accident. Suicide. Sadly, these are annual occurrences.

It is nearing three decades since there was a Lady of the Lake murder – nearly three decades since a corpse was sunk from sight.

Such might contribute to Skelgill's strength of sentiment.

Sensational news cuts deep when you are a ten-year-old boy. Not least, a ten-year-old boy with a penchant for fishing.

The memory is vivid.

A winter evening. The cosy, stifling cocoon of the Buttermere cottage kitchen. A slow-glowing fire in the small hearth. Thick air redolent with simmering hotpot; a collective leaning towards the range. The background murmur of the Bush wireless, an heirloom of sorts.

A raised adult hand.

"Hush!"

Mention of Wastwater. England's deepest lake. *And a body.*

Ears cocked.

Bound and weighted, a young woman. Found by blind touch by divers in dark depths beneath plunging screes. Amongst the wrappings, a scrap of a magazine dated twenty years earlier. The conversation: elder brothers euphoric, ghoulish; parents restrained, deflecting. The inevitable questions.

"What'd a body be like after twenty years in t' watter?"
"Would there be worms in t' eyeballs?"
"Will pike have ate t' fingers off?"
Skelgill junior had ventured one of his own.
"Would it just be a skellington?"
A skelp – a yelp.
"It's *skeleton*, thou girt donnat!"
"Daft apeth!"
"Plonker!"
Skelped ear burning, a silent vow.

Then his mother's judicious intervention. The clank of ladle upon cast iron.

"Thee'll all be skellingtons if thee don't get this down thee."

And the last word from the arl fella, fork poised.

"At least it int on us doorstep."

But it is, now.

18

MONDAY

28ᵀᴴ APRIL

2. LIFTING THE LID

Police HQ – 11.30 a.m.

THEY WATCH SKELGILL eat his bacon roll. Unusually, he is standing, and paying little heed to his sandwich, chewing mechanically. He has his back to them, and peruses the map of Cumbria on the wall behind his desk. His gaze, if it roves at all, perhaps shifts between the various pale blue bodies of water, the ribbon lakes that radiate from the high fells, a knobbly massif shaded in brown and grey to indicate relief.

'Close to home, eh, Guv?'

Skelgill does not directly acknowledge DS Leyton's observation – but he turns, and glances at his sergeant, his bulk distributed in no great comfort on an inadequate plastic chair beside the grey filing cabinet – and perhaps he does admit the smallest of nods, in recognition of the sympathetic tone.

Aye, the dead woman has been pulled from Buttermere.

His old stamping ground; the family seat.

He does not, however, relay whatever else it is that might be troubling him. He smears his hands together and absently wipes them against his thighs as he sits. He regards DS Jones for a moment; she is something of a silhouette against the bright bars of sunlight that infiltrate the tilted venetian blind, her bronzed fair hair fringed by an imperfect halo.

She seems to understand he is inviting their input. She yields, however, with an upturned palm directed towards DS Leyton, as though it is more natural that he should begin. Accordingly he shifts his plate with its unfinished roll from a broad knee to the safer landing of the top of the cabinet.

'I just got back from speaking with the diver that actually found her. He's a geezer by the name of Bob Tapp, lives at

Pooley Bridge. Works as a self-employed plumber. Him and his mate belong to the Cumberland Diving Club. I checked that out and they've both been members for over five years. They dive most Sundays between April and September – he reckons more because of the daylight than the temperature.'

Skelgill nods at this explanation. But he has a question that cannot wait.

'What were they doing in Buttermere?'

With a groan DS Leyton pulls down his pocket notebook from the cabinet. He mutters to himself as he finds his place.

'Yeah – he reckoned it was kind of random – arbitrary, at least. Him and his mate had decided this year they'd dive all the main lakes, one each week, in alphabetical order, for want of a better reason.'

'So, it's their third week.'

DS Leyton glances up sharply.

'That's right, Guv. He says they've done Bassenthwaite Lake and Brotherswater. The previous two weekends.'

Skelgill juts out his jaw and rests it against the tips of his fingers, elbows on his desk. He moves his head to-and-fro in the vertical plane, feeling the abrasion.

Was he on Bassenthwaite Lake three Sundays ago? Surely he was. But likely it was too early for divers. Besides, he was moored for a good time over at Scotch Wyke, out of sight.

'What did they say about it? Buttermere.'

DS Leyton checks his notes.

'Flat sandy bottom and a lot of perch. That's fish, right, Guv?'

Skelgill is tempted to add that he has caught trout, char and pike, and the occasional salmon.

'Aye – but to what purpose? What took them to the find?'

Now DS Leyton shakes his tousle of dark hair, overdue for a trim. He pushes it back from his forehead with his free hand.

'Sheer fluke, he reckoned, Guv. Seems they didn't have anything particular in mind. They'd come across a power cable and were following the line of that – and there it was.'

DS Leyton hesitates, and looks about at his colleagues, perhaps expecting another question. But instead they are hanging on his words.

He raises his notebook like it is a hymnal.

'I'll give it to you from the horse's mouth. "I don't know why, but I knew straightaway. You read about these things, but you never think it'll happen to you. It was the right length for a person, and the way it was tied – round the ankles, waist and neck. That gave it a human shape. When we got up close – you could see through the plastic. A face, like a ghost."'

He lowers the book.

'They marked the spot with a float on a string and raised the alarm from the public bar at the inn. I'm still to interview the mate – Abel Ketch. He lives over at Whitehaven. Runs a little boat repair business. He was the number two on the dive. I thought I'd wait to see what we all thought.'

DS Leyton leans a little towards Skelgill, but it is DS Jones that interposes.

'What are his domestic circumstances? The Tapp chap.'

DS Leyton nods compliantly, and again refers to his notes.

'Yeah – here we are. He's thirty-two. Been married for seven years. Both locals. The missus is an early-years teacher at the village primary. Got a couple of nippers under the age of five.'

There is a moment of collective reflection. DS Jones's question is not merely for casual interest. Thanks to incontrovertible statistics, the unfortunate person who finds a body also finds themselves among the early suspects – though this is more likely where it may be deemed that a purported searcher has led the police to a victim.

DS Jones seems to know to break the silence with her own report.

She has to hand an electronic tablet but she does not immediately refer to it.

'The top line is a white female, five feet three inches, about seven stones, long black hair, estimated age between twenty-five and thirty-five.

'The preliminary assessment is that the body may have been in the water for up to two years. They are going to need to do tests to be more precise. Decomposition can be arrested by a range of factors. The fact that it was effectively sealed, combined with the stable low temperature – about seven degrees Celsius ...'

Skelgill interjects.

'That's between forty-four and forty-five Fahrenheit.'

DS Jones regards him patiently for a moment, then she swipes at her tablet to reveal her notes.

'There has been a process called saponification – a soapy layer forms under anaerobic conditions. They refer to it as corpse wax. It preserves the tissue below – but they're now worried, because there is a sudden acceleration of putrefaction upon exposure to oxygen. So it's a bit of a race against the clock.

'Prima facie – we have no identification or obvious probable cause of death. But we can rule out accident or suicide, at least as far as the disposal in Buttermere is concerned.

'They're taking all the steps to identify her. Primary – dental, DNA and fingerprints. Secondary – such as implants and unique marks. And they'll be making various scans and pathological tests to try to establish cause of death. Then we've got tertiary detail. There was no clothing or jewellery – but there is the mode of concealment. The polythene sheet and ropes. However, it's going to take a few days before information starts to trickle down to us.'

There is another round of silence. After a while Skelgill repels looks of disappointment with a stern countenance.

'Where are we on missing persons?'

DS Leyton gives a small intake of breath that is indicative of guarded progress.

'DC Watson is setting up some filters on the national database. With so little information at this stage, there are literally thousands of records. That will come down a lot once we get a more precise fix on a probable time of death. Then we can start with locals or known visitors, and work outwards.'

Skelgill regards him for a moment and then rises, turning to take down a windproof shell jacket from his fish-hook peg.

'Reet, then. Do what you can.'

He might have urged caution – but he is not comfortable sitting on his hands.

3. FATHOMING

Red Pike – 2.20 p.m.

IT HAS BEEN a while since Skelgill scaled Red Pike above Buttermere (there being a twin by name over in Wasdale), and he is reminded that, were he a mountain guide of sorts, it is the outing he would choose to showcase the classic features of his native district. And he could hardly be any more native, hailing from the hamlet now just a blur of grey stone and slate, lying below him in the picturesque dale. The ascent is short, sharp and unrelenting. From the wooden footbridge over the sedate underfit stream of Buttermere Dubs, the walker climbs over two thousand feet in hardly a mile. Rising first through ancient oak woodland, a haunt of the elusive redstart and its jaunty melody, thence onto open fellside where pipits parachute in more plaintive song, the path follows the evocatively named Sourmilk Gill, a tumbling rivulet that after heavy rain beats itself into a white froth that is visible for miles, like a great strand of ectoplasm streaking the misty backcloth. By strict nomenclature, a gill is a steep ravine, and its stream is a beck, but on occasion the former noun doubles up. The source of Sourmilk Gill is Bleaberry Tarn, a teardrop of a pool that rests in its glacial comb. At two-thirds of the way, a pause is apt, to take in the atmosphere of the mountain amphitheatre, to let the imagination loose, and perhaps search about the banks for bleaberries, a fruit more widely known as the bilberry, despite that 'blea' is the local word for blue. Onwards and upwards towers Red Pike and no mistake, so-named after iron-rich syenite, a granite that colours the screes beneath its summit. The return route, arcing to the north along Lingcomb Edge, takes in Scale Force, Lakeland's highest waterfall, Coleridge's *"white downfall"*.

Thus, all these features in one short stretch of the legs; a good outing for the lungs, to boot. And the reward, a chocolate-box view of upper Lorton Vale, carved out by ice, and now dominated by the residual lakes of Buttermere and Crummock Water, the collective source of the River Cocker.

Aloft, Skelgill ponders.

First, a small conundrum.

Should he dunk the Welsh cake, or savour its inherent, buttery melt-in-the mouth quality?

He shrugs, he can afford to experiment. He has a baker's dozen.

While stopping off at his Ma's, Great Aunt Renie had wandered in from just along the way, armed with Tupperware and her signature girdle scones. Naturally there were entreaties made as to the latest Lady of the Lake – an indulgence he had avoided. Instead, he had charged his thermos with strong, sweet tea and made his apologies, indicating with an eyebrow to his Ma that he would return when gossip could be precluded. It would have been rude, however, to refuse a marching ration of Welsh cakes.

Clearly the grapevine has been twitching. That word leaked out almost as soon as the alarm was raised from the local inn introduces a small but unlikely element of risk. This being, that whoever deposited the body intended for it to remain undiscovered. News of its finding may prompt panic. Panic may put someone in jeopardy. At the very least the perpetrator may move to cover their tracks.

In such circumstances the police like to keep their cards close to their chest. And they like to control the message. However, to assuage local concern – that a killer might be on the prowl – they have been obliged to announce the gruesome nature of their find: that the unidentified female has been under water for up to two years. Accordingly, the media are thirsting for more information. *What are the lines of inquiry?*

But it is clear to Skelgill and his sergeants that they must wait for some salient detail; to launch an investigation without direction or compass will not serve them well.

But it does not mean he can do nothing. They are not entirely at the mercy of Forensics.

There is a bigger picture, and he is looking at it.

The bird's eye view.

Intuitive analysis – an oxymoron, yes, but also a singular habit of his.

He muses.

A quick dunk just has the edge. One, Mississippi.

He is glad of his windproof top. The day is bright and ostensibly mild, but there is a fresh southwesterly that chases scudding shadows like great ragged sheep across the fellsides. Throw in the updraft and the altitude (deduct a degree for every two hundred feet) and there is a spring chill in the air. Arrive at the ridge sweating and exposed, and you will soon be shivering.

Out on the water, through his inherited field glasses he can see – about halfway along and midway across – the divers' RIB with two black figures aboard. Their teammates are searching the locus of the find for personal items or anything else that might have been sunk with it, or used for weights. Occasionally a glistening seal-like head bobs up beside the boat and hands in something or other.

But mainly it is just the solitary craft.

It strikes him: a boat on Buttermere is a rare sight.

There is no public launching place, be it slipway or jetty.

Nor is there even an easy pull-in.

At the head of the lake, the vehicles of the police diving team cause an obstruction where the B5289 briefly kisses the shoreline before it begins to wind up into Honister Pass. They are coned off; an officer in hi-vis yellow has been posted to direct traffic and chivvy on any rubberneckers. There is a spotlight, too – a TV news crew filming a report, he guesses.

Officially, stopping here is proscribed. Both sides are marked with double yellow lines and there are warning signs on posts – and, if these are not enough of a deterrent, boulders have been rolled into position along the verge.

To reach the shore elsewhere would mean trespassing onto the land of a farm, or a private property that has some lake frontage, and there are few of these. Getting a boat down to the water would be challenging. It would probably require the toting of a lightweight inflatable dinghy.

So, for this practical quality alone – inaccessibility – Buttermere is spared of water sports. Even bank anglers are few and far between. Besides, they can choose so many other lakes. Lakes that hold a wider variety of specimen fishes. Lakes that have slipways and jetties and boats, motor and row, for hire. Lakes that have hotels and pubs and refreshments, with views directly from the shore.

He inhales reflectively.

Aye, Buttermere is a lake for looking at from on high.

On a rare occasion Skelgill has seen leisure divers. But he could count such sightings on the fingers of one hand. They park at one of the inns at Buttermere or use the adjacent public pay-and-display car park, and tramp the public footpath, six hundred yards or so to the northern shoreline. Here are shallows, a gently sloping beach that can be waded out from.

But as Pooley Bridge man Bob Tapp had suggested to DS Leyton, Buttermere does not hold a great attraction for the diver. It is a comparatively bland basin. Thus, combined with the faff factor, like anglers, divers tend to go elsewhere.

Not least, Wastwater, scene of his boyhood Lady of the Lake. It has almost unlimited roadside access, and is England's deepest lake. It has almost thirty fathoms on Buttermere – and thrilling sub-aquatic topography.

Diving is not his bag – there is claustrophobia that stills the senses, more extreme even than caving (or even climbing, which involves too much looking in, when there is so much looking out to be done) – however, he has experienced a couple of dives, and he knows and respects folk for whom it is their overriding passion. And divers' groups are much like others – they do it for camaraderie, banter, adventure, exercise, for the pioneering spirit, and to escape from domesticity and the day job. It is a sport growing in popularity.

Wastwater is threaded with a web of diving routes. Some have guide wires to make following easier for first-timers or when conditions are murky. Such thoroughfares reflect the local divers' humour – they are embellished with road signs, traffic cones – there is a gnomes' garden, and even a model dog and kennel. On the famed pinnacles a divers' memorial looks like something you would see in a churchyard, engraved brass tributes to friends long passed.

There is a misconception about lakes. It is a thesis Skelgill has occasionally deployed in arguments with fellow anglers. The blanked fisherman, rueing his bad luck, bemoans that it is like looking for a needle in a haystack. But this is to consider volume, when it is area that counts.

The arl fella had once come home raging about a lost bet in the local bar – that the population of Britain, laid out, could fit in Windermere. *Nay chance!* Except it could. (At fifteen gallons a person, the answer had been closer to the world population at the time.)

Skelgill's case is that, when you are looking for fish, most of them will be where the food is. In deep water, that is at the surface, where hatches take place, and flying insects land to lay their eggs, and often to expire; it is where edible windblown debris collects, and where floating weeds grow.

In deep water, fishing is not about volume, but area.

Divers, likewise, have their favoured *area* – they spend their time exploring the lakebed.

Nowadays, he doubts a body would remain hidden for long in Wastwater.

Buttermere, however ...

He starts, his reverie ended by the realisation that he is eating the last girdle scone.

He pours another flask-top of tea.

With one hand he takes up his field glasses and begins to scan the eastern bank, starting from the point where the diving unit is parked.

A public footpath circumnavigates the lake; it keeps generally close to the shore, though at times deviates for easier going. There is mainly private land between the waterline and the road, much of this wooded, concealing the occasional property. Top and tail there are ancient homesteads that farm the small but rich glacial moraine pastures where dairy cattle have long been grazed and, in turn, butter churned. Butter mere.

Close to the rounded promontory Skelgill knows as Hassness a person has left the path to stand and watch the divers. He puts down his cup and takes hold of his binoculars two-handed for extra steadiness. He can make out that it is a woman – the wind picks up her long black hair in wayward strands, and occasionally she raises a hand to brush it from her face. Though she might be clad in close-fitting outdoor gear she does not look like a walker. She has none of the accessories – backpack, poles, nor even a cagoule tied around her waist. She seems to wear only a thin top, and indeed now wraps her arms as though she is beginning to feel the spring breeze off the cool water. However, she continues to stare out, rather forlornly would be his impression – though he is conscious that is his imputation.

A couple of hikers – fully equipped – pass a little behind her where the path runs – and perhaps they call out something, for she turns and seems to engage them for a moment. Maybe they are exchanging news and details of what they think is afoot. The pair move on, and now instead of turning back to the lake, she walks away, unhurriedly – not following the path – but disappears directly into the trees.

*

No matter that it is only just past four p.m., in the time capsule of the Buttermere cottage kitchen Skelgill works his way assiduously through his second dish of hotpot. His Ma has hovered little – instead she has busied herself about the place, saying others of her brood are expected later.

He has appreciated her taciturnity, much as she must be curious – and much as she is relied upon by neighbours to be 'in the know', having a son in the CID.

She has, however, provided him with some up-to-date biographical detail. While he is never far away, his visits here tend to be fleeting – calling in at the cottage, rather than hanging around the village, or even frequenting the pub. The last census has a hundred and twenty-one inhabitants in the parish, spread across some forty-five households.

On the face of it, even this modest population offers a challenge to the investigator – but Skelgill runs filters across the hamlet's occupants. Recent arrivals can be discounted, just as may be the long-standing majority – for had any local, most notably the farmers, gleaned the faintest hint of suspicious goings on, his Ma would know about it. Indeed, anything of a remotely serious nature, the locals would report to the police.

The farms excepted, only a handful of properties have proximal access to the lake. Closest to the village on the rising fellside, the flank of High Snockrigg, is Buttermere Hikers' Hostel. Set well back from the wooded lake side of the road, first is a B&B, 'Ellerbeck', run by an established couple from Blackpool. Beyond, spaced apart by several hundred yards, are three cottages. The nearest, 'Catthwaite Cottage', is a holiday let, which the absentee landlord manages through an agency in Kendal – though charlady Jean Thackthwaite bides in the village. The next, 'Pike Rigg', is inhabited by a single male of retirement age, something of a recluse about whom little is known, despite that he has been there for a good five years – oh, but he is a birdwatcher. Further down the lake, just before Hassness Point, two young females occupy the remaining cottage of the same name. Finally, on high ground above the point, stands Hassness Castle, now a residential outdoor centre.

Skelgill had noted just the slightest sniffiness when it came to mention of the two women.

"What, sisters, like?" had been his enquiry.

His Ma had turned to stir a pot of soup that was already well stirred.

"Happen not," had been the extent of her reply.

He had chosen not to ruffle feathers.

"I spotted a lass, from the fell – long black hair. Could that be one of them?"

"Aye, it might."

They had left it at that; they were comfortable though, when for some the silence might be awkward.

Skelgill had pondered for a few moments, but the ladle had descended in his direction, and he had swayed back accommodatingly. Now, mopping gravy with home-baked bread under an appreciative eye, he is reminded of the time before – the Bush radio still murmurs from the mantelpiece – of the shocking news, the excitement and dread, the questions. His thick ear.

And his little vow.

It was not an avowal to avenge the fraternal cuffing – that when he was as big and strong as his elder brothers he would give them a good hiding (much as this was a regular mantra) – no, his pledge to himself was more esoteric. Yes – he would 'show them' – but he would show them one day by righting such a wrong. Albeit he could not have foreseen where life's winding path would bring him – to his very own Lady of the Lake – with hindsight it was a harbinger of his vocation.

He senses his mother's gaze upon him, as if she reads his mind – and that she, too, feels his time has come.

But, as always, there is her singular take on the matter.

'So ... were she a *skellington*, Daniel, lad?'

4. LENA

Hassness Cottage – 4.30 p.m.

HE DOESN'T SOUND like a police inspector. He has the local twang, albeit superficially moderated. Though she suspects dialect words lurk beneath. He had seemed reticent at the door. It had taken her invitation. She didn't need to let him in at all. But the offer of tea seemed to swing it.

She can see him now. The twisted multicoloured strips of the flyscreen form an incomplete barrier. He stands motionless, staring out from the little conservatory. Partly manufactured kitchen noises combine with local radio ads to conceal that she watches him.

He is a little above her age. His apparel is of the fell-walking variety, including boots. He looks fit, in a lean, slightly rangy kind of way. A good deal taller than her. His hair could do with a cut, and his jaw a shave. Though the unkempt effect is in keeping with the craggy features. Strong cheekbones. Wide-set eyes of an interesting grey green, the dominant hue hard to discern.

The kettle reaches its crescendo.

She checks her reflection in the little mirror. She tugs at her curtain bangs, patting them into place. She adjusts her outfit, smoothing out any creases so that the Lycra sits like a second skin. From an atomiser she sprays perfume sparingly onto her right wrist and rubs it against the left, and then reaches beneath her hair to anoint the sides of her neck.

She pushes the tray ahead of her through the flyscreen.

'Sorry to keep you. Our gas is from a cylinder.'

It takes him a second to turn.

Then there is a little battle – the grey-green eyes and where they should look.
She smiles. She had sensed his gaze as she led him through. Though the long-sleeved top and ankle-length leggings and yoga socks expose no flesh, she is fully aware that the figure-hugging material does not leave a great deal to the imagination. There is a small satisfaction in attracting a man's eye.
A single long settee faces out from the original external wall, with a low table, so they must sit side by side.
She notes that he chooses a respectful distance.
'Shall I pour?' She does. 'Help yourself to lemon or honey. I actually like both.'
Now he squints – the afternoon sun is slanting across her.
'Aye – I'll, er – thanks.'
He watches as she slowly stirs in a spoonful of honey.
But having taken instruction, he makes no move. Instead he seems to realise he should begin.
'Sorry to disturb you – er, madam.' He gestures loosely about the lean-to. 'I didn't intend to intrude.'
Cradling her mug, she sinks back against the couch, accustomed to its cushioning.
'It's fine. I've finished for the afternoon. I'll work again later.' She gives a little cough, conscious of the huskiness of her voice. 'Call me Lena, please.'
He seems a hint troubled. But he addresses her point candidly.
'Folk can get uppity – if you're over familiar.'
She plies him with another smile.
'I shan't.'
'Aye.'
He takes what is plainly an uncomfortable sip of his tea. Now he looks again at the honey. She takes the initiative.
'We've been expecting you. Well – *someone* – since the news on the radio.'
He still seems apologetic. Awkward. As if she has found him out.
He gives another indeterminate flap of a long-fingered hand.

'We probably shall need to send someone round with a questionnaire. Round to everyone, like.'

'Oh – so I'm not so special, after all.'

She leans towards him, to be sure he understands she is lightly ribbing him.

Now he definitely looks conflicted.

'I – er – reckon I might have seen you – looking at the lake. I was across the other side. About half-two, it were.'

She contrives a satisfied shrug; this is why she has been selected.

'Ah. I was practising my yoga. Now that spring is finally here.' She gives a little tug to a cuff of her elasticated top and stretches languidly. 'You can't swing a cat indoors. I can just about lay out in front of the hearth.'

Now he is looking directly ahead, his irises perhaps picking up the fresh green of the newly unfurled foliage of the oaks. She is waiting for him to elaborate upon what he said at the front door – about making inquiries in relation to the incident. But perhaps he feels there is no need. He seems a taciturn sort.

He frowns.

'There's no view of the lake – from upstairs?'

It is barely a question – it is obvious that the cottage is too low.

'We have privacy from walkers on the path. But at the cost of the trees obscuring the water.'

She contemplates her pale tea, a hint of steam rising. He has not asked who lives here, or for how long. So he must know this. After all, he knew her surname, albeit he stumbled over its prefix. He would have information from local residents. The electoral register. And the police will have other means.

When she looks up, he averts his gaze, and makes small movement of self-reproach with compressed lips, as though his attention has slipped off piste.

He takes another token taste of tea and clears his throat.

'We could be talking the thick end of two years. Folk tend to get in touch if there's owt to report. But it's our experience that they don't always know what's significant.'

'Or perhaps they're just waiting to be asked.'

He looks surprised – a little shocked even. As though he thinks she has a revelation.

'Sorry – I don't mean to suggest – that I –'

Still holding her mug she crosses her wrists over her breast; the dark maroon varnish of her nails now draws his eye. She wonders if he notices that it matches her lipstick.

His movement might be a shake of the head.

'Mind, if it's been a regular thing – your yoga – you might have seen, say, a rowing boat or an angler making a disturbance. It's the sort of sighting we would check out.'

She brings the mug up to her lips, but simply inhales the aroma.

'I go to the shore when I can. Sometimes I yearn for the greater vista, the sound of the ripples and the smell of the water. But it would depend on the time of year.' She notes that he nods – that he understands she would not be an observer in winter. 'And at weekends, holiday periods – there can be walkers. Then I use the lawn – when it's not raining.'

She murmurs a throaty chuckle, and he reacts, taking the offered side track.

'You're not originally from the North West?'

It must be obvious. But she indulges him.

'London.'

She injects a hint of diffidence into her tone, though her accent in reality betrays little of her provenance.

'We were in Seville for two years – we tried unsuccessfully to settle back into Hammersmith.'

Gently she flexes her spine and raises her gaze to the outdoors.

'We decided we'd give the Lakes a try. That will be three years ago, in May.'

He is looking at her now, perhaps wondering, since she has volunteered a sliver of back story, whether to inquire further.

'The work's mostly seasonal.'

His statement is intriguingly obtuse. But she plays along.

'I am an author. I'm footloose. It meant we could move together.'

He must have noticed the framed photograph on the bookcase perpendicular to her end of the settee, beside the careful arrangement of paperbacks. Now his gaze settles upon it. Head-and-shoulders selfie style, *La Giralda* crazily steepling into blue sky behind them, the two young women laugh as – apparently unbalanced – they attempt what might be a tipsy kiss: the fair-skinned short-cropped blonde and the sultry raven-haired brunette. Yin and Yang.

Perhaps now he is seeking to 'out' its narrative.

'Valentina works at Paige Turner's in Cockermouth.'

She reads his uncertainty.

'The bookshop – it's in Market Street.'

He remains vaguely baffled.

'I believe it used to be called Confluence Books. It's modernised now, with a café.'

He seems to perk up at this.

'Do they stock OS maps?'

She finds herself grinning, although she is unsure why. She allows her hair to fall further across her face. He might be offended.

'I should think so – but I can ask her, if you like?'

Perhaps the suggestion jars with him, though he plainly tries to conceal his reaction. She determines that she should elaborate. There is a small, brightly coloured souvenir Spanish ceramic wall clock to his left. She leans closer to look past him, blinking her dark eyes. He sits stock still, though he must inhale her aromatic perfume.

'Almost five. I'm not sure when she'll be back – they often have events in the evenings – readings and Q&As with visiting authors – book launches, and suchlike.'

He nods, now pensively.

She waits patiently for his next question – although it is increasingly evident that direct inquiries are not exactly his style.

Indeed, now he makes a two-handed gesture of concluding, and begins to rise. She sees that he has barely touched his tea.

37

'I should leave you be. Thanks for – er –'

But he moves swiftly ahead of her, ducking through the flyscreen and the low-beamed kitchen into the narrow hallway. Only when he is over the threshold of the traditional planked front door does he halt and turn. She has had to hurry, and folds herself against the jamb, perhaps a little melodramatically. He makes an instinctive lunge as if to catch her at the waist, anticipating a fall, and though he checks himself, his gaze seems to linger before meeting her eyes.

'Inspector. She *was* ...?'

'Murdered.'

He completes the phrase mechanically, as if it is top of his mind – and immediately seems to regret doing so. He grimaces and draws back his hair with the fingers of one hand, a distant look in his eyes.

'We're still waiting – for forensic reports.'

She nods obediently, but perhaps she regards him just too intensely – for now he casts about, as though he is seeking a distraction in their surroundings that will offset the macabre nature of his purpose.

His best effort is something of a platitude.

'It must be an inspiring spot – for a writer.'

'Oh – well.' She feels herself affecting a little cough of apology. 'Actually, I travel away a good deal – for research. Cathedrals, castles, catacombs.'

Now she has him narrowing his eyes.

'What kind of stuff do you write?'

'The genre?'

'Aye – that.'

She answers inscrutably.

'Horror.'

5. INCOGNITO

Kirkstile Inn, Loweswater – 8.15 p.m.

'WHAT MADE YOU think of meeting here?' Skelgill gestures about the beamed surroundings with his pint of pale IPA – he makes a two-pronged point.

'But there's real ale at Buttermere, is there not? And the ambience is good.'

'Aye – and a dozen locals who want to buttonhole us.'

DS Jones nods, accepting the point.

'Especially right now, I guess.'

'Double the mithering I'd normally get. And it's not like I can do owt about most of it. I made the mistake of trying for a quiet pint in the February school week. Then, it were tourists driving like Lewis Hamilton. Abandoned barbecues and rubbish. Dogs worrying sheep. Old Joan Todd even wanted to know what the police were going to do about mating foxes keeping her awake at night. Trouble is, with the Arl Lass living there, I have to humour folk.'

DS Jones chuckles.

'I'd like to know your fox answer.'

Skelgill dunks his nose in his pint.

'I said I'd put in a request for a dog handler to patrol the village. The foxes only make a racket for a few weeks. Then they shut up of their own accord.'

She makes a small upward movement of her head, an acknowledgement of his crafty rejoinder.

'And how was your sleuthing?'

They are side by side on the settle, and Skelgill twists and leans back a little, as if he means to contest the assertion. But her smile is disarming, almost but not quite ingenuous, though enhanced by her girlish lack of need for make-up. Competing thoughts converge to jam his immediate response.

He yields, however, and sinks back into position. He runs a finger in mid-air around the rim of his glass.

'Do you know, there's not a single property that actually looks onto Buttermere. And only a short stretch of road beside the water – and it's double yellows, with boulders along the verge.'

DS Jones regards him briefly; it is an interesting admission, for there can hardly be a person with more local knowledge than he.

'There's a footpath, though, isn't there?'

Skelgill takes a sup of beer.

'Aye. A circuit. Most folk start and finish at one of the pubs.'

She nods. This would have its draw.

'So it's not like it's totally secluded.'

Skelgill makes a face, just a touch sour.

'It's a long chalk from the likes of Derwentwater, Windermere – even Ullswater. You've got all manner of goings-on, lakeside. Villages – small towns – boatyards, hotels. Ferries, pleasure boats, rowers – folk on the water all the time.'

'Anglers.'

'Aye.' His omission goes without saying.

'What about Buttermere?'

'Fishing?'

'Yes.'

Skelgill shrugs.

'It's alreet for what it is – but you'd struggle to put a boat on it. And the path's mostly by the shore. You wouldn't get much peace on the bank.'

'What about at night?'

He tilts his head from one side to the other. He is half inclined to accept her point, but his specialism tells him otherwise. It begs the question of what to fish for at night. He voices his doubt.

'Most fishes are visual hunters – especially where there's not a lot of plant life or bottom feeding. Most night anglers are after specimen carp, grubbing about. It's not a fish of these fresh waters.'

DS Jones nods but does not offer a comment.

After a few moments he adds a concession.

'I'll have a word with Jim Hartley. The DAA will know if there's a member who fishes it regularly.'

DS Jones has correctly surmised what Skelgill has been up to – and the general gist of his approach. They will almost certainly be seeking potential witnesses, and he has plainly apprised himself of the impediments.

But now he surprises her with a question.

'Do you pay much attention when you're doing yoga?'

She is sipping her drink and takes a second to answer.

'In what way?'

'Do you get yourself into a trance, or summat?'

Now she laughs.

'Into knots, perhaps.'

She waits, leaving him to open up.

'I spoke to a woman who's got one of the cottages, near the head of the lake. Reckons she does yoga, sometimes by the shore. That's how I came across her.'

'Ah, now I see.'

DS Jones injects a hint of intrigue into her tone. But rather than tease him she is forthcoming.

'I'd say you'd be pretty alert, *Savasana* aside. That's when you lie supine with your eyes closed – it's called the corpse pose.'

He shoots her a quick sideways glance.

'And you'd do it outdoors?'

'Certainly. Where it is conducive to mindfulness.'

Skelgill nods.

'And for more room?'

DS Jones hesitates.

'No – not really – you rarely move far from your mat.'

This point causes further reflection on his part.

It takes DS Jones to prompt him.

'But there's nothing controversial – else you would have told me.'

He starts – and looks to see she is grinning – and in reprising her words he recognises the irony in her tone. He takes momentary refuge in his beer.

'Happen the conversation will jog a memory. I said we'd likely be following up.'

But when DS Jones does not immediately reply he moves to head off what is perhaps an undeserved line of reproach.

'She lives with a woman.'

'Ah.'

He realises she is looking at him in the amused manner of one watching another venture onto creaking ice. He reverts to firmer ground.

'She reckons she's an author.'

This at least has the effect of piquing his companion's interest.

'Would I know her?'

Now Skelgill shrugs, and takes a drink. There is the suggestion that there is no point asking him.

'Horror stories.'

'Does she have a penname?'

Though it never occurred to him to ask, he realises he may have the answer to this question. He can picture the little stack of new-looking paperbacks on the bookshelf. The woman's actual name is Lena Longstaff.

'Going by the books I saw – it could be L.L. James.'

DS Jones regards him quizzically – though she might well be thinking: so it was not just a passing lakeside conversation.

He interjects.

'You've heard of her?'

'Hmm. Not exactly. But *James* – you might say it's shorthand for horror. *The Turn of the Screw* – you know?'

He shakes his head.

'It's a classic – just a novella. Henry James. He was followed by M.R. James – he wrote mainly antiquarian ghost stories. Then, more recently, James Herbert.'

Skelgill is looking baffled.

'*The Rats, The Fog, Fluke* – they were some of his novels that were made into films.'

Skelgill makes a face that at best suggests agnosticism.

'I thought it were a writer called James that wrote that bonkbuster, *Fifty* summat?'

DS Jones bursts into laughter.

'*Touché!*' She likes his answer. 'Let's say some genres have their overlaps. Bram Stoker's *Dracula* has been described as thriller, romance and horror rolled into one.'

'Good for sales – if it gets you in three departments.'

While DS Jones pauses, as if to ponder his insight, Skelgill realises there is a small segue here.

'Her partner works in the bookshop in Cockermouth.'

'A recent relationship?'

Skelgill shakes his head, but his glass is on its way to his lips, and he makes her wait for clarification. He pictures the selfie taken in front of Seville's great cathedral.

'They moved up from London three years ago. They were in Spain for two years before that.'

DS Jones reflects upon information received.

'So they fall within our time window.'

Skelgill is nodding.

'I got the low-down from the Arl Lass. Locals, offcomers – recent arrivals.' He makes a gesture of frustration, of futility, like he is waving away a cloud of midges. 'Not that I'm pinning any great hopes on finding witnesses. There's a chap lives alone in one of the cottages – birdwatcher. Name of Woodcock. I called there, an' all – but there was no sign of him.' He claps his hands. 'Better to do it properly, I suppose.'

DS Jones chuckles. His conclusion must have a name – a contradiction in terms, an impractical paradox. But she knows him well enough to understand that following his nose has long stood him in good stead. Let the country dog out of the back door, and it is unlikely to wait on the step. And there is the personal connection in this case. There is pride at stake. It does not take pointing out. But earlier DI Alec Smart had sidled up to her desk. *What's this about a corpse floating up under Skelgill's nose?* Feigned ingenuity, of course. He will be the first to twist the knife if they do not make spectacular progress.

She opts not to relate this facet of her afternoon.

'While we're waiting for Forensics, I did some research.'

She turns her glass with delicate, carefully manicured fingers. It contains just clear mineral water, but in its tiny rising bubbles and shifting reflections of the bar's subdued wall-lights there is the suggestion of a small world of mystery within.

Skelgill shifts in a way that indicates acquiescence.

'First of all, assuming we have it correct that she was in her early thirties, I think it will dramatically narrow down the pool of potential missing persons. Many women of that age are in a dependent relationship, often with kids. It's not a usual age for someone to go missing. The typical runaway is in her teens. A drug user, early twenties.'

Skelgill does not contest her logic.

'Secondly, there are more Ladies of the Lake than I imagined. And not just official records, but online documentaries, some more diligent than others – in the UK and abroad. There are striking commonalities, you know?'

She offers the implication that there might be an application to their case.

'I'm sitting comfortably.'

'I say *ladies* because invariably the victim is a woman. A woman in a relationship that's gone off the rails – notably infidelity, often both partners. There's a drunken bust-up, a confrontation – a taunting of inadequacy, even. As the weaker party, she dies.

'Sad to say, *husband kills wife* is commonplace in the ranking of domestic fatalities. What makes these cases exceptional is the attempted cover-up. He decides he can get away with it. The death is unpremeditated, but the concealment involves calculation. In almost every instance, it's clear the killer believed a body in a lake would never be discovered. So much so, that they didn't worry about leaving clues.'

Skelgill offers a snippet from his own memory.

'Wastwater – it was the engraved wedding ring.'

'That's right. And a fragment of a special-interest magazine that her husband subscribed to. Other cases have involved clothing with sewn-in name tags or store labels, and unique materials that could be matched to a particular workplace, or even a domestic property.'

She pauses to have a drink.

'Another common feature is that the body was often transported a considerable distance.'

She glances at Skelgill to see that a frown has captured his brow. He shakes it off – and drains the last of his beer, and cranes to get a look at the clock behind the bar.

However, when he speaks, it is to corroborate her point.

'Wastwater – it were the south of England.'

'Over three hundred miles.'

Skelgill leans his elbows on the table and presses his fingers together.

'Folk know the police will drag local lakes when someone's gone missing. The cut, rivers, ponds, flooded quarries.'

His tone is somewhat fatalistic – such a fact would not favour the investigator. But DS Jones has qualifying data.

'Perpetrators have demonstrated prior knowledge of deep and isolated waters. And in one case the killer had regular access to a boat. A hobby that enabled him to dispose of the body in plain sight. He carried it aboard unseen after dark – and went sailing during normal daytime hours so as not to raise suspicion. He just picked his moment to roll it overboard at the deepest part of the lake. What he didn't know was that a courting couple were smooching in long grass on a secluded stretch of shoreline.'

Now Skelgill's interest is aroused.

'What happened?'

'One of them heard a splash. Ironically, they thought it was a guy dumping rubbish off his yacht. But a decade later the body was found and they responded to a public appeal. Their evidence wasn't definitive, but they were able to act as substantiating witnesses.'

Skelgill taps the tips of his fingers together five or six times, the final time decisively, making a cage as if to trap an invisible creature, a fish or a bird.
'Interesting.' He takes his empty glass and begins to rise.
'You said they were a courting couple, aye?'
'That's right.'
'I bet it were the lass that noticed.'
DS Jones is shaking her head.
'You can be surprisingly witty, when you try.'
He smirks and turns for the bar.

TUESDAY

29ᵀᴴ APRIL

6. VALENTINA

Paige Turner's Bookshop, Cockermouth – 10.20 a.m.

'GIDDAY, INSPECTOR SKELGILL. Whole milk latte and Cumberland soda cake.'

She sees that he starts. At the serving counter he had given only his name. She has found him in the little mezzanine area, facing out from a corner. He has a map spread over his table. Hurriedly, though with a cardsharp's practised aplomb, he refolds it into its glossy cover.

'I'm Valentina. You asked to speak with me. Should I sit? Or I can come back when you have finished.'

The benign grey-green irises feel deceptively penetrating. It takes will power not to falter – but she knows that in her own deep blue eyes is a weapon that can exude both allure and self-confidence. Yet she feels her hand drift up to adjust her coordinating blue-rimmed spectacles, and brush needlessly at her spiked white-blonde pixie cut.

Just briefly, his gaze appraises her outfit – not in a critical way, but if anything it is a flicker of puzzlement that crosses the hewn countenance. Perhaps he thinks she is too old for it. Though her fair skin and colour has always placed her on the girlish side of her actual age. Or perhaps he does not recognise that the washed-out, loose-fitting white hoodie and wide white flares that cover platforms, the pre-owned look, is *à la mode*. Fashion does not appear to be his forte.

As an afterthought, it seems, he gets up rather clumsily; the heavy oak furniture of the café does not slide easily on the stripped floorboards. He gestures to the chair opposite.

'Obviously ... you know who I am. I met your ... housemate.'

He seems to be explaining for his own benefit.

She feels herself relax as she settles carefully into the chair. She rests her hands on the edge of the table. He glances at them for a moment, as if small details like her neat unvarnished nails interest him. The hands of a person who needs to be dexterous with books.

He resumes his seat and scrutinises the generous portion of soda cake.

'Miss – er – Ms Longstaff – I thought she said you were from London. You sound Australian.'

She gives a little shake of her head, though he is not looking.

'New Zealand. Auckland. Lena and I met in London. After college.'

'Are you still studying? I mean – part-time, or summat?'

So he does think she looks like a student.

'I don't actually work at the café. I was in the storeroom checking a delivery of new titles when they called me. I deprived your waitress of the pleasure.'

He glances at her but quickly withdraws his gaze. He has picked up his fork in his left hand, but does not commence eating.

From a small patch pocket in her top she produces a business card branded with the logo of the bookshop and personalised to her: Valentina White, Assistant Manager. She slides it across the surface.

He frowns, squinting to read the small type.

She cannot suppress a smile. There is an irony about the little vignette. An interview with a detective in a bookshop; close by, shelves lined with crime fiction from the last hundred years and more, the best efforts of the finest writers, every evil under the sun at the tips of his fingers – if only he knew which one to reach for.

He looks up from his perusal of the card.

She broadens her smile, inviting his response.

But again his gaze shifts away; he gives a casual wave of the fork.

'Must be a nice working environment.'

It seems to be his habit to skirt his main purpose.

49

'Provided you like literature, eh?'

He makes a face that might be of regret, or ruefulness. With the back of the fork he taps the cover of the map.

'Does this count?'

There is something plaintive in his question; his tone seeks approbation.

'Why not? You *read* a map, don't you?'

He regards her quizzically. This time the look is more prolonged. There is a just-perceptible constriction of his pupils. Does he doubt her?

She reaches to touch the map – and draws his gaze.

'Is this for your investigation?'

It takes him a moment to answer. He inhales, as if he is about to sigh.

'Happen it does cover Buttermere. But a lot else, besides. Any road, I'm due a replacement. I get through one every six months.' He makes a face that she judges to be of discontent. 'They're good for what they show – but they're not well designed for actual use. Bit of a gap in the market, really.'

He has procrastinated again; meanwhile she is gaining in confidence.

She moves her hand from the map and leans closer to touch the cuff of his shirt, her cool fingertips feeling the warmer flesh of his wrist. Now they have eye contact. She lowers her voice, though they are alone in the little atrium.

'Lena said you are seeking witnesses.'

After a moment he releases the fork and sits back and folds his arms. His gaze is lowered again.

'It's early days. We're waiting on a definitive time frame – from Forensics, you know?'

So why has he come to the bookshop? Why did he visit the cottage?

'She mentioned a questionnaire – an interview, in due course?'

He gives a non-committal shrug, his arms still crossed and both hands tucked beneath his armpits.

'Sometimes it can be a bit of a jigsaw. Different folk supply different pieces. They don't know individually they're important. Put them together and you've got the makings of a picture.'

She slides her hand slowly from the table and brings both palms up behind her head. Her top is oversized, but nonetheless the action reveals something of her figure.

'I think Lena is more likely than I to help. Since she works from home. And – you saw her – doing her yoga?'

She smiles, hinting at conspiracy, and that she will keep the secret.

There is a dab of scarlet at his cheekbones. He makes an ineffectual hand-gesture towards her, eyes averted.

'What about you –' She can tell he is stumbling over what to call her. 'Do you get outdoors?'

She lowers her arms and flexes her spine; a languid movement, almost a little yoga exercise in itself.

'The lake?' It must be what he means. 'I'm a booky type. But on a fine day we'll take a walk – occasionally all the way round. I don't jog. Or swim –'

Abruptly she shudders, simultaneously inhaling – an audible hiss.

'You alreet, lass?'

She grins apologetically and pushes back her blue-rimmed glasses onto the bridge of her nose.

'To think we stroll for pleasure – around a – well, a watery grave – is that the saying?'

He looks like he thinks she has not quite got this right, but refrains from correcting her. She continues.

'A murder – so close – a woman.'

Now he is plainly moved to respond. He begins with a cluck of self-reproach.

'The wrong cat was let out of the bag when the alarm was raised. Aye – she didn't get there by accident – or of her own accord. But it wouldn't be the first time that someone has done a private burial. So it doesn't quite make it murder, not yet. And you shouldn't worry – the pair of you, I mean. It's not the work of a killer at large.'

A shadow darkens their little alcove. She turns to see her manager Ronny standing at the head of the short flight that winds up from the main café and bookshop floor. Perhaps he thinks this is a little liaison of some sort; after all, the wild-looking visitor did not announce himself as a police officer.

She is about to say she will only be a minute, when Ronny pre-empts her with a telephone hand-signal and mouths the word "wholesaler". Valentina raises an index finger, which seems to satisfy him – and he retreats.

'I shouldn't keep you from your work.'

The inspector seems sensitive to her situation.

'I shouldn't keep you from your elevenses.'

She smiles – but makes no attempt to move.

He clears his throat. Then he picks up her card and turns it over. He frowns when he sees it is blank on the reverse.

'Do you have a mobile number?'

'Neither of us have a mobile.' She sees the grey-green eyes narrow. 'There is no point – you see, there is no signal at Buttermere. Did Lena give you our landline number?'

Now he shakes his head – though it is plain he is still mulling over the notion.

She takes a biro from her thigh pocket and writes carefully on the back of the card. As she forms large cursive numerals she senses his gaze – lefties like her look so uncultivated to the right-hander.

'I can be contacted here, of course – during opening hours, sometimes after. Lena is probably a little harder to get hold of – she unplugs the phone when she is writing.'

His gaze drifts past her, unfocused.

'It's a nice setting. Pretty cottage. Cosy, though – you must have to tiptoe about.'

Now she affects a throaty purr, and rises, and reaches again to touch his sleeve.

'There are certainly times when we are on top of one another. But you are welcome to call in – perhaps we can help with your jigsaw, eh?'

7. CONFLUENCE

Brewery Lane, Cockermouth – 11.10 a.m.

SKELGILL SEES THAT the Cocker is outrunning the Derwent this morning. Overnight precipitation on the northwestern fells has not reached Cockermouth simultaneously. Such are the vagaries of the local watershed that this can happen. A raindrop that falls one inch to 'his' side of Honister Pass drains due north via Gatesgarthdale Beck through Buttermere, Crummock Water and down Lorton Vale into the small market town. Conversely, a raindrop landing one inch to the Hopes' side of Honister Pass is destined via Hause Gill to join the Derwent; it must sweep in a wide easterly arc into Borrowdale, thence easing through the much greater bodies of Derwentwater and Bassenthwaite Lake, and the meandering flood plain between Ouse Bridge and Cockermouth Castle – in all, nearly twice the distance.

Like a latter-day Kitchener of Khartoum surveying the confluence of the Nile, he stands sentinel at the tip of the isthmus. To his left, the rushing slate grey waters of the Cocker; to his right the browner, more majestic Derwent. He squints, pondering the conundrum of the coming together. Those twin raindrops, born of the same cloud, identical in shape and size, skydiving in tandem, falling just two inches apart – now separated, never again to meet. Or maybe there will be a reunion? Somewhere out in the green depths of the Irish Sea. There is a children's story in this!

He surprises himself with the notion, and grimaces, casting it off. He spent too long in that bookshop. The kiddies' section was booby-trapped with new-fangled pushchairs and random toddlers running riot, while a mothers' meeting was convened over carrot cake and cappuccinos.

He pats his jacket. His new OS map offers satisfying resistance, crisp in its shiny cover. Though, as he had intimated to Valentina White, the first thing he will do when he gets it home is to tear off the cover and refold the map to suit his own purposes. He scowls again – that was his other marketing idea of the morning.

He reflects on his unease. Maybe it stems from being surrounded by books. A deep-seated, longstanding aversion to those pages of impenetrable, dense black type, running with their dizzying rivers of white. The urge to up and run. Flight prevailing over hopeless fight. Normally he buys his maps from the safe haven of outdoor gear shops. Though, he has to concede, Paige Turner's offers a wider selection.

Besides, there was the girl – *young woman*. Though not so much younger than he. She just looked it, with her student outfit and trendy blue specs and short blonde hair; quite a contrast to the sultry Lena Longstaff with whom she is shacking up.

But what *about* the girl? What is he saying to himself?

Did he detect nervousness beneath her veneer of antipodean confidence? Or is it just the way the Aussies – *Kiwis,* rather – speak? Upfront, and yet with an inflexion that turns every other phrase into a question. They seem to probe when maybe they don't mean it. They seem forward when they are just being conversational. And the persuasive gaze from those blue eyes was disconcerting.

But there was innuendo in her replies. She even touched him. Is *that* a Kiwi thing? She leaned close enough for him to smell her light, grassy fragrance. Had she sprayed that on for his benefit?

He makes a conscious effort to stop this line of thought in its tracks.

He shakes his head. He doesn't know. He hasn't asked himself, grilled himself – about what he is up to. He is doing the things that he can. Because he can. But also because something tells him it is the right approach. Despite that their anonymous Lady of the Lake might shortly prove to hail from Liverpool or

Looe or London, his inclination is to make these rounds of the locality. To brush against its likely denizens, however oblique their interface might be.

He stoops and dips a hand into each of the rivers.

He allows himself a murmur of satisfaction.

Rain falls on the fells at about forty Fahrenheit this time of year, eventually warming maybe ten degrees by ambient conduction. His left hand feels a good couple of degrees cooler than his right.

But before he can celebrate further his theory, his phone rings: DS Jones.

He rises awkwardly, at once wiping wet palms against his thighs.

For a moment he sways to the beat, 1970s soul by the water – a distant watcher might question his sanity – is he about to topple in?

He answers.

'Jones.'

'Where are you, Guv? You sound outdoors.'

He casts about, a little panicked for an answer.

'By the Jennings brewery.'

'Cockermouth?'

'I thought I'd have a word with the char who does the holiday let by the lake – the Arl Lass told me she cleans a rental property up here on a Tuesday.'

'Oh, have you seen her?'

DS Jones waits patiently.

'Not yet. I needed a new map of Buttermere. I called into the bookshop. Killed two birds with one stone.' Three really, there was the soda cake. 'Had a blether with the other lass that lives at Hassness Cottage.'

He wonders if he makes it sound too casual.

'Ah. How was she?'

Skelgill stares unseeingly across the Derwent where a small party of swallows swoop for hatching mayflies.

'Taller. Blonde. Short hair. I didn't like to pay too close attention.'

55

'Sure.' She seems to go along with his affected discretion.
'Anything of note?'
He shakes his head – but his expression remains conflicted.
'She reckons she's more of an indoor type than her writer pal.'
DS Jones inhales – as though she might wish to question his loose descriptor.
'But nothing evidential.'
'She's from New Zealand.'
His response infers that this would hamper the woman from recognising anything of significance – but DS Jones takes the opportunity to introduce her purpose.
'Well – we have a starter for ten. A possible date.'
There is a public viewing bench just a few yards behind Skelgill, and now he takes a seat.
'Fire away.'
'The lab have completed an analysis of the stomach contents. Certain foodstuffs have survived intact – they would naturally preserve well. Raisins, figs, fragments of orange peel – zest – sliced almonds, stem ginger, and ground nutmeg and allspice. A mixture blackened probably with treacle.'
Skelgill is frowning.
'What was she – some kind of fanatical veggie?'
DS Jones chuckles.
'Guv – it's the recipe for Christmas pudding! All that's missing is an old sixpence.'
Skelgill is silent for a moment.
'I might have got it if you'd said the sixpence first.'
But DS Jones is eager to press on.
'And how often does anyone eat that?'
Now he is nodding. Never mind that the answer is *not often* – for the vast majority it is one day of the year. Most folk don't even like it – an aspect that has served him well, yuletides past.'
DS Jones has more.
'And you know the stats – domestic rifts spike over Christmas.'

Skelgill leans to rest his elbows on his knees and gazes out again across the rippling waters. He reaches for a dried grass stem and fits it between his bared teeth.

DS Jones specifies the scenario.

'It suggests she was killed sixteen months ago. Potentially on Christmas Day. Afternoon or evening. I've chatted with Dr Herdwick and he accepts that the timing fits with the pathology to date. But there is no obvious cause of death – no signs of injury or physical trauma. Suffocation or drowning may be impossible to establish. They're running chemical tests, including for alcohol and recreational drugs – but a toxin may have long degraded or dissolved away.'

Skelgill clears his throat, as if the latter scenario disturbs him.

'If it were a Christmas Day bust-up, it would be physical, spur of the moment.'

'I agree, Guv. And I do doubt that anyone would eat Christmas pudding alone. They've also established that the woman had not given birth. That she wasn't a mother – it's easier to understand why she might not have been reported missing.'

Skelgill performs another unseen facial contortion.

'I take it there's nowt on DNA?'

'Nothing on DNA – and they've not been able to extract fingerprints. But I suppose we shouldn't be surprised if she's not on the national database – and, in a way, it helps with elimination. The majority of mispers have a criminal record – younger females previously picked up for the likes of using or soliciting –'

In her slight hesitation, Skelgill detects that some unwelcome thought has interrupted his colleague's flow.

'Aye?'

Now it is she that is reticent.

'Oh – it was just – DI Smart was angling for gossip.'

'Gossip?'

'Well – you know? He's saying it's an outside job – that she'll be an undocumented Romanian – that it will be linked to an international drugs-and-people-trafficking gang.'

Skelgill spits away his grass stem.

'He's angling for the case, more like. He'll be in the Chief's ear, you can bet.'

They share a small silence. First in Mancunian Alec Smart's playbook is that, when it comes to organised crime, home-grown detectives cannot be expected to see the wood for the trees.

Skelgill shifts the subject.

'What's your next step?'

DS Jones gives a little cough.

'I know this sounds offbeat – but I thought I'd contact the supermarkets about their Christmas pudding recipes. Allspice, in particular, is an uncommon ingredient. It's a long shot – but it might get us something for future cross-reference. There must be a chance that the purchase is on a storecard record – that she bought it and took it home to have with her husband or partner for Christmas dinner.'

Skelgill does not demur; but he checks the time on his handset and rises.

'Reet. Don't forget Booths.'

'Guv?'

'The supermarket in Keswick. That'd be their kind of thing – a bit different, quirky.'

'Okay, sure. I'm impressed that you know.'

'They do a good line in frozen meals for two.'

Skelgill hears an ironic laugh as his colleague ends the call.

8. CHARLADY

Castlegate Mansions, Cockermouth – 11.25 a.m.

SHE WOULDN'T HAVE recognised him. Never mind that he doesn't look owt like a detective – he casts quite a different figure to the skinny bairn she shooed from outback many a time when the apples were ripening. Reet terrors they were, as la'al 'uns, Minnie Graham's lads. Who'd have thought the shrimp would turn out to be a tall policeman. Still, if no longer skinny, maybe rangy. And he's got his Ma's eyes – they won't miss much, that's for sure. There's no one pulls the wool over arl Minnie Graham. And Minnie Graham must be how's he's tracked her down.

'It's Jean, aye? Jean Thackthwaite?'

She nods, conscious of standing to attention with her mop, and that now the boot is on the other foot.

But she rouses herself for a reply.

'Thou're Minnie's lad. Young Daniel, int it? Scallywag.'

She sees that she has momentarily disarmed him. At very least, he affects a sheepish grin.

'I've been called worse.'

Aye, by her. She steps back, conscious of passers-by nebbing from the narrow pavement.

'You'll tek a mash?'

'Are you allowed?'

His tone sounds hopeful rather than reproachful.

'I'm allowed a break. Besides, I have to clear out all t' food that's left. Health and safety. Replace it wi' a new welcome pack. There's tea, milk and sugar – and chocolate digestives – it's all to go.'

In fact there is a small trove of foodstuffs that she has already packed in her cooler bag. But she won't mention that.

'Don't mind if I do, then.'
She beckons him to pass her and closes the door.
'Carry on – the kitchen's through t' back.'
She watches as he proceeds, glancing about. The Georgian townhouse is deceptively large, easily overlooked on the steep terraced street. Though its internal scale is its downfall; to refurbish the tired décor and furnishings would break the budget; it is trapped in slow decline.
He makes an exclamation – the long kitchen table has eight chairs on either side.
'How many does this place sleep?'
'There's seven bedrooms, all ensuite. There's four public – it's across four floors – and never mind the mess they leave in this kitchen. I've just put three bags o' beer cans in t' yard.'
'You've got your work cut out, Jean.'
His compliment seems genuine, though she keeps her back to him as she makes the tea.
'Aye – it can tek all day, and I'm not getting any younger.'
He inhales as though he might be about to reply – but then thinks the better of it. She stirs in milk and sugar and places the two mugs on a small tray with a plate of biscuits. They settle at one end of the table, facing each other. He seems hardly inquisitive, and his eyes follow the movements of the kitchenware.
'Help thesen, lad – I'm counting calories.'
He needs no further invitation. He breaks a biscuit in half and dunks it, quickly followed by the second piece. He obviously feels at home. She decides to have just one biscuit.
He takes a gulp of tea.
'I believe you clean the holiday cottage – Catthwaite.'
She notes he does not reveal his source.
But now she can ask.
'Is it the body – the lass in t' lake – is that what it's about?'
He nods. At least he doesn't try any trickery – asking why does she think he's here? Then again, it's all round the village – he must know that. He's probably irked that it's common knowledge. All trussed up like a turkey, she were. And her Bert

were at the bar when the divers came bursting in, still in their wetsuits, gasping and shouting and wanting to know where's the landline. He'd plied them with stiff whiskies and extracted the full story by the time the pair of constables arrived from Cockermouth. He knew she'd give him hell if he didn't bring home the gossip. But not before he'd had a few extra pints on it.

'Christmas before last – were it occupied?'

She is not expecting the question. He has shifted the time frame altogether. She has to think for a moment.

'The cottage? It's not let out at Christmas and New Year. The owners keep it for themselves.'

'For when?'

'They block out two weeks.'

'Starting when?'

'It depends on how the days fall. But always afore Christmas Eve. And past the Second – of January. They tek the extra Scottish bank holiday.'

'Are they from Scotland?'

The questions feel quickfire – though he is casual in his manner.

'Edinburgh. Name of McLeish. They're solicitors – summat like that – they have another word for it.'

She wonders why he asks her. He could get all this from the Cumbria Cottage Company.

'And they were there, Christmas before last?'

'Aye. They don't miss a year.'

He is nodding, looking a little more pensive now.

'Did you see them?'

She struggles to recall; one Christmas is much like another.

'I usually go in, mid-way – to change the beds and do a bit of a – a *re-fresh*, it's called.'

She is conscious that she has not yet answered the question, but he continues.

'Would they have had any visitors?'

Now she shakes her head; about this, she can be more certain.

'Not as I know of. Not to stay, any road – there's only two bedrooms. And they've got two teenagers, as it is.'

She watches as he despatches another biscuit. He seems to know exactly how long to dunk for – it can make you anxious, watching a person dunking a biscuit.

She reaches for another. But then she suddenly finds herself raising it, as if illustratively.

Wait. That were when we had the bad snow. It were a reet White Christmas, weren't it? T' village were more or less cut off. First they shut the Honister, then the next day the Newlands. And you could only get by Hause Point in a four-by-four. Jack Nicholson brought supplies up from Lorton in his tractor.'

He is looking at her now as if he thinks she has something more to tell – something has occurred to him and he is perhaps waiting to see if she reveals it. But she has nothing to hide, does she?

'The McLeishes – they were running low on basics. I mind I had to wear Bert's wellies to get there. I took a frozen loaf and powdered milk, some eggs and bacon, and a few tins of beans.'

He seems interested – but he makes short work of another biscuit and she is not sure if he is satisfied with her answer. Then another biscuit. His appetite is one thing that's obviously not changed since he were a bairn.

She gives a little chuckle – affected, but she feels appropriate.

'Funny thing was – they had plenty o' fancy food. Mrs McLeish, as a thank you, she gave me a Scotch Christmas pudding – Black Bun, she called it.'

Now he definitely conceals a reaction, rubbing his left eye as if a mote of dust has got into it.

'This Black Bun – were it homemade?'

'Walkers.'

'Walkers? I thought they made crisps.'

He is straight-faced, but he might be being ironic. She plays it straight.

'Aye, they do. But there's a Scotch Walkers, an' all – them as makes that tartan shortbread.'

He grins.

'I've heard of tartan custard.'

So he *is* joking, in the midst of seriousness.

'What did you do with it, Jean?'

It strikes her as a little curious that he pursues the subject.

She makes a flamboyant gesture with her biscuit, noting that his eyes follow it, and then she gives a disdainful scoff.

'I hoyed most of it. Bert said it were only fit for building walls. It gave him reet bad indigestion – kept him up all night – reckoned it near killed him.'

9. THE HINDLEWAKES

Ellerbeck B&B, Buttermere – 12.30 p.m.

'WE'RE FULL UP, I'm afraid, love.'

How plain does "No Vacancies" have to be? Yet folk still try it on – as if they think by turning up before pre-booked guests they can steal a march on them. This one has a determined look in his eye. She's glad they're full; lusty hill-walking types are not her cup of tea. They stomp in with muddy boots and string up washing lines across the bedroom. Besides, single occupancy doesn't command the full price.

The man seems undeterred.

Perhaps Ted's forgot to turn the sign on the gate this morning.

'Madam, I'm actually from the police, Cumbria CID.'

Elizabeth Hindlewake finds herself squinting at his credentials. *Skelgill?* Isn't that the married name of the elderly widow she sees careering about the village on an old boneshaker? The one locals call Ma Graham.

'Can I trouble you for a quick word?'

He seems content to ignore her flour-smeared apron and that she persistently wipes her hands on a tea towel – surely signs that she is busy. Then again, she can guess why he's here. And she is curious.

'You'd better come through, then. Will you want to speak to my Ted, an' all? He's just changing the beds. We've only got the three rooms. All doubles.'

She is conscious that she adds the rider out of guilt – and to suggest that any negative reaction towards him, mistaken for a potential customer, was for practical reasons rather than in any way discriminatory. You can't be too careful, these days.

She pushes open the door to the residents' lounge and steps aside.

'Have a seat, love.'

She can hear Ted banging about – he always gets a cob on when all three rooms have to be done at once. She leans over the banister and cranes her neck.

'Ted! Come down. The police want to see you.'

The thumping ceases. There is a moment's silence, then his footsteps creak across the floorboards – he must be in Room Two, it's the creakiest. They've thought about getting them fixed, but have concluded it's better to know when folk are prowling about. Now he creaks down the stairs.

'What's that you say, Betty?'

'The police are here. A detective.' As he reaches her level, she leans closer and lowers her voice. 'Says his name's Skelgill – like that woman in the village. Must be related.'

She is a little disappointed that this mysterious snippet does not engender more of a reaction. Ted merely makes a face of indifference. He pushes past her and enters the lounge.

'Right-ho. What can we do for you, officer?'

He doesn't beat about the bush, her Ted. Whenever she's shy of mentioning a matter of protocol to a guest, he's never slow in coming forward. He'll point out minor misdemeanours – such as leaving lights on when they go out, or running the hot water while they're brushing their teeth (although how he knows about that, she never can fathom). He insists he saves them a small fortune in electricity bills, but she's never quite sure what it does for trade.

The detective is unmoved by her spouse's offer. He is literally unmoved – he remains seated in the fireside armchair, and he waits until they have felt it necessary to settle obediently side-by-side on the sofa opposite.

Ted tries again.

'Is it this Lady of the Lake malarkey? It could hit us in the pocket. Mind, there's some as saying it'll bring in the ghouls. It

65

were all the talk when I picked up the papers from the shop at Lorton this morning. The Gazette's got a front-page splash. *Hah!'*

Betty glances anxiously at the detective. Folk can't always tell when Ted is joking. She notices his gaze as it takes in the contents of the room, dwelling on the fire irons (as potentially lethal weapons?) and now rests on the reproduction landscape above the mantelpiece, a painting of Haystacks that she bought from an antique shop in Cockermouth (though she never told Ted exactly how much she paid).

He shifts a little, as if to stretch his spine, and makes a bit of a face.

'Aye. We think the incident might have occurred over Christmas – the one before last. It gives us a focus for finding possible witnesses.'

She feels Ted jolt and he turns to her.

'Huh. We didn't see owt, did we Betty? We were up to our eyeballs.'

She feels herself frowning. Ted always says this, no matter how quiet or busy they are. But the detective looks like this doesn't matter to him, or he disregards the comment.

'So, you were open for business?'

She leans forwards and nods vigorously. She does the bookings, and she makes sure she answers before Ted interjects.

'We're always full at Christmas – we have regulars that come every year. We do them a special three-night package – full board, when usually it's just B&B.'

He is looking at her intently, yet casually. How can it be both? She worries that she has said something out of place. But, if so, Ted seems oblivious. She can tell he's bursting to ask questions.

The detective responds quickly.

'Your Christmas package – what does that cover?'

She is surprised that he has asked.

She finds herself reciting her little sales spiel – not that she ever has to sell it to anyone – but one day, she supposes, she'll need to.

'Arrive on Christmas Eve. Fish supper – we serve that in here, by the fire. Full English breakfast on Christmas Day. They get a full English every day. They're free to use the lounge – for them to have their presents and whatnot – they're free to come and go. Christmas Dinner in the dining room at five o'clock. Then the same on Boxing Day, except we do a turkey hotpot with bubble-and-squeak – you know, to make the best of the leftovers?'

She can't be sure, but he might be looking hungry. She wonders if she should offer a brew and a cheese-and-pickle barm – she's got them ready for their own lunch. But Ted would probably complain afterwards – saying they get their lunch on expenses, these coppers – he'd probably only double claim it.

'And you say you've got regulars?'

She feels a little unnerved, on the defensive.

'They've been coming to us for seven or eight years, isn't that right, Ted?' She turns to him, but he seems not to be listening. He's probably thinking that they don't charge enough – what with the price of food inflation these days. He was bemoaning that they're not a chuffing charity when they last discussed it. She presses on. 'They used to come to us in Blackpool, and they stayed with us when we moved up to the Lakes. That'll be four years this June.'

The detective appears sceptical.

'They're couples, are they – that take your three doubles?'

So he did pay attention. She begins to nod, but corrects herself.

'Two couples – and Mr Black. He brings Napoleon. They all get on like a house on fire.'

Now the detective certainly frowns – and she feels obliged to elaborate, lest he think there is something amiss going on.

'Two *married* couples. And Napoleon's a Frenchie. We don't normally take pets – but we make an exception for Mr Black and Napoleon. He's very well housetrained, and friendly for a bulldog, isn't he, Ted?'

Now Ted is also scowling, and he declines to answer. He's probably remembering the last time Napoleon bit him.

But the detective seems satisfied with her explanation.

'And are they all booked in for this Christmas?'

'Aye. They get priority, and they always book for the next year just as they're leaving.'

He is nodding pensively.

'We may need to speak with them.'

Now Ted harrumphs.

'I don't see what good that'd do you – they can't have seen owt – they would have told us, eh, Betty?'

She is a little surprised that he delegates corroboration to her.

'Well – happen they would have.'

The detective persists, though he gives a casual shrug, as if the answers to his questions are not of great interest – that he is going through the motions.

'Are they walkers? Outdoor types?'

She gives a brisk shake of her head to emphasise the definitive response to follow.

'No – not at all. They're in their seventies now, the Greens *and* the Browns. Mrs Green, she's troubled by arthritis, and Mr Brown – he's been waiting above two years for his hip replacement.'

'How about the chap with the dog?'

'Mr Black?' She glances at Ted; he is grimacing again. But she decides to continue. 'Well, of course – he goes out – Napoleon has his business to see to. But he usually just takes him into the back garden – it's quite big enough for a little dog, and it's all fenced in, to keep the Canada geese out – so he can't chase them and fall in the lake – owt like that.'

She is sure she feels a little dig from Ted's elbow, though she might have imagined it. Perhaps it is just one of his nervous twitches; he seems to get them more often these days.

And now, to her relief – although she is not quite sure why – the detective rises.

'Perhaps you could give me their addresses, if it's convenient.'

She has a vague idea that there's something about "private data" – but that's probably to do with the internet. Nor does

Ted produce an objection. She finds herself rising, too, and stepping across to the sideboard.

'It's all in our visitors' book.' It lies open, and she flicks back through the pages until December dates begin to appear. 'Here they are, all together, look.'

The detective peers over her shoulder, and she steps aside, realising he is preparing his phone to take a photograph. She can't help feeling a little swell of pride.

'See how they all say they can't wait to come back. Great company and fine food.'

The detective squints at his camera, as though he can't quite make this out. He does comment, however.

'You must look after them well. Do you give them all the trimmings? The likes of Christmas pudding?'

'Ooh, yes – Christmas pudding, especially. I get it every year from the charity Christmas fair in the Old Schoolroom. And rum butter. There's an elderly lady that sets up a little stall, with her homemade local recipes. She does these scrumptious Welsh cakes – they're always first to go.'

The detective does not answer – and though he is staring at the photograph he has taken, he seems not to see its contents at all, as if his gaze has been taken over by some distant thought. Then he snaps out of it. He slips his phone into his back pocket and moves towards the door.

'Reet, then – sorry to take up your time – I can see you're busy, now the season's coming on.'

She notices that Ted does not get up – and he is still sitting when she returns from seeing the visitor off the premises. He is staring at the door, awaiting her return, his lips pressed shut in a tight line. It's not like him to hold his peace.

'What is it, Ted?'

He makes a face which could be what they call 'conspiratorial'. He lowers his voice, even though they are the only ones home.

'That Christmas – it were when we had all the snow.'

She relaxes.

'Aye, that's right – and everyone stayed in. And they all had to leave by way of Cockermouth, when the snowplough cleared the road the day after Boxing Day.'

Ted is shaking his head.

'Everyone stayed in. But that damned dog went missing, didn't it? On Christmas Night. Did a runner – climbed a snowdrift and got over the fence, according to Roger Black. Remember, Betty? Black was gone a good hour in the dark.'

10. KEVIN

Buttermere Hikers' Hostel – 1.10 p.m.

HE'S TAKEN HIS time to get up to the entrance. Kevin Pope spotted the man when he picked up the mail from the porch five minutes ago. He was standing halfway up the steep gravel drive facing away from the building, staring down the slope and back across the road. He seemed to be looking in the direction of High Crag, or maybe Haystacks, beyond the trees and the lake. He's dressed for hillwalking, though he doesn't even have a day-bag. And he's not driven a car in. Perhaps he's been poking around.

'Are you the manager?'

Kevin subconsciously raises a hand to touch his name badge.

'Acting manager. Do you want accommodation? It's too early to arrive.'

'DI Skelgill.'

Kevin finds himself confronted by a police warrant card. It is not an unfamiliar sight and it triggers just a hint of what might be PTSD, the urge to run. The chap doesn't look like a detective, though. What if he's found it lying in the road and is trying it on. What's he up to?

'You don't – erm – you don't have a car?'

'I'm parked at the Fish.'

He doesn't elaborate. Kevin supposes he's making inquiries on foot. It must be about the body in the lake. But he doesn't feel he can ask. There's something intimidating about the man's taciturnity. And he's an inspector – that's senior.

'Oh, I see.'

The silence persists. Kevin wonders if he should invite him in – but they ask, the police, when they want to come inside.

'Do you open at Christmas?'

Finally, a question. It catches him unawares. He feels a tremor run down his spine and a tingling in his toes and fingertips. His stress reaction. He flexes his hands, but then quickly shoves them in his pockets, thinking the officer might have noticed.

'Christmas?'

'Aye.'

The detective must realise he is struggling to find his words.

'I don't want to book, or owt – I just want to know if you open for business.'

He finds his tongue, albeit his words begin disjointedly.

'D-do we open at Christmas? N–no, we d-don't. It's so staff can – can get home to their families. But – anyway – between November and February – we only open weekends. The days are too short – for there to be many long-distance walkers. And the weather –'

The inspector is scowling at him. He looks the sort that wouldn't be bothered by the weather – he looks *weathered*, as if by exposure, like a shepherd. He looks the sort of person who's come down from the fells, his face like a rock formation, his hair like windblown heather. But don't stare at him.

'How long have you been the manager?'

Kevin's hands ball up in his pockets. He tells himself there's no reason why he should be so nervous. But he gets the feeling the policeman knows the answers to the questions he is asking – that he's testing him out. He could already have checked with head office. *Acting* manager – but he won't correct him again.

'It'll be two years in October.'

'Where were you working before that?'

'Shrewsbury.'

'On the Severn?'

'That's it. Though I think there's only one. *Ha-hah.*'

He doesn't know why he laughs. It comes out as a pathetic giggle. It's not even a proper joke.

'They say it's good for chub and barbel.'

'I'm sorry?'

What does he mean?

'Types of coarse fish. Fishes.'
'Oh – I see. I wouldn't really know. We don't often get – well, anglers. Just walkers.'
The inspector's eyes are penetrating. Does he know something – and is waiting for it to slip out?
'You sound like you're from Manchester.'
He finds himself nodding. At least here is something.
'Wythenshawe.'
He doesn't get the usual reaction – the grimace of distaste or the glance of sympathy.
'You'll know why I'm here.'
He stares back. He feels like he's a boy again, accused by the headmaster – innocent, but desperately trying to think up some minor misdemeanour to confess to. Or that time the police came to the hostel at Shrewsbury after the complaint but wouldn't tell him at first what it was. Then they showed him the peephole in the unisex shower compartment. It must have been another guest that was looking at the woman – he was on breakfast duty that day. But in the end he was transferred up here to the infernal rain – as if he needed reminding of showers.
'I h-heard about the b-body – on the radio.'
What does the detective know about him? It feels like he can read his mind.
'Female, early thirties, small and slim with long black hair. Does that ring any bells?'
He feels – what is it? A lump rising in his throat? He wants to speak – or does he? Perhaps it's best that he doesn't.
'W-was it Christmas? Is that why you were asking?'
The officer seems reluctant to answer this. He cranes his neck, squinting into the angled eaves of the Victorian building, where the martins are back at their mud nests, making repairs. It's supposed to be an omen of good luck to have martins. He thought he had good luck, for a while.
The policeman suddenly responds, and it makes him start.
'It's a possible line of inquiry. Christmas before last.'

Kevin feels like he knows what's coming next – but without warning the detective steps back and turns away as if to leave. Doesn't he want to know his answer?

'Was there – was there something wrong?'

'Eh?'

'I noticed you were looking at something – down the driveway.'

The detective gives a half shake of his head.

'Wrong? Nay – you've got a pair of pied wagtails nest-building – where the wall's part-collapsed – by the gate. There's nowt wrong – so long as you don't disturb it while they've flown.'

Kevin feels a wave of relief coming over him.

'We have a property department that deals with all that. It can take forever to get anything done. The wall's been down since before I arrived. I wouldn't dare touch it – I'm hopeless at practical jobs.'

The detective seems disinclined to humour him; he merely glances at his watch and gives a dismissive wave as he departs. Kevin retreats into the porch and closes the door. It is gloomy inside, and the detective won't see him standing here if he looks back.

But now the man moves purposefully – he doesn't dwell this time – just a glance at the crumbling wall at the entrance. He said he was parked at the Fish Inn – at least, that's what the locals still call it. Except he turns not right, towards the village, but left along the road to Gatesgarth and Honister Pass. There are other places to call at, he supposes. So perhaps he's not been singled out.

His gaze drifts. The weather might be changing. A strip of low cloud has condensed over the ridge, levelling off the uneven summit of Haystacks. He can just glimpse a sliver of the lake above the treetops; it looks dark now, and uninviting.

He replays the detective's words.

Female, early thirties, small and slim with long black hair.

It can't be.

There're thousands of women like that. There's one fits that description staying here most days.

But what if it's her? What if it's Tina they've found?

Do the police secretly know who it is? Do they know she used to come here?

He mulls over that no one ever came asking for Tina – he's always assumed because she never told anyone – that she was perhaps a married woman who liked getting high when the fancy took her.

Though she never told him that. She hardly told him anything. Just that she could get away from time to time. What he didn't know couldn't hurt him. What was it she used to say? Consider her enigmatic, like the Mona Lisa.

But that she could 'get away' suggests something. If she'd been a totally free agent she wouldn't have put it like that.

He always feared she'd stop coming. For a loser like him he couldn't believe his luck when the woman fancied him in the first place.

Then there was the Christmas where it all went wrong.

Hand shaking, he fumbles in his shirt pocket for the joint he rolled earlier.

11. SCOUTING

Buttermere – 1.25 p.m.

SKELGILL MUST KEEP his wits about him. The road south is narrow – it barely accommodates two car-widths – with no appreciable verge, and irregular bends. Tourists from the suburbs are not used to the idea that around the corner there may be sheep in the road; local bus drivers – gung-ho – are used to the idea that mainly there are not. To his right, dry stone wall doubles-up with stock fencing. To his left, the fellside rises thick with bracken, its green shoots unfurling snakelike through the crackling brown litter of last year's growth. To the left is the easier bet if evasive action is required, though there is impenetrable gorse in places.

The gradient he traverses is moderate, sliding eventually into the lake. Through gaps in the trees of Ellerbeck Wood he gets occasional glimpses of the water, its surface mirroring a greying sky. The ridge has disappeared into cloud, and for now birdsong seems subdued. Only clumps of pale primroses offer a cheery reminder of the season, and occasional jousting pipits that still vie for territory or mates.

Striding out, he passes at intervals of two or three minutes the driveway openings of Ellerbeck B&B (Betty and Ted Hindlewake from Blackpool) and the three more modest dwellings, Catthwaite Cottage holiday let (cleaner Jean Thackthwaite, owners the McLeishes of Edinburgh), Pike Rigg Cottage (the hitherto unmet twitcher by the name of Woodcock), and Hassness Cottage (the intriguing pairing of author Lena Longstaff and Kiwi Valentina White), where his step momentarily falters. But he does little more than note that none of these properties is visible from the public highway, and only the B&B advertises its presence by name. The local postie needs no such intelligence.

It takes him twelve minutes to walk the stretch of lane from the Hikers' Hostel to Hassness Castle. Though it is a commercial enterprise, it does not proclaim its wares by roadside billboards and, set on a sharp bend on raised ground before the road dips to Gatesgarth, the entrance would be easy to miss when travelling by car.

For Skelgill, of course, this is not an issue – never mind that as a youngster he secretly penetrated its wooded environs on many occasions. In those days it was still a private residence, a substantial country seat, its lone inhabitant the last of a long line, a retired military officer by the name of Bletheroe, commonly referred to by locals as "Colonel Blimp", the aging man a throwback to times when small village lads like Skelgill were considered fodder for shoving up chimneys or down mines, or beating for grouse in the line of fire and the consequences be damned – and, while Skelgill knew he was never in danger of being caught by the collar, more than once he found himself retreating through the undergrowth beneath a shower of shotgun pellets loosed off into the skies.

The signboard merely identifies the property, though on close examination there is a small reference to the organisation that leases it out – a website address. He supposes that, unlike say a B&B which can attract passing walk-up trade, a business that targets corporate outward-bound group activities will probably find its customers by remote electronic means of advertising.

His understanding is that the facilities are of a self-catering nature – like a giant Airbnb – and that management takes the form of a travelling overseer or caretaker who arranges maintenance and repairs at arm's length and is responsible for a portfolio of such properties owned by the group across the north of England.

Spring weeds are sprouting from the gravel of the curving driveway, and under mainly oak and sycamore a swathe of bluebells sends out a waft of hyacinth that contrasts with the pungent reek of ramsons – the white-spiked wood garlic that has set up in competitive patches. Here, the still air is resonant with arboreal birdsong and the buzz of insect life. He wipes his brow, perspiring a little from his brisk march. Pressure is falling and the humidity rising, amplified beneath the leafy canopy.

The castle appears. Its antiquity is belied by its rather stark frontage, two wings extending symmetrically from a central atrium, its exterior distempered white with a regular arrangement of undersized windows – Art Deco might be guessed at, when in fact by that era it had long been in its heyday as a country sporting estate.

But Skelgill does not trouble himself with any such appraisal. Notwithstanding its familiar look, more salient to him is the absence of any vehicles. And the ground-floor windows have internal wooden shutters drawn. Evidently it is not currently let.

He cannot help staying in cover at first – the old memories are fresh. And it is boyhood habit – boyhood understanding – you were always up to mischief; you were always on your guard. Another wild animal – like the fox – predatory, but never free of jeopardy.

The feeling is mitigated in that the residence nowadays has a commercial role; the assumption of trespassing cannot be so easily charged, when he might be inquiring of availability, an authorised scout making a recce armed with the company chequebook.

That there is no one here to interrogate does not trouble him.

He breaks from the shadow of the trees and skirts the property. At the rear, lakeside, only the upper floor will have a glimpse of Buttermere, as the sweep of woodland lies in between.

The immediate grounds are set to lawn; it is long and dewy and well overdue for a cut. Presumably there is a local contractor who swings in every so often; quite likely the warm moist spring will have him chasing his tail; shepherds are rueing the surfeit of grass right now, and vets busy with bloated yowes.

Skelgill notices a recent extension – it looks like a kitchen – just high horizontal slit windows to afford maximum internal wall space, and there is an elaborate silvered extraction unit and flue, and an emergency exit door – all to comply with red tape, no doubt.

Extending from the newbuild is another smaller set of foundations, just footings and a concrete base with plumbing in place – he deduces it is intended to be a pair of outside toilets, but evidently this part of the project has been mothballed. There is some uncleared builders' debris – and on a decaying pallet a stack of concrete blocks and maybe some timbers, the whole thing wrapped in translucent polythene and tied and weighted down with rotting logs. He would guess these materials have lain untouched for a good time. Rainwater has pooled in depressions in the polythene, and these puddles are thick with green algae and blackening leaf litter and accumulated windblown silt.

He muses, his expression tending towards nostalgia. Not enough places have outside toilets. He is reminded, he must time it right to call in at his Ma's; she'll complain at the lack of notice, but be affronted if he doesn't eat. Then again, when doesn't he eat?

He makes a backward movement and accidentally slips off the edge of the foundations, needing several stuttering dance steps to regain his balance. But it snaps him out of his reverie, and he turns and heads into the woodland fringe.

He ponders heading directly for the lake. It is a good three or four hundred yards to the shore, a plunging descent in places, over rough terrain that is rocky and moss-covered, beneath birch and larch and through an understory of blackthorn, hawthorn and hazel. There is no obvious path – indeed it is not an appealing prospect outside of an emergency. But in reverse it provides a satisfactory deterrent to lake circumnavigators who might decide to scale the boundary wall and explore the grounds.

After a moment's hesitation he eschews the declination, the pull of gravity, and sets off on a traverse along the contour, in effect commencing the return journey to the village. He moves without apparent caution and yet silently, following a narrow badger path, placing his feet with care and ducking and weaving to avoid branches that would impede the upright walker's progress. When he comes upon a pair of roe deer stretching to browse fresh sycamore leaves, a dozen yards to his left, he clicks his tongue and displays a palm in a calming motion. The creatures do not take flight; the doe resumes feeding, though the ivory-antlered buck is watchful. Skelgill passes otherwise uneventfully.

Just a few minutes more find him reaching a wire fence of three rusted strands stapled to listing posts. Hassness Cottage would have been the abode of an estate worker – gamekeeper, most likely – and the token barrier erected when it was sold off separately from the main house, its purpose merely to stake out the change in title. His estimate is that each of the cottages in the woods has a couple of acres, stretching between the road and the shore of Buttermere.

While the fence is merely cosmetic he hesitates, now confronted by the practical reality of his approach – it is unconventional, even for a detective of his proclivities and provenance. It verges on the Peeping Tom – and the mere fact of him encountering the notion tells him that he must harbour some guilt in this regard. He reminds himself there is a new reason to speak with the occupants of the cottage – the potential Christmas disappearance – though he vacillates for a second time when he emerges upon the patch of lawn. Strung across a washing line – exhibited flagrantly, it seems – he recognises the black figure-hugging yoga outfit worn yesterday by Lena Longstaff, the Lycra leggings and long-sleeved top, along with what might have been her unseen underwear, a tiny scrap of black silk. There are also two pairs of the billowing white jeans of the type sported this morning by Valentina White, and other items of pale cream lingerie economic in their use of fabric.

He blinks his way past the display of laundry, ducking under the line, self-consciously playing to an unseen audience – which quite likely does not exist. He detects no one in the conservatory, although there is a small kitchen window, and the bedroom window up in the gable beneath deep eaves.

The rear access is now via the little sunroom extension – he decides it is inappropriate to knock here, and he rounds to the front. He is unsure why, but intuition tells him the property is empty; perhaps it is that he has brushed against a leg of the jeans, and the material is stiff and dry.

And when he knocks, and waits, and knocks again, and waits again – his prophecy is proved correct – unless Lena Longstaff is inside but declining to be disturbed from her writing. And yet she would surely at least peer out to see who is calling. Yesterday she had seemed – how can he put it – alluring? Is that the word? He strains his lexicon but can come up with nothing better.

He steps back and casts about.

There is no car parked – but there had been none yesterday. If they have just one perhaps it is used by Valentina White to commute to her job in Cockermouth. But he doubts even this idea. The driveway surface comprises compacted earth and stones, more like a farm track – but there are no wheel ruts. The paved hardstanding near the cottage is uniformly encrusted with hundreds of small discs of lichen, in colour from pale aquamarine to vibrant lemon green, and fleshy liverwort inhabits the cracks. A car regularly parked inhibits such primordial colonisation and leaves instead a ghostly trace, a bleached outline and dark eyespots of engine oil.

He makes a face and inhales through bared teeth, in the way of a reformed smoker unable to kick the last vestige of the habit, though it has never been his bag. It is as if the sudden intake of oxygen provides the means of propulsion, when a burst of energy is needed, and a change in plan is called for. He fishes his mobile phone from his back pocket. There is no signal, but he picks out a calling card from a slot in the case and digs for the stub of a pencil that he keeps in the capacious map pocket of his trousers. Leaning against the front door, methodically he prints out a short note, and posts the card into the letterbox.

Now he exhales deeply. It cannot be the same breath, though it might seem that way – he has conducted the manoeuvres with lips compressed in grim concentration. He turns and strides down the driveway towards the lane. The next property he ought to approach more formally.

12. WOODCOCK

Pike Rigg, Buttermere – 2.20 p.m.

IT'S HIM AGAIN. The snooper he caught on camera. Royston Woodcock adjusts the focus of his Leica binoculars. He surely can't be a burglar – otherwise, why didn't he just ruddy well break in yesterday? And there was milk he could have nicked, that was left untouched on the step. Is he a vagrant looking for an empty property? Why doesn't he just go up to the Hikers' Hostel? They do a cheap rate for bed and board.

Could he be from the council, or the electricity, or the water people?

He must have tried at the front. And, to give him his due, he did knock twice at the back and stand to polite attention before he started peering through the windows, shading his eyes with both hands to get a better view. Well, he won't see much. Just bird books on his desk, and photos on the side wall.

Now he's looking this way.

Royston keeps perfectly still.

He knows he blends in. He'd damned well better do – his wildlife photographer's camouflage gear cost a right royal packet. He'd tried it himself – placing the outfit like a scarecrow and retreating a distance, then trying to convince himself he couldn't see it. Trouble is, he knew where it was. Still, look at the photos he gets. If sharp-eyed sparrowhawks don't spot him, why would a person?

Except the bloke's coming straight at his hiding place.

Maybe he's seen the glint of his lenses.

Or is he just following the lie of the land in the direction of the lake?

Royston holds his nerve for another twenty seconds or so.

But it's no good; he caves under the pressure. He rises stiffly from his log seat and disentangles himself from the undergrowth. He totes his camera and tripod and steps forward to adjust the red squirrel feeder that has been his object. Maybe that's what the bloke saw – the feeder, not him.

Royston now looks up, affecting surprise that the bloke is here, that he is so close. He knows it can't seem natural – it contradicts – how could he have missed his approach when he's been sitting here watching?

'Mr Woodcock? I'm DI Skelgill from Cumbria CID.'

There is the flash of a warrant card. He does not doubt its authenticity; perhaps this is how country detectives look. More like mountain goats than prancing city ponies.

Unnerved, Royston shoots out a hand, and the sharp action prompts a reflexive if unwilling reciprocation. The grip is ironlike, disconcerting.

'Call me Roy.' He feels he squeaks the words.

'Sorry to intrude on your birdwatching, sir.'

It seems he ignores Royston's invitation to be informal. Is that something he should worry about? Royston manufactures a shrug, as if to suggest there is no intrusion.

'I'm sure you're aware, sir, that a woman's body has been recovered from the lake.'

The detective regards him casually – but there is something in the unblinking grey-green eyes that smacks of watchfulness. And he waits. Royston finally feels compelled to answer. His free hand drifts to touch his Leicas.

'Yeah – I've seen the divers – and the report on *Lakes Live* last night.'

The detective is looking at his binoculars. Then his gaze moves to peruse the camera with its indecently extravagant telephoto lens. Royston wonders if he should be saying something about the body, that it is a terrible thing.

'That's decent kit, you've got.'

Royston finds his tongue.

'Yeah – well – pricey, right enough – but it's what I do, see?'

'For a living?'

Now the detective narrows his eyes. This is to be expected.

'Nah – I'm a retired papermaker, me. Used to work in a wadding mill down in Kent. We used to churn out lavvy rolls by the million.'

The policeman's reaction is slow-to-non-existent. He is hard to read. He doesn't seem engaged by the idea of toilet tissue. So often in telling of his former profession Royston has been the butt of jokes, like the bottom falling out of the market, and getting a bum deal, or that it must have been a crap job, or that he's flush with cash. People think they're the first to say it and are pleased with themselves.

In the silence that ensues he feels obliged to elaborate.

'I get the occasional photo published. RSPB magazine. BBC *Countryfile*. *Cumbria Life*. Only a few quid, like – beer money.'

The detective's gaze has drifted away, towards the copse that shields sight of the lake.

'There's a chance someone's witnessed summat. Some folk are more observant than others.'

Ah. So this is the implication. He's being consulted. He might be an amateur, but he's a trained observer. However, he contrives a face expressing doubt. He doesn't want to create any false hopes. He doesn't want to draw too much attention to himself.

'I would have reported anything – obviously.'

The detective remains stolid.

'It wouldn't necessarily have looked suspicious.'

The ball is back in Royston's court.

'Yeah – well – I suppose – if you were disposing of a body – you'd make it look like, what – fishing from a boat?'

The detective scowls at this suggestion. But no explanation is forthcoming.

Royston rows back on the idea.

'Can't say I've ever seen a boat on Buttermere.'

The taller man casts him a sharp glance.

'Aye. It's National Trust. Water sports are prohibited. Diving's allowed. And fishing.'

Royston shifts a little uneasily from one foot to the other. Sitting for so long – and no squirrels – has given him pins and needles.

'It's mainly walkers, that I see. Picnickers. It's just a nice distance round the lake, so they say.'

The detective scrutinises his camera once again. Royston tries to imagine what he is thinking. Has he said the wrong thing – a hint that he might photograph people?

'Do you photograph at night?'

Royston doesn't know why – but he gets a feeling he ought not say yes to this.

'I've tried – there's a badger path crosses my back lawn.' He inclines his head towards the cottage. 'They'll stop if you lay food out. Grated cheese, especially. But they don't like the flash.' He casts his free hand loosely over his shoulder. 'Birds are my main area of interest – but there's only really owls active at night, and they're silent hunters – they're almost impossible to locate – more trouble than it's worth.'

The detective is pensive. His eyes move about, settling here and there, but nowhere long enough to give Royston a clue as to his underlying motive. It is as if he suspects something has recently happened and there might be traces of it. It prompts an involuntary objection from Royston.

'But – they said on the news – the body – it was two years ago?'

To Royston's surprise, his little outburst yields an unexpected release of information.

'We have a line of inquiry. Under two years. Christmas before last – Christmas Day.'

Royston feels the old tingle creep up his spine – though he is not quite sure why – not just yet. He wants to speak, but he feels like he will squeak again, that his voice wants to rise by an octave against his will. He forces himself to respond.

'That was The Big Freeze – when we had that great dump of snow. The place was cut off. The lake partly froze over. I even got photos of a cracking drake smew – now, there's a bird I ain't previously seen outside of Kent. Cliffe marshes used to be a

85

reliable spot for it – winter visitor from the Arctic Circle. I remember thinking, what a nice Christmas present it was, to myself. Being on me tod, like.'

The detective sighs, as if he has been holding his breath during Royston's little speech, and that now he feels sorry for him.

'Did you move up alone?'

Royston seems to be nodding too eagerly. It's strange, how the police make you feel – like they've checked your tyres in the drive, and they've got something on you.

'I was divorced ten years ago. The missus moved to New Zealand. Our daughter's out there – a doctor, she is. I was offered redundancy at sixty and took advantage of being a free agent.' Royston looks about, wondering if he is being over-wistful. 'Who wouldn't fall in love with this spot?'

The detective seems to bridle proprietorially. He issues an abrupt question.

'I take it you can get through to the lake?'

He is staring again at the trees.

'Yeah – I've got a gate onto the footpath.'

'Can you show me where you took the photos from – of – what did you call it? Smew?'

Royston feels the tingle once again. Is it excitement, or should he be alarmed?

He leads the way. Just short of the shoreline, as the water begins to appear though the thinning trunks, the detective suddenly halts. There is a disturbance on the surface.

'Goosander.'

'Close – but no cigar.' Royston has blurted the unintended rebuke before he can stop himself. The detective is looking thunderous, like he might land one on him. 'No – I mean – well spotted, like. And you ain't far wrong. Just that it's a red-breasted merganser – female – the females are hard to separate from goosander. And you'd be right to think goosander – they nest in tree holes, so they're more frequent inland. In fact, red-breasted merganser are almost entirely maritime in winter. Look – see – over there – just surfaced – a drake – see how different that is to a drake goosander. They're both members of the sawbill family – so are smew, come to that. They dive for fry and small fish – not the angler's best friend.'

He dares to look back at the policeman – but the cloud has passed and he is watching the pair of narrow-billed, long-bodied birds as they trail parallel wakes and then submerge in synchrony. It suddenly strikes him that the man is probably an angler himself. Dear, dear – another two trout about to be accounted for.

'And you don't recall seeing owt – when you were here? On Christmas Day. Besides your smew.'

Royston can hear the thump of his pulse in his temples.

'But – I thought the body was further down the lake – off the point, where it's deepest?'

He realises this might seem like a gaffe. How would he know these things? He scrambles to recover.

'I mean – like I say – I've seen your police divers. I bet they're still there, ain't they?'

Without ado he crosses the public path and in ungainly fashion clambers down onto the rocky shoreline to the water's edge.

'Yeah. That's it – I see them. Still plumbing the depths, they are.'

The detective follows him. Royston notices he suffers no such trouble in crossing the unforgiving terrain. He shades his eyes with his left hand as he looks along the lake.

Neither does the man have any difficulty with pregnant pauses, and Royston finds himself uttering another question that might be off limits.

'I take it you ain't got no – no identification – not yet?'

It is a few seconds more before the man replies.

'Female, early thirties, small and slim with long black hair.'

This time Royston's tingle is more of a tremor, and there is a palpitation in his chest – so much so that he sways unsteadily, and the lake seems to tilt.

'Ruddy heck. They never said that – on *Lakes Live*, I mean.'

13. ALLSPICE

Buttermere – 2.50 p.m.

WHEELING LEFT TOWARDS Buttermere village, in short order Skelgill strides past the entrance to Catthwaite Cottage, the holiday let. Jean Thackthwaite has advised him that a couple with pre-school children are in residence for the week. He would like a deek – about the grounds, as much as anything – but it can wait until the place is being cleaned on changeover day.

Passing the Hikers' Hostel, his eye is drawn by the industrious pied wagtails. They will often nest in a fellside cairn, and the part-collapsed corner of the wall is a fair imitation, a fortress vulnerable perhaps only to a marauding weasel, a merciless assassin the size of a small Cumberland sausage. The cock bird settles suspiciously on the rusted wrought-iron gate, which hangs on just its lower hinge, permanently open, tilted back and long overgrown by rambling roses and an untrimmed hawthorn hedge that borders the rising driveway.

He moves on, experiencing inner rumblings that are hard to define. In meeting a succession of people – he can't say *suspects* – it is hard to know which if any of them might be responsible for the sense of discord – because it may not manifest itself at the time. He glances up at the hostel. There was an air of the delinquent about Kevin Pope – and of holding something back. Royston Woodcock, the fresher in his mind, was also on edge. The balding little man might be substantially overweight and asthmatic, but he was sweating metaphorically. The small beady birder's eyes could not conceal inner machinations. And there is something unsavoury about Royston Woodcock.

But this is what folk can be like in the presence of the police. He has learned that, well enough. Even his pals in the pub are guarded at times, hoping he's not noticed they've had one too many to drive home, or got wind of an MOT or road tax that has run out.

Inner rumblings. They could of course be of the Pavlovian variety. That, before he is consciously aware, he is detecting the invisible tentacles of some baking aroma that ride the breeze to draw him towards his Ma's place. Then again, *baking* – that is more likely to be Aunt Renie – and it is she whom he has in mind.

Indeed, when he finds his mother's kitchen silent and abandoned, he follows his nose along the little terrace to Renie and Ernie's place – correction, now the *late* Ernie – to discover the venerable widows with an open Tupperware of Buttermere biscuits and a large pot of tea between them. He notices a mug and side plate at a spare seat and a glint in his mother's eye. Is he so predictable when he's in the vicinity? The church bell strikes three and salivation ensues.

'I were just telling Renie – weren't I, Reen? How oor Daniel's out to solve this lass-in-t'-lake case.'

Skelgill affects a show of modest awkwardness, of not counting chickens, and accompanies the little performance with a growl of exasperation. He finds it slightly disconcerting that his Ma refers to him in the third person.

However, he sits and holds steady his mug before the proffered teapot. No eyelids are batted here as he liberally spoons in sugar.

'There's lovely.'

Renie beams at him, admiringly but somewhat ingenuously for his liking. And that she employs a phrase of endearment from her sing-song Welsh vernacular for what is a macabre topic is additionally disconcerting. But he knows she intends encouragement.

He eyes her benignly; it is an expression that belies the underlying motive of the question he is forming.

'Aunt Renie, do you put allspice in your Christmas pudding?'

The watery blue eyes widen, though she answers candidly, and without hesitation.

'Well, now – I do. Is it a Christmas pudding, you're wanting? I can make you one – but it's a long way to Christmas – we've only just had Easter.'

Without looking at his Ma, he detects scepticism in her demeanour: he will not have changed the habit of a lifetime and suddenly developed a culinary interest that extends beyond consumption. But perhaps she also understands that he treads carefully. Renie, unlike his Ma, lacks prudence, dear arl lass though she is.

'What else do you put in it?'

With a little difficulty – such that Skelgill leans to help to shift her chair – Renie half-rises and reaches for a ring binder from a shelf beside the sink. Once seated, she finds the page – a small sheet of notepaper in faded handwriting inside one of the plastic sleeves.

'Oh – now – it's an old family recipe. I got it from my Nanna Ebbw Vale – that's what we called her. There was Nanna Ebbw Vale and Nanna Brynsadler. Where they lived, you see? *And* she gave me her recipe for Welsh cakes.'

Skelgill is affecting interest, though he doubts he convinces his Ma. Renie pores over the words, plainly missing her spectacles.

'You soak raisins and figs overnight in brandy, and next morning mix in suet, flour, sugar, salt, breadcrumbs, egg – and then the flavourings – orange zest, almonds, ginger, nutmeg and allspice – and a good helping of black treacle.'

Skelgill frowns. It is a long list of ingredients, and he will have to take a photograph.

Now he listens patiently. He begins to appreciate that the skill in Christmas pudding owes far less to the recipe than to what is a tortuous method. Its mere relating is a lecture. However, Renie finishes with a flourish.

'And a nice big dollop of your Ma's melting rum butter – and you lap it up, don't you, bach?'

He grins, sheepishly.

'And you have your stall – Christmas – in the village hall?'

'Of course – I never miss a year, do I, Minnie?'

Skelgill glances at his mother – she certainly harbours an insight into what might be afoot. He casts a hand towards the little kitchen window that looks upon the rising fellside behind the cottages.

'It was the Christmas before last – we had the bad snow – they called it The Big Freeze. Do you remember how many you made?'

Renie seems absorbed by the challenge.

'Half a dozen, normally – I'd make more – they're popular – but you have to prepare them four weeks ahead – and I haven't got the space, see?'

He nods obligingly.

'And how about who bought them?'

'Well, now –' She regards his mother, apologetically. 'You took one, didn't you, Minnie? You always insist on paying – though I wouldn't charge you – but it is all for charity. Then Doreen next door always buys one, and so does old Mrs Johnson from the farm – and they were both in early – before the snow started to get too deep. And the lady from Blackpool who runs the B&B – she took two – they had guests staying over Christmas.'

Skelgill is feeling a frisson of anticipation. This is too good to be true. Renie is systematically cataloguing her customer base.

But now she reaches for a biscuit and dunks it pensively. Sucking her teeth, she shakes her head.

'I really don't recall who had the other one. That's strange.' She raises the surviving half-biscuit. *Wait a minute* – I didn't stay till the end – did I, Minnie? Remember – because of the snow – and what with Ernie being gone – I slept at yourn on Christmas Eve, didn't I? I came back early and Edna who organised the fair waited and sold off the last of the stock – for a few of the stallholders.' She looks at Skelgill and then lowers her eyes. 'Course – she passed away last December – and her daughter Janice had to step in at the last minute.'

Skelgill drinks. He can't say why, but he feels a curious sense of relief. His mother is staring at him – but perhaps she misguidedly reads disappointment. It is tempting to spill the beans – to elaborate on the investigation. But he reminds himself there is no need, and winks at her.

He reaches for another Buttermere biscuit by way of complimenting his Aunt Renie on their moreishness.

14. VOICEMAIL

Passing Crummock Water – 3.20 p.m.

BRUSHING CRUMBS FROM his lap, Skelgill keeps his eyes on the winding road as he passes through Hause Point, Crummock Water perilously to his left, were it not for the retaining wall. He is thinking how much easier it would be to deposit a corpse here than in Buttermere. There are stopping places aplenty, and the lake is larger and deeper than its near neighbour. Though it is true to say that for the same reasons divers come here more often. With all their gear, they want to be able to park their vans by the shore and get on with their hobby.

He is keeping half an eye on his mobile in its cradle. He intends to phone Jones. He is waiting for the signal to come in as he descends Lorton Vale. However, he is past the great green bulk of Grasmoor when a single bar appears. And before he can search her number an alert tells him there is a voicemail waiting.

It might be her.

He presses play.

"Inspector, hello – it's Lena – you know?" A pause, a throaty purr. "I'm sorry to have missed you. I got your note. I'll be home for a while, if you are able to call back round. I have been wondering – if perhaps I do have a little piece of your jigsaw. I'm alone – at the moment."

The carefully enunciated English accent conjures an image of their meeting – of the long veil of hair shading the sultry eyes and dark complexion; of the shapely form – and then of the flimsy yoga outfit shifting in the breeze.

The message ends with what sounds like an intake of breath, before the woman hangs up. On the screen he recognises the landline number that her housemate Valentina White had written on her business card. The call is timed at just under an hour ago. He must have narrowly missed her.

And now the little morsel of dangled bait.

How long is *home for a while?*

He drives, unseeing. The road is above familiar. Every second takes him further away. He feels stretched on elastic.

It breaks.

DS Jones's ringtone.

He grimaces. If he turns now, he might lose the signal.

He punches a finger at the handset – but finds his mouth dry.

'Guv?'

He swallows with difficulty. He puts it down to that last biscuit. He clears his throat.

'Happen I've saved you a job, lass.'

'And which one would that be?'

She has a smile in her voice.

'You can forget the supermarkets. The Christmas pudding was made in the village. It's bang on Aunt Renie's family recipe – right down to allspice. I've photographed her kitchen cookbook.'

'Wow.'

Skelgill is conscious of having cut to the chase; pleasantries dispensed with. But he might as well continue.

'They hold a charity fair every Christmas Eve in the Old Schoolhouse. There were six Christmas puddings. Three went to locals that we can write off, two to Ellerbeck B&B. One's unaccounted for.'

DS Jones has hit the ground running.

'What about the B&B – did they have guests?'

'All returned alive the following year. I'll text you a photo of the visitors' book when I stop. They were older folk that stayed indoors because of the snow. But one of them's a single chap with a dog. He must have gone out. Better check he's not wanted for serial murder.'

DS Jones laughs – but in a way that indicates she will do just that. The methodical approach is their stock fallback. Skelgill continues.

'Have you got a pen?'
'There's more?'
It seems she can tell he has more.
She is right.
'There's a bit of a raft of stuff.'
'I'm actually on the move – but I'll remember.'
Skelgill hesitates. He makes a doubtful face. Then he proceeds.
'Call the Cumbria Cottage Company. Check that it was the owners that stayed at Catthwaite Cottage over the Christmas period. Name of McLeish from Edinburgh. Lawyers. Speak to them, if you can. The cleaner spun me some yarn about them giving her black bun.'
'*Black bun?*'
'Seems it's a Scotch Christmas pudding.'
'Okay. I think I see where you're coming from.'
'I collared the manager of the Hikers' Hostel. Shady bloke in his thirties. Manc. Hiding summat – I didn't press him. He reckons they were shut – that they close at Christmas so the staff can get home.'
'I'll contact their head office, and then see if we've got anything on him.'
'I flushed out the birdman. Royston Woodcock. Southerner – sounds like Leyton. He was sitting in bushes with a long lens, pretending to photograph squirrels.'
'Pretending?'
Skelgill exhales in frustration.
'Gave us a load of flannel about birds on the lake. I wouldn't put it past him that people are his preferred prey. He was out taking photos on the Christmas Day in question – he admits to that.'
'But he saw nothing?'
'A smew.'
'It sounds like a strange marsupial.'
'Cross between a duck and a crocodile.'
DS Jones murmurs with amusement.
'Okay. I'll see what I can do. Anything else?'

'Aye, maybe. Find out whether Hassness Castle was occupied. They host outward bound courses. I doubt it, over Christmas. And find out when their last building work was done. Looks like a kitchen extension. Depending on timing, we might need to get Forensics in to take some samples.'

'*Samples?*'

It is plain that – to DS Jones's mind – Skelgill has suddenly upped the ante.

'There's an abandoned pile of blocks and timber out the back – wrapped in polythene and tied down with rope.'

'Oh.'

There is gravity in her single word, such that Skelgill makes an adjustment, his rejoinder tending towards the lukewarm.

'Don't get your hopes up – that kind of stuff's ten a penny.'

'Still – you never know.'

'Aye, well – we'll see.'

'You've been busy.'

'Keeps us out of temptation.' After a moment, he adds a qualification. 'I'm reliving my youth – sneaking round all these places.'

DS Jones has a question on her mind.

'You didn't call at the writer's cottage again? To ask them about Christmas.'

Skelgill makes an involuntary face, unseen by his colleague and of uncertain meaning to himself.

'I knocked in passing. There was no one home. We'll need to go back.'

DS Jones murmurs again – a reflective precursor to a suggestion, for which he has provided a small opening.

'Guv – I'd find it useful – you know, to get the lie of the land?'

'Aye.'

It does not sound like an objection.

'Why don't I get onto these points – get the team moving – and maybe tomorrow I could meet you there – Buttermere – and bring you up to speed?'

'Race you round the lake, if you like.'

She chuckles.

'Will I need boots?'

'Trainers are fine. It's mostly flat and no wading's required. Unless you want to cheat and swim across.'

*

A bookshop twice in a day. It must be a record. DS Jones would be impressed.

It strikes him now that his colleague never said why she rang. That he had intended to call her had formed reason enough for their conversation. Striding the short distance from his favoured parking spot on the isthmus, Skelgill now replays in his mind the voice message from Lena Longstaff. The sound, the tone, the timbre – the impression is fading – supplanted by his colleague's mellow Cumbrian brogue.

When he might have turned back, he had driven on.

He was already past Low Lorton, well on the way to Cockermouth – and keeping going had seemed the thing to do. Lena Longstaff's *home for a while* had surely expired. Besides, Valentina White is just as likely to be able to enlighten him regarding the Christmas Day in question.

He enters Paige Turner's to see that the cash desk is unstaffed – but it suits him to approach the food counter. It is the same waitress as this morning. She appears to recognise him – and is, he detects, a little intrigued. On this occasion, he waits for his order.

Receiving his tray, he hands over a ten-pound note.

'Stick the change in the jar, lass.'

His offer receives approval, and he moves to capitalise upon the enhanced goodwill.

'I was wondering – is Valentina still about?'

His question engenders a conspiratorial smile.

'I haven't seen her since she had the bacon-and-lentil soup for lunch. She went to the book depository.'

Skelgill plays down his interest.

'Where is that, again?'

The waitress names a street in Gote, the conjoined settlement on the flood plain, just across the Derwent. He knows the cluster of industrial units.

'We keep all our spare stock there. And rarer books that are in the online catalogue.'

Skelgill nods.

'Would you like me to pass on a message?'

There is just a hint in her tone of some hoped-for salaciousness.

'Nay – nay bother. Thanks, all the same.'

He meanders with his tray. The café and bookshop facilities are intermingled, with clusters of tables in sections by genre. He gives the kiddies' zone a wide berth and finds a secluded corner marked "Natural History & Gardening".

He lays down his tray but instead of sitting turns to a shelf labelled "Ornithology". After several false starts he settles on a fairly hefty tome that, by weight, seems to contradict its own jacket claim to be *'The definitive field guide to British Birds'*.

Now he settles down. He flicks. Squints. Scowls. Absently, he works his way through his slice of Kendal ginger cake, washing down each mouthful with strong sweet tea.

He finishes the tasks simultaneously.

He closes the book – and with his cuff rubs at finger marks on its glossy cover.

He rises and replaces it, and departs, his expression contemplative.

Incongruous as it seems for a species so ungainly on land, the goosander does nest in tree holes. Red-breasted merganser is maritime outside the breeding season. And smew is a scarce winter visitor, mainly to reservoirs in southeast England.

It's said a person knows their onions; certainly, Royston Woodcock knows his sawbills.

WEDNESDAY

30ᵀᴴ APRIL

15. ABEL KETCH

Whitehaven – 9.20 a.m.

NOT ANOTHER DAMNED reporter. That fancy dan from the *Gazette* had come close to getting a knuckle sandwich. Abel Ketch grinds his teeth. If only Bob hadn't started yatterin' in the bar at Buttermere. But he supposes it was shock, and the double whisky that local bought them. And it drew a crowd, that they'd burst in wearing dripping wetsuits and demanding to phone 999.

'Alright, mate?'

The man, short, stocky – a little well padded, actually – speaks with an accent that announces he is not from around here. A Londoner, by the sound of it. A suit that's not a great fit. A certain air of determination. Looks like he could ride a punch. A little black notebook in one hand. What if he's from one of the nationals – *The Sun* or the *Daily Mirror*?

Just as Abel is beginning to wonder what a national newspaper might pay, there is a deft flourish and he finds himself glowering at a police warrant card.

'DS Leyton, Cumbria CID – I spoke with your diving oppo. It's Mr Ketch, right?'

'Aye. Aye, it is.'

Abel softens his face of discontent and loosens his grip on the wrench he has been holding and lays it down on the workbench. He shifts a little uncomfortably from one foot to the other, conscious that the police officer's gaze has taken in the surroundings, and that there are centrefolds pinned to the wall of the dank workshop that do not garner unanimous approval.

However, the man grins affably.

'Sorry I didn't give you any notice, sir. Looks like there was an error transcribing your mobile number. We need to take a witness statement, as you were among the first to find the body. I shall only be five minutes, if you can spare the time.'

Abel knows this has been coming. He may as well get it over and done with. He's quiet today, until he collects the Maxum powerboat at lunchtime. But he feels obliged to throw in a token objection.

'Have you not got the story from Bob?'

'Yeah – he's given a statement, has Mr Tapp – but two people never see quite the same thing. Sometimes a small detail can make all the difference to an investigation.' Now the detective looks at him a little apologetically. 'Besides, we have to tick all the boxes to keep the powers-that-be happy.'

The man seems genuine enough. Abel realises he is beginning to scowl, and counters the impression with a compliant nod.

'I've not heard who she is, yet – there's bin nowt on t' news.'

The policeman regards him with a wide-eyed look.

'Truth be told, sir – we don't know, not yet. There's tests being done that might identify her.'

Abel affects a shiver – it might come across as a shudder, he's not sure – but he turns away and grabs his oil-smeared denim shirt from a hook and shrugs it on. He tries to do it casually, but senses the detective is observing his movements.

'Do you want to come into t' waiting room? It's not much, but there's seats and a kettle.'

'I'm fine for a drink, sir – but if there's a table I can lean on, that would help.'

Abel points the way through the side door into the lean-to. With its windows onto the boatyard it is brighter, and the detective is still blinking as he takes a seat and flattens out his notebook. Abel watches as he begins to write the date in tiny, neat print that is incongruous with his bulk and demeanour.

'Down to brass tacks, then, sir. We've got your name and date of birth from the officer who spoke to you at the scene. If I could just take your address. And correct this mobile number.'

Jenny's name's still on the rent book at the flat – and he's never bothered to fill in the electoral register forms. Abel gives his Ma's address. It's where his driving licence is registered. He'd better call round on his Ma later to tell her.

'I believe you chose Buttermere because you'd had this idea to dive all the lakes in alphabetical order?'

Abel feels himself frowning. Is there a second point embedded in the broader question?

'Aye – it were Bob's idea.'

The detective seems briefly to hesitate, but he does not write anything down.

'And I believe you drove there separately?'

'We were coming from the complete opposite directions. We met at the car park at Buttermere. Got us gear ready, walked round the public path to the north end of t' lake. It's like a pebble beach. Just waded in from there.'

The detective does note this description. Abel supposes he'll ask him to sign it at the end.

'Did you have a plan of what you were going to do?'

Abel rubs the stubble beneath his jaw with the backs of his fingers.

'Not especially. Decided we'd swim to t' end and back. It's not much above a mile. It gradually shelves down. We were following a comms cable – power cable – summat like that. There in't much to see in Buttermere. That's why it's hardly ever dived. That and because you can't park up close by.'

The detective is writing. He looks up, and glances about outside.

'Why wouldn't you use a boat?'

The question sounds sincere. And, he supposes, why would a Londoner – a city type – know the answer? He finds himself grinning, if a little acerbically.

'Ever tried getting aboard a boat wearing a wetsuit and Nitrox tanks?'

The detective splutters.

'Nah, mate – I ain't even tried getting *out* of one. I like water like cats like water.'

Abel feels a tinge of empathy – and is encouraged by the man's candid admission.

'You need at least another person. Even then, there's a danger you'll just capsize. Most hobby divers like us don't use boats – not for freshwater dives.'

The detective takes notes accordingly.

'Anything about what you saw – or where the body was – from your diving experience – that struck you as unusual?'

Abel is thinking that a body is unusual – but he knows that is not what the man means. In this respect he honestly can't think of anything to say. It was dark at seventy-five foot and they were getting close to needing a decompression stop before they could surface. Then there was the grisly moment when Bob beckoned him forward and they lit up the ghostly face under the polythene with their torches. He knew he hadn't wanted to look.

The detective is waiting, pen poised.

He shrugs.

'Nowt, really – except I suppose it weren't t' deepest part of t' lake.'

'No?'

'Further towards the southern end – it's a hundred foot. If you look on a diving map, it's called The Hole.'

The detective seems interested in this point. He presses the end of the pen against the centre of his clean-shaven chin, forming a dimple in the ample flesh.

'So, what you're saying, sir – is that if you knew the lake, that's the spot you'd pick – The Hole?'

Abel shrugs again, more theatrically.

'I reckon so.'

Now the copper makes a mark in the margin – it is not a word Abel can identify upside down.

'I take it you've dived the lake before, sir – that's how you know the lie of the land?'

Abel nods.

'When you're starting out – you tend to go round them all – then find your favourites – some are a lot easier to reach, and more interesting than others. Wastwater's probably t' best – but it's a bit of a pain to get to – especially for Bob, for where he bides.'

The officer is nodding appreciatively; but Abel knows he has not entirely provided the desired response. He waits for the direct prompt.

'Can you recall when you were last at Buttermere?'

He has a ready answer.

'It were in our first year in t' club – above four year ago. Bob were a novice, you see – so we picked the shallower lakes that posed fewer risks.'

The detective seems a little surprised by this explanation. His confusion becomes clear.

'I thought as Mr Tapp was leading the dive he was the more experienced?'

'I were in t' Royal Navy. That's where I trained – I were a mine clearance diver.'

The detective exhales – it seems with genuine admiration.

'Cor blimey, rather you than me, mate. Deep water's bad enough – but chuck in explosives. Jeez, I take me hat off to you.'

Abel affects a degree of modesty that he doesn't feel.

The detective casts a hand beyond the grimy glass of the waiting room.

Abel follows the indication. There stand two craft, one on chocks and the other upended. His Toyota pick-up has seen better days and will likely fail its next MOT, and the trailer tethered to it needs new tyres.

'Is that how come you got into this business? The navy, I mean.'

Abel detects no ulterior motive in the question.

'Aye – I were thinking of starting up a diving school. But you'd need to be lakeside. Plus there's more year-round trade in fixing boats – and no customers getting the bends to worry about.'

The detective flashes him a somewhat chary look – and he realises his throwaway remark is not in the best possible taste. But before he can make a correction, the officer's mobile phone rings.

The detective makes a face, indicating he must take the call. He remains seated, however, first listening to what might be a male voice, though Abel cannot make out the words.

'Alright, George? Yeah – I'm just finishing off a witness statement. Be a couple of minutes.'

He listens again.

'Yeah – well, he probably ain't got no signal. Neither of them – if they're together.'

Another pause.

'Yeah – right you are. I'll drive straight there.' He checks his wristwatch. 'Tell the lads I'll be no later than eleven.'

He hangs up and frowns at his notes – though he does not appear unduly alarmed by whatever news he has received. Certainly it seems to have nothing to do with Abel. He looks like he's trying to remember what else he ought to ask. Then he taps his pen on the open page.

'The diving club – would they know who else might have visited Buttermere?'

Abel sees no harm in answering the question to the best of his ability.

'Maybe if there'd been an organised trip – but I'm not aware of it – they're more likely to go to Windermere, or Wastwater. There's some who keep their own logs – but there's folk as come t' Lakes from all ower, not just locals.'

The officer nods evenly – quite likely the police have already worked this out. Clearly, it is an inconvenient reality.

'What about yourself and Mr Tapp – what's the next one on your list?'

Abel finds himself scowling again. It is not an objection to the question so much as what he considers to be the right response. He's thinking it must be Crummock Water, a mere mile from Buttermere – and it would seem disrespectful – until he remembers Coniston Water is next – but that was where Donald Campbell died breaking the water speed record in 1967 ... and where his body lay undiscovered until 2001. What must it have been like, after thirty-odd years?

105

'You alright, sir? You look a bit pale. I understand if you'll be giving it a break for a while – it must have been a shock for the pair of you.'

When the detective has gone, Abel finds himself absently rubbing at his forearm as he reflects on their meeting. He pulls down the sleeve. The officer seemed straight enough – but he remembers a crafty Cockney or two from his time at sea.

16. LAKE WALK

Buttermere – 10.20 a.m.

SKELGILL AND DS JONES, in coming together, look like they do not quite know how they ought to greet one another, their surroundings – the two Buttermere inns and a walkers' café, a confusing arrangement where farmyard and public parking collide without obvious demarcation – being populated by the occasional hiker, or small group thereof who might ogle them. Indeed, were they about to make physical contact – which is how it may have seemed to an onlooker watching the rendezvous – any such intention is rudely interrupted by the roar of a quad bike – which has Skelgill both hopping backwards and heaving with him the five-barred farm gate that he may have been about to open in a more considered fashion. DS Jones, for her part, skips nimbly aside in the opposing direction.

'Alreet, young Daniel, lad!'

Skelgill begins to salute the gnarled gap-toothed rider who, without any intent to decelerate, swerves through the narrow aperture, lifting onto two wheels and remarkably losing neither the bale of straw that must obscure much of his view nor the sheepdog perched perilously on the pillion. Skelgill's hand action becomes more like the flourish of a chequered flag.

Cackling, the farmer speeds away. They observe as he recedes from view, leaving terrorised unsuspecting walkers and a cloud of dust trailing in his wake.

Skelgill flashes a grin at his colleague. Now chivalrously he waves her through the gate. Hauling it to, he leans over to fasten it diligently – though he knows that despite hand-painted entreaties referring to the lambing season this status is unlikely to last for long.

They follow the route taken by the quad. The farm track doubles as the public right of way to the lake. There is a dry crunch as they trudge the alluvial plain – such flat ground a rare commodity in the Lakes, which Skelgill points out. How often do you have both feet on the same level? They pass tiny black Herdwick lambs in pastures – DS Jones coos over one nesting amidst ample fleece on its recumbent mother's back. White blackthorn blossom is just going over, while beneath the hedgerows fresh bursts of lemony primroses punctuate thrusting herbaceous greenery. Astride a golden spike of a gorse, a pink-breasted chaffinch belts out a hearty if not entirely mellifluous ditty that ends in a tumbling crescendo.

DS Jones is prompted to comment.

'Isn't that supposed to be like the tempo of a cricketer running up to bowl?'

Skelgill relays his opinion via a frown. He prefers to believe he has a silkier approach to the wicket.

But they are each content to take in the spring morning – they look a sight more like a pair of walkers than murder detectives – even DS Jones, who is more prone than Skelgill to appear in an outfit befitting of her role is this morning clad entirely in outdoor gear with a sports influence. A slinky Nike top when Skelgill makes do with well-worn Berghaus seconds.

It is DS Jones that first seems pressed by their progress – the lake is heaving into sight, along with the suggestion that it is a landmark that will require an alternative agenda.

'Before we start – I took a call from the station on the way here. There's possible misper. A thirty-two-year-old woman from Manchester who fits the description, in general appearance. Martina Radu, said to be of Eastern European descent. She had no criminal record – there's no fingerprints or DNA. DC Watson is trying to trace relatives with a view to obtaining a familial DNA match. But she may have been living under an assumed name. She was last seen in October before the Christmas in question, but not reported missing until the following June, approaching a year ago – by a housemate, when it came to paying a factoring bill. The report states that the address had been raided for drugs, although it's not known if she had any involvement. The property is a large old villa divided up, with individual rooms rented out. The housemate believed she regularly visited a relative in Kendal by train – and may have gone there and never came back.'

Skelgill has listened unemotionally – but his concentration is betrayed by his unfocused gaze.

'What makes her a missing person?'

'I know – I thought that myself. It's not as if she has abandoned a relationship or a job. But she is on the system, she matches the description, she has background irregularities, and she could have been coming to the Lakes.'

Skelgill is silent as they close in on the shoreline.

DS Jones sounds a note of optimism.

'It would be a neat solution.'

He chooses to answer obliquely.

'If Smart gets a sniff of the words Manchester and drugs he'll be here like a rat up a drainpipe.'

DS Jones inhales – hesitates – then speaks.

'The word is that he's struggling to make any progress with a county lines case that has its roots in the Greater Manchester area.'

Skelgill growls.

'Exactly.'

The path trifuricates. There is the option of the route north to Crummock Water, or straight ahead the scramble skywards up beside Sourmilk Gill, to Bleaberry Tarn and Red Pike beyond. They take the third prong, a sharp left towards the northern shallows of Buttermere. The ground hereabouts is of an indistinct nature; it has an intertidal look of short turf, exposed roots and shingle, and stranded logs.

For Skelgill this is a familiar scene, but less so for DS Jones. One of the most photographed views in the Lake District, it graces many a calendar. The near-perfect pyramid of Fleetwith Pike thrusts centre stage between the twin V-shaped valleys of Gatesgarthdale and Warnscale, its sharply crested ridge seeming to rise from the plane of the lake, its inverted image captured in perfect symmetry in Buttermere's mirrored surface.

He watches, a little reluctantly, as she takes out her mobile phone – is it such an Instagrammable spot that here comes the inevitable selfie? But instead she uses the camera conventionally, and stoops low, resting upon a beached log to compose a shot that begins with a foreground of shattered grey Skiddaw slate, and takes in a series of semi-submerged smooth black boulders, Borrowdale volcanics, hard rocks brought intact by the long-melted glacier.

He hears her murmur of satisfaction – and what she has seen is revealed when she approaches with the handset.

'Very clever.'

He cannot suppress a grin – she has produced a more-than-passable rendering of the Loch Ness monster, its four slick humps with the trace of a wake caused by a light zephyr that gives the impression of movement.

'That's all we'd need, lass.'

'You mean another crowd-puller?'

'Aye.'

'I'm surprised there aren't spectators about. It was on the TV news again last night – and the radio this morning. But I don't see the diving unit. Perhaps they've called it a day.'

She gazes down the lake, shading her eyes.

When she looks back at Skelgill he has turned ninety degrees and is staring intently. She follows his line of sight. Visible above the trees that fringe the shore, low on the fellside there is a cluster of grey stone gables and angular rooftops of darker slate.

'What is it, Guv?'

'Mind Kevin Pope reckoned he's from Manchester. And he said he came in the October.'

'The year before last?'

He nods.

'Two more little coincidences.' DS Jones pauses reflectively, then resumes. 'But I did uncover some background relating to his previous position.'

Skelgill cocks his head.

'Let's walk and talk. Else we'll never get round.'

'Sure.'

They cross the foot of the lake and scramble up onto the shore path, distinctive now as it weaves between bankside alders. A denser stand of trees, birch and oak and mixed conifers, rises gently to their left.

'You suggested Kevin Pope was shady.'

'Just a feeling I got, like.'

'I checked our records before I contacted his employer. At his previous post there was an unsubstantiated complaint of voyeurism made against him – and a peephole was found in the showers. When he was questioned they found marijuana in his possession. He was cautioned, but it's not clear from the Shropshire police report why it was taken no further – but it might explain why he was transferred to Cumbria. I couldn't get through to anyone in the company's HR department who had authority to release his personnel records. However, they did confirm that the Buttermere hostel is always closed over Christmas, and that staff take mandatory leave.'

She looks at Skelgill.

He speaks after a while.

'I didn't press him on where he was.'

Uncharacteristically, Skelgill sounds a little crestfallen – but DS Jones is quick to correct any misapprehension.

'It's okay – I get why you wouldn't.'

Skelgill throws her a sideways glance and possibly the hint of a secretive grin.

She understands such unobtrusiveness. He is sniffing out lairs, building up a picture of the area, and of what might be possible. He has directed her to investigate behind the scenes. He will have left an impression of casual disinterest – his method he describes as the 'daft country copper'. Though she wonders – it is perhaps not as convincing as he thinks. A certain steel underlies even his most affected mild manner.

Now he waves a hand to their left; she sees only trees.

'Beyond – there's a fence and a gate to Ellerbeck.'

He points more precisely and she discerns a faint path – though not one in regular use.

'The bed and breakfast itself?'

The name, like many hereabouts, doubles for the local landform as well as the property that occupies it. Indeed, a brook trickles through; it is the beck in question. Eller meaning alder; ergo the stream through the alders. The stretch of woodland, too, is known as Ellerbeck Wood.

'Aye.'

Now DS Jones appears amused.

'What?'

'Oh – Dr Herdwick – he was most entertained by your theory of the Christmas pudding. He said you made it sound like we've got a Conan Doyle mystery on our hands.'

Skelgill seems offended by such flippancy and prepares to counter – but she interjects.

'Don't worry – he thinks you're right. Not least that they've found a tiny piece of glitter in the shape of an angel, amongst the stomach contents. Even better than a sixpence.'

Skelgill clears the beck and turns to offer a hand – it is a sign that he relents.

Accordingly, DS Jones continues.

'He likened it to a partial DNA profile. Subtract the foods that would either have been quickly digested at the time, or naturally dissolved or degraded by bacteria – the suet, flour, sugar, salt, breadcrumbs, egg – and what's left is exactly your aunt's family recipe. The fact that there is no additional ingredient is particularly telling. I've searched recipes online – I stopped after about a dozen – and every single one has something extraneous, some spice or nut or fruit that would likely have survived.'

She glances at Skelgill. They are having to prop and cop as the path contracts in places, and winds, and rises and falls over protruding rocks and roots. He looks both pleased with himself and perhaps also alarmed by the prospect – as if he did not really believe this aspect could have been so telling.

DS Jones reverts to the next item in her itinerary.

'Mr Black?'

'The serial killer.'

She casts him a reproachful glance.

'DC Watson is still trying – but yesterday she had no joy in locating him. The address he had written in the B&B's guest book is incomplete. The street exists – Bannockburn Drive in Fylde – but there's no house number and his name is not coming up on the electoral register. She's running more checks this morning – DVLA, DWP, et cetera.'

'Fylde's part of Blackpool.'

'Yes.'

'He's an old customer – and they used to have their B&B in Blackpool. They were on his doorstep.'

'I realised that. I mean – I know I'll need to speak with him. But I assumed if he's a single older chap – no relatives to go to at Christmas – the appeal of a regular home-from-home is understandable. They move – he follows.'

Skelgill has stopped and is staring at a stranded shoreline alder – where there was once earth bank the ground is now eroded to leave a myriad of exposed roots. There are logs washed up by winter floods in what is a tiny bay. A wyke.

But now he nods and moves on, seemingly accepting her explanation; it is more or less what he was told by Betty Hindlewake.

'Aye – we should talk to him.' He casts an arm about. 'He might be a witness – if he walked the dog here – he'd have been one of the few folk about. It'd be dark by four – and he'd need to let it out last thing.'

DS Jones is nodding in agreement.

'The other guests seem bona fide and pretty harmless – and the owners are certainly longstanding in the trade.' She smiles to herself. 'There are one or two entertaining reviews on Tripadvisor. I think mainly down to the antics of Mr Hindlewake.'

Skelgill's interest is piqued.

'Such as?'

113

'Oh – well. I get the impression he's a stickler for rules and likes to get his money out of every bar of soap. There were separate references to the Gestapo and the Spartans.'

Skelgill raises an eyebrow. Thinking back to his encounter, what would he say about the man? Indignant, uppity – and also a little cagey? But he did not detect sinister – which he couldn't say of either Kevin Pope or Royston Woodcock.

But they have made progress and DS Jones notices another path and, through a gap in trees, fifty yards distant a gate and something of a fence. There is a wild cherry in full bloom that endows a quaint ambience.

'Which property is that?'

'By the gean?' Skelgill uses the country name for the tree. 'Catthwaite Cottage. The holiday home.'

It seems to DS Jones that it will be convenient to relate her findings as they pass each residence in turn.

'I found out about black bun.'

'Aye?'

'You were right about the Scots origin. It's basically a very dense fruitcake, packed with currants and baked in a pastry case.'

'What, like a pie?'

'It seems so.'

'A cake in pastry?'

'Scotland is the land of the deep-fried Mars Bar. I seem to remember you showed me.'

'Aye, well, there is that.'

'That it was a branded product helped. I found the ingredients list online. There was some overlap with your aunt's Christmas pudding recipe, but not enough to be mistaken for it. Apparently black bun is popular as a first-footing gift.'

Skelgill revisits his conversation with charlady Jean Thackthwaite. It had not been a hit with her husband.

DS Jones waits a moment for his attention to return.

'The cottage rental company confirmed that no public bookings are taken over the festive period. Then I got hold of the co-owner, Mrs McLeish. She said they've come for nine Christmases in a row. It's the family tradition. The year before last, she confirmed they were snowed in – and didn't leave the property between Christmas Eve and the day after Boxing Day. The kids – a boy and a girl, twins who were then aged twelve – had a ball, making snowmen, snowball fights, sledging. There's a big enough garden with a good slope. They forbade them from going near the lake – by strict instruction when they were playing out on their own.'

As they proceed Skelgill has taken to staring across the water, a flickering view between the attenuated bankside alders. He makes no response.

DS Jones offers a prompt.

'You've not asked me if they bought the missing Christmas pudding.'

'Did they?'

She shakes her head.

'They brought their own – they had a hamper. Same make as the black bun. Anyway – she said they arrived too late on Christmas Eve to go to the local fair. They only just made it through the snow – despite that they have a long-wheelbase Defender.'

'New Town tractor.'

'I'm sorry?'

'It's what Cammy calls them. Edinburgh New Town – the posh part – it's got more Defenders than the surrounding county.'

DS Jones waves a palm abstractedly.

'I was thinking of him – in case we should need a local enquiry.'

Skelgill seems to smile fondly – but perhaps becomes self-aware and replaces it with a small grimace.

Shortly, he extends his left arm – the sudden action perhaps puts to flight the hen pheasant that simultaneously bursts from the undergrowth and glides low over the bracken and bluebells that carpet the glade.

'Woodcock.'

DS Jones hesitates, a little startled.

'For a second I thought you were identifying the bird.'

Skelgill shrugs.

'You occasionally get them, woodcock. It's a wader – but classed as game. Got a bit of a tack to it, like partridge.'

She nods, not quite sufficiently diverted.

'So, that's Pike Rigg Cottage through there?'

Again, there is the semblance of a path. A worn line of exposed leaf mould snakes between trunks and disappears from sight.

'Woodcock's place.'

'What's he like?'

'Funny-looking bald guy, sixty-mark, short, tubby, little beady eyes. Wheezing – weighed down by clobber – whacking great telephoto lens.'

It is not quite what DS Jones is after.

'You weren't convinced he's a genuine twitcher.'

'Cancel that.'

Skelgill offers no further explanation.

'Okay. Then what about your suspicion – that he spies on people?'

Now he is more considered in his response; indeed, guarded.

'What did you get?'

She turns out her bottom lip.

'He's completely clean, as far as all the basics go. An expired disclosure certificate from Kent Constabulary – he was cleared to give wildlife talks to local groups. A few minor motoring offences; that's it. We also checked with HM Land Registry – he bought the property freehold five years ago. There's no mortgage. No debts registered, no CCJs.'

Skelgill makes a face that might be a small admission of misjudgement.

'Happen it were just the long lens that mithered us.'

His use of the full vernacular makes DS Jones look hard at him – it is a form of regression she recognises when he is testing out a proposition on the hoof.

She holds her peace.

They continue circumspectly, not hurrying as Skelgill might normally appear to do, in the way of a person that habitually listens to audio recordings at one-and-a-half speed.

After a minute or so, she introduces her deferred point.

'He told you he took photographs on Christmas Day.'

Skelgill looks across at her.

It is a knowing glance – they do not need to exchange the words – such material might be worth looking at. It would not be the first time a crime has been captured in the corner of an innocently taken photo.

Skelgill casually indicates again.

'Hassness Cottage.'

She notes that while he has once more signalled left, he is looking right, where a patch of open ground extends into the shallows, a small grassy islet like a fairy stage.

She cannot see any more through the trees here than at the properties passed thus far. Nor has Skelgill asked her to do any background digging on the two young women who live there.

Indeed, he has quickened his step.

He stops and turns and although she inhales to make a query he pre-empts her.

'Howay, lass. Come and see this.'

They have reached Hassness itself, the wooded spur of high ground that juts out into Buttermere. Ness being Old Norse for headland, then Hass was surely its erstwhile Viking overlord. Commanding the high ground, Hassness Castle likely rests on the foundations of a much earlier stronghold. DS Jones sees that the path, hitherto meandering along a relatively broad strip, suddenly narrows as it approaches the rocky bluff – and seems to disappear. Then as Skelgill moves ahead she realises that a dark shadow on the fellside is in fact the entrance to a tunnel. He waits at the cleft.

'Wow – is this for real?'

'Unless you want to swim round the point.'

'How long is it?'

'Under a hundred paces.'

There is a small wooden sign affixed to the left of the entrance, its words just legible: "BEWARE Tunnel Roof is low at points."

Skelgill leads the way. She notices he automatically stoops, to be sure of not catching his head.

'Who made it?'

'Folk'll tell you it were some distant owner of Hassness Castle – when this land were part of the estate. Put his workers on the job when they were idle in winter.' Skelgill scoffs, as if this seems an unrealistic proposition. 'My arl fella reckoned it were nowt of the sort. There'd be a time when they needed to bring slate down from the mine at Honister. He reckoned they probably put in a little tramway – carts drawn by pit ponies – in the early 1700s. Gravity wouldn't let them go over Hassness – the obvious route was to stick it beside the mere. The pitmen would know how to handle gunpowder. It came from local savin charcoal at Sedgwick – it were ideal for blasting slate because it's a low explosive – doesn't shatter the rock to smithereens.'

She knows there are miners among his antecedents. And with the mountain rescue he trains for cave extractions. He moves confidently, but darkness begins to envelop them and she activates her mobile phone torch. It reveals roughly hewn walls; she can touch both sides and the ceiling easily, where in places there are braced pit props that look none-too-secure.

'How safe is this?'

Skelgill presents what in the shadows is a ghoulish face.

'A sight less likely to fall on you than the average old oak. And you don't think twice about walking under a tree.'

She murmurs unconvincingly.

He offers reassurance.

'We used to play murder games down here as bairns. Used to dare us selves to walk slowly through at night with no torch – or just a candle – that were almost as scary – you'd see shapes, imagine vampires and werewolves.'

Now she chuckles, if apprehensively.

'I understand what you meant when you said you were revisiting your childhood.'

'Aye – except the only thing that's missing is we've not been chased yet. Let's see if we can change that.'

And as they emerge from the passageway Skelgill veers off the path, away from the lake and attacks a steeply rising mossy cliff. He gains a ledge and offers a hand up. She accepts, though she would make it untroubled.

'Where are we going?'

'You said you wanted to get the lie of the land. May as well have a deek at Hassness Castle.'

It takes them several minutes to break through to the patch of overgrown lawn at the rear of the converted mansion. They arrive blinking at the white walls reflecting the morning spring sunshine that slants into the dale. From the ground beneath a branch-hung feeder, a couple of woodpigeons take flight in a battering of white-flashing wings.

Skelgill reaches to touch DS Jones on the arm – it is a warning sign, and she stops dead. Then she sees what he is looking at.

'*Oh – yes.* That's lovely.'

A red squirrel hunches on the shelf of the feeder, expertly shelling peanuts. They sidle away judiciously, so as not to disturb its breakfast.

'That was empty yesterday.'

DS Jones casts a backwards glance. So there was more to Skelgill's reaction than the sight of the cute native rodent.

'Do you think there's someone staying here?'

Skelgill takes a moment to answer.

'Might be one of Woodcock's. I shan't be surprised if he's got feeding stations secreted about these woods. Hidey holes nearby. Might be watching us now.'

But he is not entirely serious and he leads the way unhesitatingly. The lawn ends in a steep slope, almost like a ha-ha, and they reach the new extension and the incomplete foundations. He turns, his expression inquiring.

She understands it is for her to elaborate.

'I have an explanation – and one that probably suits us. I got through to the property director of the holding company.

Christmas before last, the place was closed for renovation – for the whole of December. That was when the kitchen extension was built. So there were no guests or staff here.'

'What about the builders? What about this?'

Skelgill gestures to the gaping soil pipes clogged with leaves. He strides over to the stack of materials roped under the polythene and gives it a tap with the toe of his left boot.

'It's a small local contractor based in Cockermouth. Alfred Lord & Sons. I spoke to the owner. He says they weren't on site. They were scheduled to wrap up on Christmas Eve and not come back until the first week of January. They didn't even work on Christmas Eve because the snow began to fall – and after New Year there was a thick crust of frozen snow and they were further held up.' Skelgill inhales to object – but she anticipates his question. 'It seems there is some enduring dispute over a bill – and that's why the remainder of the job has been mothballed.'

Skelgill is scowling.

'It's a long time to be mothballed. More like suspended animation.'

She is nodding.

'We can look into it, if you like. I considered the key point to be that there was no one here over the Christmas period. You know – a house party of twenty, plus staff? It would give us a headache.'

Skelgill tugs at the rope that secures the weathered polythene sheeting.

It is plain to his colleague that he is turning over in his mind the inevitable comparison with the way the woman's corpse had been wrapped.

'I did ask Mr Lord who supplies their materials. It's a builders' merchant in Whitehaven.'

Skelgill gives a parting kick to the pile of blocks and turns away.

'This isn't going anywhere in a hurry.'

She murmurs agreement. He means should they yet decide to take samples for comparison.

They are mainly silent as they regain the shoreline path. After a while, it is Skelgill who raises what might be on his mind.

'Yesterday – when I phoned you. Are you sure you didn't write all that down?'

She smiles sweetly.

'Maybe I recorded our conversation.'

'Did you?'

She makes a sound of disapproval.

'That's the sort of underhand thing DI Smart would do.'

Skelgill grimaces.

'He'd do owt to gain an advantage.'

They each reflect in silence. They are nearing the point where the narrow road from Buttermere up to Honister Pass briefly approaches lakeside. DS Jones is first to make an observation.

'Oh – there's the divers' boat. That's why we didn't see them out on the lake.'

The craft, a RIB of twenty feet or so, is beached. A uniformed officer is managing the cones and directing occasional traffic. Part-blocking the lane are the divers' truck and trailer, a second marked police car, and a haphazardly parked civilian vehicle.

Now Skelgill exclaims.

'That's Leyton's motor. What's he doing here?'

There is a small group of figures on the shoreline. They seem to be clustered around some object at their feet. It is DS Jones who answers.

'That's him – speaking with the divers. They've found something.'

17. SLATE POST

Buttermere – 11.15 a.m.

'WHAT IS IT, Leyton – a record pike?'
DS Leyton must have warned the divers that the wild-looking walker approaching (with the lithe young woman who, frankly, is the primary source of their curiosity) is his boss, and they might do well to make themselves scarce – for they retreat muttering to their boat and begin making ready to disembark.

What Skelgill imagines, might well be what he describes – upon a blue plastic forensic mat an elongated object, some thirty inches by twelve, glistens wet and shows flecked colours of ochre and olive on a charcoal substrate. In shape it is crudely rhomboid; in all, not so far from a decently sized jill pike. To complete the impression a two-foot length of thin nylon rope trails from an eyehole. It might indeed be a specimen laid out by a trophy-hunting angler for a souvenir photograph before returning it to the water.

DS Leyton has moved to intercept his colleagues, like he might want first to get in a word of explanation. He nods a greeting to DS Jones, knowing Skelgill will not trouble with such niceties.

'The station couldn't get you, Guv. I said you'd have no signal – but I thought I might find you. The divers radioed through – and George called me to pass on the message. I was coming east from Whitehaven, anyway.'

Skelgill does not break stride and DS Leyton has to make an abrupt turn and scuttle over the shingle to keep up.

'They found it about thirty feet from where the body had been lying. They reckon it could be what was used to weigh her down. Looks like it was tied on, and the knot eventually came loose. The body was maybe shifted a bit by currents, but by then it had lost its buoyancy.'

Now they all surround the object, inert and strangely sinister. At close quarters it is less of a fish and more of a rock, a shard of even thickness, perhaps three inches.

DS Leyton casts an arm in the direction of the frogmen.

'One of the divers – seems he's a bit of an amateur geologist in his spare time. He reckons it's Westmorland green slate – the type they mine up at Honister Pass. That's what – a couple of miles? He says there's stacks of rubble and cast-offs lying loose around the public parking area. Anyone could have stopped and grabbed a suitable rock without being noticed. I was thinking we could take it up there and see if one of the experts might recognise it. Especially as it's got that little hole chiselled through it.'

When he receives no answer DS Leyton looks from the object to his superior – as does DS Jones – to see that Skelgill's eyes might almost be boring through the stone like green lasers.

Still he does not immediately reply.

Instead he drops to his knees and begins to fold the mat around the rock and picks it up, rising with a muscular jerk and an expiration of breath, in a single movement that swings his burden under one arm.

'I'll show you exactly what it is, Leyton.'

He begins to march towards DS Leyton's car.

But after twenty paces Skelgill seems to have a second thought. He halts and turns and two-handed offers the bundle to DS Jones.

'Try it for size.'

Surprised, she takes it, bracing herself.

DS Leyton watches with a little trepidation – but she does not flinch – and nods that she can manage fine, and they continue walking. She flashes a puzzled glance at her associate.

DS Leyton offers a suggestion.

'The diver reckoned eleven or twelve kilos – enough to sink the body of a small female.'

Skelgill almost snaps his correction.

'It's two stone. Twenty-eight pound.'

He grins perfunctorily. He can gauge a pike's weight to the nearest couple of ounces. The only variation comes in the pub later, which sees the figure creep upwards with each retelling and with each pint consumed.

DS Leyton trots ahead to open the boot and lends a hand to DS Jones as they lay the object carefully in place. Skelgill makes straight for the passenger seat; he waits, drumming the fingers of his right hand impatiently upon the central console.

'Where to, Guv?'

'Just drive, Leyton. Head towards Buttermere.'

DS Leyton grunts as he performs a three-point turn in the narrow lane – he directs a nod of thanks through the open driver's window to the uniformed constable who shifts a traffic cone and holds back an oncoming van.

DS Jones watches from the rear – she suspects there will be an imminent order to turn off – but they pass the hoarding for Hassness Castle, the unmarked entrances of Hassness Cottage, Pike Rigg Cottage and Catthwaite Cottage, and the B&B sign for Ellerbeck advertising no vacancies.

Skelgill remains self-absorbed – it becomes plain that in some respect he is on tenterhooks – an uncharacteristic state of mind. But the journey is not long enough for the lack of conversation to become uncomfortable.

'Pull in after this bend – into the driveway on your right.'

They see it is the Hikers' Hostel.

DS Leyton veers across and parks parallel to the road, blocking the entrance where the overgrown gate lies half off its hinges.

Skelgill is instantly out of the car.

DS Jones is watching him closely. His gaze – a keen stare – homes in on the boundary wall at its corner where it joins the gate. The stonework is part collapsed. There might be a small bird that flits away, disturbed by their arrival. Skelgill seems consumed – by concern, or perhaps even self-doubt – but now she sees his expression subtly change, and his countenance becomes one of grim satisfaction.

But neither she nor DS Leyton quite knows what is going on.

'Have you got nitrile gloves, Leyton?'

'Yeah, sure – there's a bunch of 'em in the glove box.' He reaches inside the open passenger door. 'What do I do, Guv?'

Skelgill strides across to the wall. Where the gate tilts away from its base, it is attached only by a twisted bottom hinge hooked on a traditional cast-iron drive-pin, hammered long ago into the slate gatepost.

Skelgill merely points to thin air.

The upper half of the gatepost is missing. It is sheared clean off at a jagged diagonal.

DS Leyton makes a sound of choked epiphany.

He pulls on a pair of gloves and easily lifts the rock from the boot, fuelled by growing excitement. He needs no further instruction to carry it across and two-handed hold it in position.

'Cor blimey, Guvnor – it's a perfect fit – like a jigsaw piece.'

The fine intermeshing of the serrated edges is extraordinary. And the underlying swirling pattern of the Westmorland green slate, despite one part having spent time submerged, confirms this to be the missing upper section. While there are thousands of such ancient gateposts throughout the county, many lying broken and dispersed, no two aspiring halves could possibly match with such precision. Prince Charming meets Cinderella.

A silence now ensues.

It is DS Leyton, a little breathless from the effort of keeping the rock in place, who speaks first.

'How the flippin' heck did you notice that, Guvnor?'

But Skelgill is not basking in the glory of his powers of observation.

They see he is glaring with some consternation up at the hostel building.

'Stick it back out of sight, Leyton.'

He watches as DS Leyton obeys – and now there is something else – for Skelgill hurriedly follows.

He leans to look into the boot.

'Turn it over, can you.'

DS Leyton obliges.

'What is it, Guv?'
Skelgill is staring again. Now he shows alarm – confusion – doubt.
'That's a cowboy bowline.'
'Guv?'
Skelgill points with an index finger to the strand of rope that is fed through the chiselled drive-pin hole and tied off.
'A bowline. It's a knot. I use it myself. Watch.'
He digs into his pocket and pulls out a hank of baler twine. It takes him just a few seconds, the fingers of his left hand deftly looping and threading and tugging. He displays his product for close comparison.
DS Jones now interjects.
'Are you saying it's a specialist knot?'
He looks at her, as though his first reaction would be to disagree.
'I wouldn't say specialist. It's probably the number one knot used by climbers. But your average Joe Bloggs wouldn't know it.'
She follows up.
'Exclusively climbers?'
He shakes his head.
'Anglers – sailors – any folk that use a boat.'
There is a moment's silence before DS Leyton speaks.
'And divers?'
Skelgill narrows his eyes.
'Aye. Them an' all.'
DS Leyton looks a little disconcerted – he exchanges a glance with DS Jones, as though he wants to suggest something but does not quite have the courage of his convictions.
Skelgill meanwhile is looking again up at the hostel.
DS Jones offers to read his mind.
'Are you thinking we should pull in Kevin Pope?'
It takes a moment before he turns to look at her. It is plain from his expression that he has been thinking exactly that.

But he delays his answer, biting at the corner of a thumbnail: a clue that conflicting feelings do not yet want to resolve themselves.

'Trouble is, I can't see Kevin Pope tying his bootlaces, never mind a cowboy bowline.'

Again there is a silence while they each consider the circumstances.

DS Jones indicates the length of damp cord.

'I'm no expert, but this looks identical to the nylon rope that's wrapped round those blocks. It's the same diameter and weave, and it even seems to have weathered to a similar hue.'

Skelgill, scowling, begins to nod.

DS Jones continues.

'Forensics will need to compare this to the rope tied around the body. Why don't we give them samples from the building work, as well?'

DS Leyton combs his fingers to-and-fro through his tousle of dark hair.

'Hold on – I'm in the dark here, girl. What's this building malarkey?'

She nods, apologetically.

'There's a mothballed construction job at the rear of Hassness Castle. Concrete blocks wrapped in polythene sheeting and tied down with cord. The contractors were Alfred Lord & Sons – from Cockermouth.'

DS Leyton widens his eyes, contrasting their prominent whites against his dark irises.

'What about the builders' knots?'

But Skelgill seems to have anticipated the question; he is already shaking his head.

'Bog-standard overhand knots – ham fisted – a reet arl mess. The only similarity's the word cowboy.'

DS Jones is regarding him with a look of small wonderment – although not, perhaps, of surprise.

Preoccupied, he scowls at his watch.

'Tell you what. Leyton, we'll walk on – we're parked by the pub. You drop back to Hassness Castle and bag up a couple of samples of the rope and the poly. Then go to the builders' yard and ask for the same. We'll meet you in the bookshop café by Cocker Bridge.'

DS Leyton's expression brightens as Skelgill's order unfolds; time is getting on and mention of the word café seems to have an uplifting effect.

'Sounds like a plan, Guv. It means we can give Forensics the whole kit and caboodle. Soon as I get a signal I'll warn them to expect it – what, mid-afternoon?'

Skelgill, instead of replying, has suddenly turned to glare towards the dry stone wall that bounds the lakeside belt of woodland.

'Shut the boot.'

With a surge he crosses the lane without care for traffic and to his colleagues' amazement vaults the wall.

There comes a high-pitched cry of surprise – an unfamiliar male voice, though the hint of an accent not unlike DS Leyton's Cockney brogue.

A few moments later Skelgill emerges from the nearest gate, followed by a short and tubby man in his sixties, clad in camouflage gear and toting a camera on a thick neoprene neck strap fitted with a telephoto lens.

DS Jones lowers her voice.

'That's Royston Woodcock – the one that lives at Pike Rigg Cottage.'

Though he has not exactly been taken prisoner, there is a condemned look about the man.

He seems to be babbling an explanation.

'What it is, officer – there's a pair of pied wagtails nesting in the corner of the wall – where it's tumbled down. It makes a perfect breeding site. Look – I can show you the shots I've got.'

He tries to present the screen to Skelgill, who is not interested. Indeed, he seems to want to have no more to do with the man – and prioritises with a jerk of the head to DS Leyton that he should get on his way. DS Leyton nods, climbs into his car and leaves the scene.

Royston Woodcock makes a further attempt at appeasement.

'There – look, Inspector! That's the hen bird now – perched at the far end of the long gate. See how she's got a beak-full of wool to line the nest?'

Skelgill, however, is looking at DS Jones. As with their colleague, he makes a head movement indicating that they will depart. He begins to step away – but he hesitates and turns back to address the apprehensive older man.

'That's exactly why we'd stopped. My sergeant DS Leyton's a massive twitcher. He was telling us the pied wagtail's the British subspecies of the European white wagtail.'

Royston Woodcock opens his mouth to speak but no words come out.

Skelgill now sets off and DS Jones falls in beside him. He calls back over his shoulder.

'We'll leave you and them in peace, sir. I'm sure you're familiar with the Wildlife & Countryside Act – disturbing birds at their nest is a breach of the law. You wouldn't want to fall foul of it. You could land yourself in a lot of trouble.'

18. SHELF TALK

Paige Turner's Bookshop, Cockermouth – 12.45 p.m.

IN AN ALCOVE marked "Crime & Horror" DS Jones leans against shelves with an open paperback in hand, but though she is absorbed her gaze passes over the top of the novel and across the forest of print to where Skelgill sits upon a comfortable leather sofa they found free in the cookery section. A fashionably dressed young woman – though probably a few years her senior – is delivering their lunch of toasted sandwiches and café lattes. She bends almost to one knee to reach the low table, revealing substantial platform soles under her flapping white jeans; as she reaches over, her short blonde hair flares briefly beneath an overhead spotlight.

Skelgill watches with apparent awkwardness as she unloads the tray – but once she stands upright to back away he says something that causes her to hesitate. She seems to realise he is straining, squinting into the bright bulb – and she tentatively lowers herself into the armchair set at right angles to the sofa, settling on its edge and bracing her palms on its arms, as though it is a temporary state of affairs and she is preparing to push off at any moment.

DS Jones contemplates her options – she has deduced that this is Valentina White, whom Skelgill had asked for upon their arrival, and indeed he had said don't be surprised if she brings their order. Now listening with seemingly keen intent, she leans to place a hand on Skelgill's lower arm, and she keeps it there while she responds to his entreaty. Skelgill's reaction is not entirely pleasing to DS Jones – and she feels a pang of frustration, suspecting female guile to be at work.

She decides to observe from the cover of her book. The conversation continues for a minute or so more; an evidently lighter exchange, the woman smiling and responding animatedly – and briefly touching him several more times. Skelgill does nothing to discourage the contact, and indeed betrays to DS Jones's practised eye the characteristics of rising to compliments. When the woman stands and casually tugs down the sides of her loose top, he struggles to avert his gaze. She makes a gesture that she should leave him to his hot meal – and he aims a hand roughly in DS Jones's direction, as if to explain that his colleague is somewhere about the bookshop and will no doubt return shortly.

DS Jones steps back half a pace, so that only a sliver of her is visible. She watches through one eye as the woman turns smiling from Skelgill and heads briefly towards her before changing course and passing from sight. But in that moment the smile dissolves.

She considers Valentina White's unexpected reaction. Is it of self-reproach – for consorting in the line of duty? For flirting with a man? Or is that just wishful thinking on DS Jones's part?

She waits a little longer before she returns the paperback, taking a second to locate its original place. As an afterthought she peels free a sellotaped shelf-talker. She saunters over to where Skelgill is already tucking into his bacon-and-brie toasted sandwich.

He is quicker than she, however, and speaks through his munching.

'I saw you watching.'

She plies him with a look that is at once conspiratorial and censorious – and rounds to sit beside him and take up her coffee.

'That *was* her, I take it?'

Skelgill drinks from his mug without testing the temperature, and wipes froth from his upper lip and briskly rubs his fingers along his thigh before answering.

'What would put off a vegan that's in a Christmas pudding?'

So, he has raised the subject; and his response is typically oblique.

Two can play at that game.

'They were home for Christmas before last?'

Skelgill perhaps detects her feathers have been ruffled.

'She reckons they're both vegan – they don't buy owt when they don't know what's in it.'

DS Jones cranes around to regard the shelves at their backs, decorated with exotic cookbooks.

'You could look it up.'

'Or you could just tell us, lass.'

There is a note of defeat in his tone that makes her relent. She grins; she is not one to hold a grudge for long.

'More than you might guess. Eggs, butter, milk, honey – and a lot of traditional recipes use lard. Your aunt's – it would be the suet as well.'

Skelgill nods pensively, evidently weighing up the likely veracity of what he has learned. As it is, he is conscious of having revealed something of their hand.

DS Jones's curiosity now takes over.

'What did she say – about the Christmas?'

Skelgill makes a face that is a familiar precursor to not much. Though he generously postpones a bite of his sandwich in order to respond.

'They were home the whole time. Snowed in like everyone else. No visitors – it's a one-bedroomed cottage.'

He flashes her a sideways glance that reveals what might have been a component of his conversation with Valentina White. He takes refuge in the toastie, but DS Jones sets about her own – and waits for him to speak again.

'They went for daily walks – it were nice and festive, with the snow. There were virtually no folk about. Nothing of note to report. She can't recall seeing a bloke with a telephoto lens, a bloke with a Frenchie on a lead, or a bloke with a body tied up in polythene.'

DS Jones's involuntary laugh causes her to splutter and almost choke and Skelgill reaches to give her a sharp thump between the shoulder blades.

Heroically recovered, she poses a pressing question.

'You didn't actually ask that?'

He shakes his head.

'Nay – not about the body, any road.' He inhales and holds the breath for a second before exhaling resignedly. 'Everyone knows why we're poking about – whether we say it, or not.'

DS Jones gazes reflectively at the shelves of books lining the wall opposite. Why do they display so many end-on, when cover-out is so much easier to digest? Perhaps it is an impression that qualifies her analysis.

'With fewer people, you'd be less likely to be seen – but more likely to stand out. I imagine in a normal year the Buttermere circuit is popular for the traditional Boxing Day walk.'

'Aye. Christmas Day, an' all – afternoon, while it's still light.'

DS Jones nods pensively.

'I guess I'm sold on your theory.'

'*My* theory?'

'You've never thought the body was brought from the other end of the country, have you? She didn't even come from Fylde in the boot of Mr Black's car.'

Skelgill grins.

DS Jones continues.

'You know – in the historical report – the Wastwater case – the investigators seriously considered the possibility of the body having been dropped from a light aircraft. The prime suspect was an airline pilot, and they found a scrap of a flight magazine wrapped in the debris.'

Skelgill looks vaguely amused but lets her know with his expression that he anticipates some conclusion. Accordingly, she obliges.

'If we're right about the Christmas pudding – she died here in Cumbria – in Buttermere – on Christmas Night. It's like in a whodunit – the conveniently smashed wristwatch that marks the exact time of the crime.'

'I'm glad you've learned something from those books you bury your head in.'

She laughs.

'All I ever learn is that true crime's more unbelievable than fiction.'

But now she frowns, sufficiently to pique Skelgill's concern.

'So, what's mithering you?'

'It's just – that piece of gatepost – it tells us the body never moved far from where it was deposited in the water. Surely there had to be a boat?'

'You've seen the lake – where would you launch it?'

'By the little road section, I guess. I mean – if you had an accomplice, he could drop off you and the boat and come back later.'

Skelgill is shaking his head.

'It's not summat you could do in two minutes – even the pair of you. Unhitch a trailer. Manhandle it down the verge, over rocks and onto the shore. Float the boat, get aboard. All in sub-zero conditions. Besides – Honister Pass was closed on Christmas Eve – there was no way through from the south – and by morning the road from Buttermere village was impassable, except on foot. A boat on a trailer? There's no chance.'

DS Jones nods reluctantly, but her thoughts rebel.

'Well, what about an inflatable? What if it were Kevin Pope? He could have carried a deflated dinghy down through one of the properties and used their path through the trees to the shore.'

'Aye – and then back again for the gatepost? And what about fetching the rope and the poly? Never mind carrying the body from the hostel. It's a furlong or more – and the terrain's unforgiving – you've seen it yourself.'

Skelgill, despite his gainsaying, is however trying not to disparage his colleague's efforts. He offers some mitigation.

'But there was sixteen hours of darkness. Ample time for someone determined to move about unseen.'

DS Jones nods, and they resort to sipping in silence. They both know there is no easy explanation. Yet it must have been done. Fact can be stranger than fiction.

'Here's Leyton.'

It is Skelgill who spots their colleague – he looks a little lost in the booky maze and has stopped to gawp at a display of cardboard cutout dinosaurs in the children's section. Skelgill calls out and he stirs from his reverie.

'Ah – right you are, Guv. Emma.'

He takes the seat briefly occupied by Valentina White, and there is something in his body language that tells them his too will be a fleeting visit. He cuts to the chase.

'I've got all the gear in the motor. I was thinking I shouldn't hang about – I can get a sarnie from the canteen.'

Skelgill reads his man.

'Summat we should know?'

DS Leyton grimaces sheepishly; he makes a double hand gesture of playing down what he is about to say.

'Well – just a couple of things that have kind of come together –' He falters, but sees that his colleagues are urging him to continue. 'This morning – when I did the routine interview with Abel Ketch – I felt he was being cagey – fair enough, that's not unusual. Told me he trained as a diver in the Royal Navy. Obviously, he's got access to boats – and a trailer. Then you pointed out that bowline knot, Guv. I suppose it got me thinking – he'd learn that in the navy – and use it as a boatman and diver.'

DS Leyton pauses, as if he is hoping one of them will utter some inference. Skelgill remains tight-lipped, but DS Jones nods encouragingly.

'Then just now at the builders' gaff – Alfred Lord & Sons – I found out that Ketch's diving mate Bob Tapp worked on that unfinished job at Hassness Castle. They subcontracted him to do all the plumbing work.'

Skelgill inhales sharply – and DS Leyton, anticipating an objection, raises a palm, to be heard out.

'When I was with Abel Ketch – like I say, he was edgy. It was flippin' warm in his workshop – he had some furnace or other going. But he put on a long-sleeved shirt – I reckon to cover up a tattoo on his arm. It was an anchor on a heart – and the name, Jenny. Course, him and his mate found the body.'

Skelgill releases the breath in lieu of his intended response. He looks at DS Jones to see that she is animated.

DS Leyton concludes.

'So I thought I should look into their backgrounds, Ketch and Tapp – dive a bit deeper, you might say. Find out who Jenny is.'

Skelgill is evidently wrestling with competing thoughts. He stares grimly across the floor of the store to where the serving counter can be glimpsed beneath the low beam of an archway.

'There's time enough if you want a bite, Leyton.'

But DS Leyton is plainly reluctant to linger.

'Thing is, Guv – when I phoned the lab they told me I'd need to be sharp. It takes them a couple of hours to prep the materials and run them through the mass spectrometer. Seems DI Smart's got an urgent job booked in later – and we need to get in before that, else we'll have to wait until tomorrow afternoon. Truth be told, I reckon they're only saying they'll squeeze us in because they ain't his number one fans.'

Skelgill's expression has darkened during the telling of the short tale – quickly to be replaced by a look of resolve.

'You'd better get a shift on, marra.'

Left again to their own devices, it is DS Jones who first speaks, though she is provoked by what she evidently regards as unreasonable surveillance from her superior.

'What? What are you smirking at?'

Skelgill does nothing to mask his mocking grin.

'I suppose you're thinking that's your boat-and-accomplice theory resurrected?'

When she might be tempted to agree, instead she makes a non-committal gesture, raising her palms simultaneously. She intones sweetly.

'Actually, I'm thinking you were right in not pulling in Kevin Pope.'

Skelgill folds his arms, unprepared for such blatant flattery.

'I could argue that amounts to the same thing.'

But DS Jones is shaking her head.

'No – it makes me appreciate that any action would be premature. We need to get the forensic work done – there's information on the table. The ropes, the polythene – the piece of rock. We might track down Martina Radu. And there's more to know about these divers, Tapp and Ketch – perhaps the builders, too – and certainly the various local inhabitants.'

Skelgill relents a little.

'The likes of Kevin Pope – I reckon you only get one shot. Jump the gun and he clams up.' He shakes his head a little dejectedly. 'Mind you – another thing that puts me off – I can't see him visiting the village fair – let alone buying a Christmas pudding.'

DS Jones is more optimistic.

'But maybe a woman did – *the* woman. What if there is a connection between him and Martina Radu?'

Skelgill does not immediately answer. Conjecture is like setting off down a scree slope; it is easy to start, but much harder to stop, with always the possibility of an ungainly denouement.

DS Jones comprehends his reticence. Rather than press for an answer to her question, she poses another that is likely more palatable.

'Royston Woodcock – do you think he gleaned much?'

Skelgill scowls.

'Leyton's motor was blocking the line of sight. He might have heard us. But I don't know that we said owt that would make much sense to him.'

'Unless he's our murderer.'

'In which case, I doubt I fooled him about Leyton being a twitcher.'

DS Jones grins.

'Where did you get that from – about the taxonomy of the pied wagtail?'

Skelgill jerks a thumb in a sideways direction.

'Over there, somewhere. There's a section on wildlife.'

She seems momentarily distracted – but Skelgill takes from her the shelf-talker that she is absently turning over between her fingers.

'What's this?'

'What? Oh – it's a staff recommendation – for Lena Longstaff's latest novel. I thought I'd look it up on Goodreads.'

Skelgill scrutinises the item. He leans forward to slide his wallet from his hip pocket and extracts from it the business card presented to him by Valentina White. He lays the two items side by side.

DS Jones immediately sees what he is up to.

'It's the same handwriting.'

Skelgill grimaces, deciphering the flowing penmanship.

'*Unputdownable.* Is that a word? She's singing her pal's praises.'

DS Jones nods pensively. But she seems phlegmatic.

'I suppose, why not? You'd do the same for me.'

Skelgill chokes back a denial.

'I could maybe see you writing a book – but to save time I'd let you tell me what to say about it.'

On this note, by mutual if unspoken agreement, they begin to rise and make their way from the store. At a sales counter near the exit, they notice that Valentina White seems to be helping out, arranging Lakeland souvenir postcards and bookmarks in display units – though she appears not to see them leaving. They walk in silence the short distance to Cocker Bridge, where Skelgill inevitably stops and peers through the railings. He makes a face of dismay at the extraordinary sight where in its exuberance the river has ripped the foundations from the Old Courthouse, an edifice that has teetered on the bank for two centuries; now it is a doubly precarious sight.

'She's not so tall.'

'Eh?' Skelgill is baffled by the out-of-context statement.

'Valentina White. When you first described her, you referred to her as tall – or taller. But she's wearing three-inch platforms. Even with them on, she's only my height.'

Though it stretches the limits of Skelgill's sensitivities, he perhaps detects a certain fishing is at play – if not exactly for compliments, then maybe for reassurance.

'That's what I meant – I mean – you're a good height – above average for a lass.'

DS Jones smiles – and now she might easily be distracted by his response. She watches the grey ripples, as if she is mesmerised by the amorphous conveyor sliding beneath them, one strand in the endless cycle of sea, vapour, cloud, rain and river.

But having successfully raised the subject of the woman, she proceeds to the matter that is preying on her mind.

'Did she seem offended – about what you asked her?'

Skelgill's brow creases.

'Offended? What are you talking about?'

DS Jones realises she has let a small cat out of the bag, in trying to understand the woman's observed reaction. She rows back a little, taking more care in her choice of words.

'Oh – just that she seemed ... well, *introspective* – as she left you.'

Skelgill, too, now vacantly observes the water passing under the bridge, once a component of Buttermere, and shortly to become subsumed in the Derwent, returning to the Irish Sea.

He sighs – or at least exhales reluctantly, as if he has reached a decision.

'I didn't really ask her much. Yesterday, Lena Longstaff left me a voicemail – she said she might have a piece of the jigsaw. That, I never mentioned to Valentina White. I haven't managed to get back to Lena Longstaff.'

DS Jones is nodding; this makes more sense; it is in the nature of how he goes about things. Though it does fleetingly strike her that this morning they twice passed close by Hassness Cottage. She senses, however, that he is awaiting her opinion – her approbation, even.

'I imagine she must know all that – if they're as close as we think. Perhaps she was expecting you to ask her what it was about – and when she realised that you hadn't, she just looked a little rattled.'

Skelgill turns to DS Jones and places a hand on her shoulder.

'There you go then, lass. By now, I reckon that's pretty much everyone's cage we've rattled.'

19. BAD LINE

Pike Rigg, Buttermere – 7.10 p.m.

NO RUDDY SIGNAL. You're lucky if you ever get one up here, surrounded by the mountains. That's why they've all got landlines, when most of the country never uses them anymore. Even by the time he left Kent, he never answered the landline. The only calls were scammers and people trying to sell him double glazing.

Royston's palms are sweating; he rubs them on his thighs. And his pulse is racing; he can hear it thumping in his temples. He reaches for his whisky tumbler; perhaps he should have a refill?

But he must keep his wits about him. Dutch courage is all very well, until you can't see straight to shoot, so to speak. Not that he's going to be *taking* any photos.

He needs the loo again – but it can only be nerves; he went five minutes ago. He fumbles for his reading glasses. The time in the corner of his computer screen states that it's after seven; that must be long enough to have waited – nor too late; a good time to call.

The entry from the Phone Book is before his eyes. It's handy that they put it online. Gone are the days of that great big directory everyone used to keep; it must have taken half a forest to print every year.

And it's the number, alright. The address is a match.

He drains his glass. Did he top it up? He can't remember.

Careful, Royston old son – you ain't no drinker.

He reaches for the landline telephone.

His hands are shaking.

Starting with 141 to withhold his number, it takes him three attempts to prod the keys in the right order.

He holds his breath as the call goes through and the *burr-burr* of the GPO ringing tone kicks in.

He finds himself counting in time, in pairs, like he counts a flock of birds on the lake.

One-two, three-four, five-six, seven-eight, nine-ten, eleven-twel ...

They pick up on twelve.

The line is poor, the salutation distant.

Royston presses the handset hard against his ear.

He suddenly wonders if he should disguise his own voice. Yes – what he'll do – he'll speak in a high-pitched northern accent – as best he can.

'Hey up. You probably don't know me.'

They'll think it's a crank call. They'll probably hang up.

He might be relieved if they hang up.

But they don't.

He almost panics. He almost puts down the receiver.

He needs to make himself say it.

He hears his voice. It's squeaky. He's already lost his fake accent.

'I have some pictures you might like.'

No answer. But the crackle of interference tells him they're still there.

Then a question comes.

'I shan't go into detail. I think you know what I mean.'

There is a denial.

But still they're not hanging up. They're not telling him to sling his hook.

'If I were to say ... *Jingle Bells* ... would that make it any clearer?'

Royston grins. He was pleased with himself when he thought this up.

Another pause, just the faint crackling.

He offers a prompt.

'I was wondering – in return for them – what you'd offer?'

More delay.

Now a demand – but isn't that progress? A demand means negotiations are open.

'I understand that – that you'll want to see them. But I can assure you they exist.'

A quicker rejoinder, now.

He fights back the excited tremor in his voice.

'Of course. You can watch me delete them.'

Another question.

It's sounding promising.

'Well – I thought we could do it in instalments. Start with the prints – there's a set of four photos. It would depend on what you want to offer.'

A thrill of anticipation runs through his body.

For a moment he loses concentration – he finds himself repeating the question just asked.

When can you see them? As soon as you like. We could start tonight.'

He can't believe he's said it.

Where? I thought neutral ground. I'm open to suggestions. I'm open to lots of things.'

There is a longer pause – the longest yet.

Surely they won't hang up now?

He can feel warm beads of sweat from his armpits trickling down the cool flab of his flanks.

Then comes a proposal.

He listens intently, nodding.

'Okay – that's a good idea. Ideal spot – secluded. Fine by me.' He glances at the wall clock, though it never quite reads the same as his laptop. 'Yeah, I'll be there.'

The call is hung up abruptly.

Royston reaches for the whisky bottle. He takes a swig directly, short-circuiting the glass.

He gasps. His heart is pounding in his chest.

He lifts the bottle again – but stops himself.

Keep your wits about you, Royston, old son. You'll need them – it's going to be dark at eleven o'clock.

Pitch dark.

And a shadow seems to fill the room. Alarmed, he lifts his gaze to the window.

But it was the last sliver of the evening sun, slipping behind the ridge.

He rouses himself – he reflects on what just happened.

There was no argument.

Ruddy heck – his hunch … *it must be right.*

THURSDAY

1ST MAY

20. TUNNEL VISION

Buttermere – 5.30 a.m.

SKELGILL CANNOT REMEMBER when he last fished Buttermere. It must be donkey's years. Since he inherited the boat – and it was always moored at Peel Wyke on Bass Lake – he has hardly ever troubled to come up this way. As a lad he exhausted every nook and cranny of the perimeter; Hassness was always his preferred spot, the headland having a nice submerged shelf, when much of the remaining shoreline plunges too deep, too fast. A glance at a contour map reveals a profile like a bathtub, with steep sides and a flat bottom, most gently sloping at its foot, where glacial moraine rises to form the pastureland. And Buttermere is one of the least eutrophic of the lakes (only Wastwater and Ennerdale Water are less so); such lack of nutrients corresponds to a scarcity of fish ... and anglers.

But DS Leyton's recounting of diver Bob Tapp's description ("flat sandy bottom and a lot of perch") has prompted him to see what size of striped specimen he can winkle out with his ten-foot coarse rod and wriggling red-banded brandlings dug at a clandestine raid on his Ma's steaming compost heap. After all, he has a soft spot for perch – it was his first fish, and sometimes he thinks he can still make out the scar, when the Arl Fella's warning came a split second too late to mind its spines.

More than this has prompted him. Without really evaluating why, and merely responding to the inability to get back to sleep at four a.m., he had hitched up his trailer and driven over to Peel Wyke. By five o'clock, in morning twilight, he was rearranging the cones at Gatesgarth, reversing cursing into the makeshift police layby occupying half of the narrow lane's width. It took fifteen minutes and all his strength to get his boat afloat, and now, drifting a few yards out, he kneels upon the centre thwart to flex his backbone, tilting his face skywards.

The overhead conditions are clear; the weather is set fair. But it will be a while before the sun's rays, massing above Hindscarth Edge, overflow into the dale. It is May Day – though too cool right now for mayflies to be hatching. The calm surface of Buttermere is bereft of rises as he pulls away.

He is heading for the sheltered wyke on the north side of Hassness, keeping quite close to the shore.

Sculling – it is conducive to mulling. Thinking, but not thinking. The rhythmical swish and splash of his oars; spray in his face when he gets it slightly wrong; the earthy pungency of diatoms in the water.

The next thing Skelgill knows is a voice breaking into his thoughts.

'Hello! Hello there!'

He heaves to.

It is a woman, well spoken, a slight Scots accent revealed in the rolled 'r' and disyllabic *they-rr*. He turns to his left to see her on the bank, about thirty yards away, not easily spotted amongst shadows beneath the oaks; a dark olive Barbour jacket and matching wellingtons, and skin-tight beige riding breeches. She is waving a mobile phone in a manner that conveys futility.

'Do you have a mobile signal?'

He knows, over the water, that he hardly needs to raise his voice.

'What's the problem?'

She leans forwards but hesitates, taking a moment to choose her words.

'There's a person in the tunnel ... injured.'

'Wait there.'

Skelgill backs to starboard and wrenches the boat to port, and then propels it shoreward. The old railway track enters the tunnel on a short stretch of stone embankment, like a small sea wall; there is no easy point to beach. He comes alongside.

'Catch.'

He tosses the painter; she is adept, and hauls backwards while he scales the wall, and hands him the rope which he makes fast with a clove hitch around the scaly trunk of a silver birch sapling. He straightens. They look at one another.

At close range he sees she is slender, skinny even, with straight, shoulder-length dark hair, fair skin, narrow features and faint eyebrows that seem to be raised in a permanent state of concern. He guesses she is in her early forties.

He wavers – and decides to show her his warrant card.

'I've got no signal – but you've picked the right person.'

She looks at his ID, neither more nor less troubled.

'I'm Margery McLeish. My husband and I own Catthwaite Cottage – the holiday let. I think I must have spoken to one of your colleagues – on Tuesday evening.'

Skelgill is watching her intently; he merely nods.

There is a small hiatus – he indicates with his left hand.

'The tunnel?'

It is both a reminder of their purpose and an offer for her to decline to accompany him. He begins to move.

'I – I think it's worse.'

He stops and turns.

'Worse than injured?'

She hesitates.

'I'm afraid so. I would have said – if I'd known you were a police officer. I didn't want to alarm you.'

Skelgill gives a curt nod.

'Male or female?'

'It's a man – a little elderly – from what I could see. He's not breathing. I couldn't find a pulse.' She makes a face that might be of regret for the person's condition, or perhaps that she worries that she has overstepped the mark. 'I have basic training – I'm a volunteer first-aider at my daughter's hockey club.'

Skelgill presses on.

The mouth of tunnel is just a few yards away. He engages the torch on his phone and he can tell she does the same behind him.

'Better just double-check, first off.'

Skelgill is expecting to see a body lying collapsed or perhaps propped up against the side wall – and he is shocked by what his beam reveals. A pile of loose earth, from which protrudes rocks and rotted pit props, a heap a good three feet high, fills most of the bottom of the passage. The man lies face down with his head pointing in their direction, his torso buried in the debris, only his left arm flung forward and free, and his legs visible from the calves down. There are several large rocks around his head. Dried blood is caked on the back of his skull.

Skelgill stands for a moment, taking in the scene.

The splayed fingers of the extended arm seem to be stretching for the camera with its telephoto lens that lies just out of reach.

'I moved the rocks – they were on top of his head.'

Skelgill starts at her voice.

He stoops to verify that the man is dead.

And that the dead man is Royston Woodcock.

21. PHOTOS

Buttermere – 8.30 a.m.

'WHAT DID SHE say, Margery McLeish?'
They are afloat, anchored twenty yards offshore. Skelgill seems distracted by the state of affairs on land. A tiny but vital artery, the B5289 road over Honister Pass cannot be closed without great inconvenience, and now temporary traffic lights have been set up. In addition to police cars, marked and plain, the divers, the scene-of-crime team, there are emergency vehicles, including an ambulance. There is DS Jones's distinctive yellow hatchback. There is Skelgill's car, and his trailer tilted on the bank. It looks like a small travelling circus has come to town.

Skelgill's expression might convey a smidgeon of self-doubt. This could be described as over the top. But he is not taking any chances. If there is something to be gleaned, it must not be missed.

'Guv?'

He starts.

Slowly, he prepares to answer DS Jones's question.

It is plain that his thoughts are backtracking.

'I couldn't sleep.'

'I noticed.'

He is silent for a moment.

'Look – I weren't testing your theory – I thought I'd just do it, that's all. Bring the boat up from Bass Lake. Catch a perch or two – be back in time to start work.'

DS Jones regards him benevolently – who cares – this is what he does. She nudges him back onto the subject.

'What was she doing – when you saw her?'

Skelgill shakes his head.

'She reckoned she might get a signal once she came out of the tunnel. When she didn't, she decided to head to Gatesgarth – phone from the farm.'

'What do you think about that?'

'Makes sense. It's a quarter of the distance of going back to Buttermere. Plus there was the chance of a lift when she met the lane.'

'She didn't consider one of the properties on Hassness? Surely they're closest?'

Skelgill looks into the inquiring hazel eyes; his own are flecked with green, if seeming greyer than usual out on the water. He shrugs, but a little ineffectually.

'Along the shore's the line of least resistance. Besides, she'd have been wasting her time clambering up to the castle. Can't knock what she did.'

Skelgill knows what DS Jones is getting at. They will need to talk to her – but she is not his priority right now. A mother of two, a respectable lawyer, Margery McLeish is not about to flee the country. He throws a morsel to acknowledge his colleague's concern.

'We'll catch her later, eh, lass?'

DS Jones nods acquiescently. But Skelgill's gaze is attracted by a rise; his eyes flash like those of a hawk; his hand is drawn towards his rod. Though she can see he does not have fly gear, and she knows enough that he can't fling a float and worm at a trout.

The ripples gradually disperse, and the minor indiscretion is averted.

DS Jones does, however, cast a line.

'Sixty-four-thousand-dollar question.'

She waits.

Skelgill is surprisingly compliant.

'You mean, were it an accident?'

She nods. 'What do you think?'

'I can't believe you said those pit props looked dodgy.'

DS Jones chokes back a reproachful laugh.

'I hope you're not going to blame me for tempting fate?'

Skelgill treats her question as rhetorical. She has brought a two-way radio; it is on the thwart beside her. He gestures towards it.

'What's the story?'

'Dr Herdwick said he may have a preliminary view by lunchtime.'

Skelgill grins wryly.

'Let's hope he's hungry.'

It had fallen to DS Jones to rouse the pathologist. He had not been enamoured by the dawn call – and, like her, he probably has missed breakfast. She wraps her arms about her midriff. Skelgill has made her don a Crewsaver; beneath she has on just a sports top, and there is a cool breeze beginning to slide over the water.

'What do we do in the meantime?'

Skelgill begins to haul in the anchor, hand over hand, the blue nylon rope dripping wet into the boat.

'There used to be some decent perch in here.' His reply is poker faced – she knows he is kidding. 'Next stop, Woodcock's place.'

Skelgill rows them quite close to the shore, and in approaching the vicinity of the tunnel they attract bemused looks from colleagues – and friendly jibes.

"Ahoy there, Cap'n!"

"You'll never mek t' Boat Race!"

There is a short rendition of *Jolly Boating Weather*, and perhaps cheekiest of all, "Always obey t' cox's orders, Skelly, lad!"

DS Jones, facing forwards on the stern thwart, does not seem to mind the suggestion of role reversal.

But Skelgill is a little chagrined.

'Make sure you put in your report that we're reconstructing getting a boat in and out of Buttermere at different points of difficulty.'

DS Jones merely smiles, when she could take him up on his duplicity. She watches the wooded shoreline pass them by, noticing occasional walkers, who will shortly be turned back by the police tape and the surly constable posted at the entrance to the tunnel.

'Pike Rigg.'

DS Jones does not see any distinguishing feature to match Skelgill's announcement of their arrival.

'You'd expect a ridge rising to a peak. Or does it refer to the fish?'

Skelgill looks like he might not have considered this, taking the given name for granted.

But he brings his angling experience to bear.

'There's a steep drop-off runs along this stretch. It's a good spot to drag a toby, just beyond the edge. The pike lurk in the depths – rise to a lure like a shark seeing a surfer.'

She withdraws a trailing hand from the water and makes a face that is suitably disconcerted.

But Skelgill finds a friendly mooring, where they are able to step directly onto short dry turf. DS Jones has a small rucksack, into which she places the radio. Skelgill stows his gear, though there is not much he can do about concealing his fishing rod. There is one item that he brings, however – a large evidence bag. He has yet to explain his reason for commandeering Royston Woodcock's camera, with its telephoto lens still attached – other than stating the obvious, that it could not be left lying in the tunnel while assistance was being sought.

His navigation proves to be accurate; a short walk directly through the woods brings them to the gate that marks the boundary of Pike Rigg Cottage. The garden is unkempt – perhaps to attract wildlife. It is more a paddock of rank grasses, dock and common rush, and scattered elders and hawthorns, that joins the woods to a patch of lawn near the building.

Skelgill notices that the feeder is empty.

The detectives approach the back of the house with a sense of expectation tinged with emptiness, knowing the owner is not going to be home.

Skelgill asks DS Jones to wait while he circles the property; he is back within the minute.

'No sign of a break-in.' He glares at the door handle. 'We might need some jiggery-pokery.'

Then he notices his colleague is wearing blue nitrile gloves. She hands him a pair from her rucksack.

'It's open. The key's in the lock on the inside.'

He looks suitably chastised.

They enter directly into a compact kitchen. The impression is that it is orderly and clean. A single glass tumbler rests upside down on the drainer.

The hallway has a room off to the right and the front door ahead, facing the stair on the left.

Skelgill hands the bag with the camera to his colleague.

'I'll check up-the-way.'

He finds just a bathroom and a single bedroom. The bed is made and unslept in. He pokes about in cupboards and a wardrobe, but finds nothing that arrests him until he uncovers a framed photograph beneath vests in a drawer. He leans closer. It could be a selfie, and in fact the quality looks like it was produced on a home printer. A young blonde woman, smiling and squinting into sunlight, leans down in front of a vehicle bonnet so that the badge appears in the shot – the marque is Volkswagen. Celebrating a new car, perhaps. Skelgill recalls mention of a daughter. Perhaps the father made a contribution.

He stands back and exhales, unaware he has held his breath. But he is reminded there will be the family to contact. New Zealand, Woodcock had said. It comes as a small relief that it is not likely to fall to him to break the news. They will have to track them down, first.

He descends to find DS Jones sitting at a laptop at a desk facing the window that gives onto the rear garden. It was where he had peered inside on an earlier visit. To her left the wall is covered with prints – wildlife shots, neatly cut out and displayed – easily a couple of hundred.

He can see she is scrolling through decks of similar photographs.

'I've found The Big Freeze.'

Skelgill waits. Beside her on the desk is a mobile phone. He picks it up – but the battery appears to be flat. There is also a landline, the avocado unit likely dating from the 1980s, when the push-button replaced the dial. He picks up the receiver and listens for the dialling tone – the line is live – but he knows a device like this holds no records: never mind no microchip, it does not even have a redial button. He turns back to DS Jones.

'Any joy?'

'There are thousands of shots. For the period in question, lots of squirrels in the snow; ducks huddled on the ice.'

Skelgill watches for a moment, and then casts about for the camera. She has placed the bag on a low table in front of an armchair. He sits and methodically ascertains how to display images on the digital screen. They each work in silence, until DS Jones clears her throat, a little portentously.

'I've moved on from the winter period. I'm coming across the occasional – well – what you might call voyeuristic shot. He obviously snooped about under cover of the woods. There are female hikers picnicking – sunbathing – and in one case swimming.'

Skelgill's continued silence makes her turn in her seat.

'You'd better see this, then, lass.'

She realises he has been holding off, and there is some connection with her own discovery.

She rises and he hands her the camera.

'Oh.'

On the little screen is a full-face shot of herself.

It has to be said, it is taken in such a way, with skilled composition and timing, as to capture her allure.

'I might get one of them for my screensaver.'

She glances at Skelgill – but his remark serves to lighten the moment.

She scrolls through the deck – there are more portraits of her … and none of her colleagues.

Skelgill stands and leans close at her shoulder.

She scrolls to the first of the sequence.

'They're only from yesterday. He must have wiped the memory card each time he uploaded to his laptop. I suppose that makes sense, the number he's been taking.'

The first few images capture the nest-building pied wagtails. Then DS Leyton's car appears in the frame.

Then shots of DS Jones standing a little away from her colleagues.

Then the close-ups.

Skelgill eyes her surreptitiously as she reprises them.

She may be annoyed – but then also intrigued; there is always an interest in how another person might see one.

She moves on – and halts at a shot from a slightly different angle which has the trio stooped down around the collapsed wall.

She raises the camera for Skelgill better to see.

He understands the implication – but he shrugs in a way that seems to give the photographer the benefit of the doubt.

DS Jones is about to object when the two-way radio crackles into life.

From her rucksack comes the disembodied voice of DC Watson.

'Hey up, Sarge, do you read us? Sarge – hello?'

The detective constable is briefed to relay only urgent news. It seems the police pathologist has pulled out all the stops. DS Jones retrieves the handset and engages with her subordinate.

DC Watson wastes no time in small talk, no-nonsense front-row forward that she is in her spare time. Her thick Cumbrian brogue resonates in the still, stale air of the room.

'Sarge, I reckon you should know this. First off, Dr Herdwick puts the time of death between ten p.m. and two a.m. Second, the blow that killed him were to the base of the skull. T' other rocks must have fallen on him afterwards – they caused fractures but no bleeding.'

Skelgill and DS Jones are looking at one another as they absorb these words – but it is only Skelgill who can accurately picture the scene. He inhales to respond, but DC Watson interjects with a curious throaty growl that might be of dissatisfaction.

'So, I says to the Doc – how's that, then? Did the soil trip him up, and a girt rock just fall smack bang on the back of his head? *Did it heck as like.*'

There is derision in her tone, but spirit also – and Skelgill listens with approval. She knows her own mind, and evidently has had no qualms in challenging the eminent medic.

DS Jones plays a straight bat.

'What did he say to that?'

'He admitted I had a point – the stone ceiling would have to collapse first – before the earth above it came down. It couldn't happen t' other way round. Wouldn't be logical.'

More glances are exchanged. DC Watson, for her part, seems content to have conveyed the facts, and that she considers further conjecture to be above her pay grade. Having eschewed the protocols of two-way radio usage, now she utters a belated, "Over".

DS Jones thanks her and moves to wrap up the conversation.

The detectives stand for a few moments in silence.

DS Jones realises Skelgill is waiting for her. So she states the obvious, since it needs to be said.

'DC Watson is surely right. If Royston Woodcock wasn't lying prone when that first blow struck, he must have been standing up. In which case there's no way it could have been a rock falling on him – not impacting the base of his skull.'

Skelgill runs both hands through his hair until his fingers intertwine at the back of his neck. He tilts his head to-and-fro, experimentally.

'What are you saying, lass?'

Now DS Jones raises the camera, its screen still displaying the shot of the three detectives crouched around the jigsaw puzzle of the gatepost.

'Guv – what if he did overhear? And that he knew enough to think we were onto Kevin Pope? What if he – well – *approached* Kevin Pope?'

Skelgill remains silent. But he takes the camera from his colleague and replaces it in the evidence bag, which he puts down on the little table. He straightens – and flexes his spine with a small accompanying groan.

'Howay, lass. Let's lock this stuff up – why speculate when we can just ask him?'

22. HOSTAGE

Hikers' Hostel, Buttermere – 9.45 a.m.

'THAT'S KATYA.'
'Come again?'
'In the car – there.'

Skelgill turns to follow DS Jones's indication. A large but clapped-out estate car has rumbled past them, down the uneven slope over the gravel towards the gateway of the Hikers' Hostel. The driver brakes cautiously at the junction, and then, satisfied the way is clear, in contrast sends up a spurt of stones. The interior is crammed to the roof with blue laundry hampers; they afford only a brief glimpse of a young, blonde-haired woman at the wheel as she turns right towards the village.

'She cleans at the YHA hostel at Honister Hause – she must have the contract for this place, as well. Remember – she helped us previously? She's a refugee from Ukraine.'

'Aye, maybe.'

Skelgill stares pensively as the dust from the car's tyres drifts from sight.

'Can I help you good people?'

The officers swivel in tandem. Another woman, perhaps in her late thirties, hangs on the corner of the building. There is the suggestion in her demeanour that she heard them and has come to investigate. She wears a knee-length catering overall and has a clipboard in one hand; she could have been signing out the laundry despatch at the back door.

Skelgill considers she is vaguely familiar. She is of medium height and shapely build with short, dark hair and pleasant friendly features, and shining blue eyes that seem to convey recognition on her part. He would guess they are of an age, and it strikes him they may be former schoolmates, when he attended the local primary down in Lorton Vale. She wears a gold wedding band on the ring finger of her left hand.

As such, he is momentarily tongue-tied, and it is DS Jones who steps into the breach.

She approaches the woman and displays her police ID.

'We would like to speak with Mr Kevin Pope. He's the manager here, yes?'

'Aye – he's the manager. Acting manager. But he's not here. I'm next in charge – general dogsbody – Ann Wilson.'

The woman transfers her gaze to Skelgill, standing a few feet back – to observe his reaction to her name, it would seem. When he gives a small involuntary jerk of the head, she looks again at DS Jones.

'He went away with your officer.'

Skelgill is jolted into action. What the heck is Leyton playing at? Running some secret line of inquiry? He steps alongside DS Jones.

'Short, stocky with a Cockney accent?'

The woman seems pleased with Skelgill's intervention. She gives a precocious shake of her head.

'Nay – he were a skinny bloke – tidy, like – but mean-looking – and rude. Thought he were summat.'

DS Jones senses Skelgill stiffen – and that he is stymied for what to say. Again, she stands in.

'When was this, madam?'

The woman takes a second to turn to her. She smiles a little diffidently, as if the polite address is something to which she is unaccustomed.

'It were yesterday morning – must have been about this time – happen ... just after ten. Then later they let him phone to say they were keeping him overnight.'

It must be plain to the woman that both detectives are shocked by this news; she rocks from one foot to the other, perhaps faintly amused by the effect of her words.

For her part, DS Jones can tell that Skelgill, first mildly stirred by the woman's identity, has transitioned to an altogether more volcanic mode. He is not far from blowing his top.

She reaches to touch his sleeve.

'We seem to have a crossed wire, at our end. We'll need to make a call.'

With her other hand, she gestures in the direction of the road, though of course it is not as if they have a vehicle sitting there, and the suggestion might seem peculiar. Nonetheless, she begins to back away, and Skelgill for once is the follower.

'We'll leave you to your work. We'll call if we need more information. Thanks for your help, Mrs Wilson.'

'It's Johnson – my married name. I were Wilson before.'

She beams, looking directly at Skelgill – offering him the chance of formal recognition – but it is the most he can do to manufacture an unconvincing simper.

They halt at the roadside, once they are immediately out of sight of the hostel building.

Skelgill is seething.

'What the devil is Smart up to?'

DS Jones wrestles the walkie-talkie from her rucksack. She does not attempt to reply, but instead, while Skelgill flings stones viciously at a No Parking sign, she succeeds in raising Desk Sergeant George Appleby. She steps a little away, better to hear her colleague under the clanging of Skelgill's angry hits. She returns to Skelgill's side when the conversation is concluded. She hesitates, in the way of a messenger fearing the proverbial fate.

'You were right, Guv. DI Smart has detained him in connection with his county lines case.'

Skelgill is still spitting feathers, and his immediate rejoinder is not entirely coherent. He struts round in a circle, taking a kick at a spear thistle and sending an unopened flower head sailing over the roadside wall.

He returns to face her.

'He's been prying into our reports. Didn't I say it? He's put together the missing Manchester woman, and Pope being from Wythenshawe, and drug-running – and made five.'

161

DS Jones stares at her superior, troubled by his torment. And she has not yet conveyed the full story supplied by DS Appleby. She steels herself.

'Word in the canteen is that he's going to lay the murder charge on him. But how can he do that – there's no evidence?'

Skelgill turns away, and DS Jones fears for the wall – or Skelgill's toes, whichever is about to come off worse – but instead he merely leans on the copings and addresses the trees beyond.

'Of course he is! Smart couldn't give a monkey's about evidence. It's page one of his playbook. He'll use it as leverage to get a confession to drug dealing – that's all. He knows yon soft donnat Pope will cave.'

He pushes off from the wall and flails an arm in the direction of the Hikers' Hostel. DS Jones waits patiently for the metaphorical dust and an accompanying hail of literal expletives to settle.

'Just one thing, Guv – we've been sidetracked.'

Skelgill regards her intently.

'Aye – I know – Pope's been in custody since this time yesterday.'

DS Jones is startled. His fury over DI Smart has subsided almost as quickly as it blew up. And – it seems – he has not been sidetracked. She double-checks his understanding.

'Irrespective of whether Royston Woodcock's death was an accident – Kevin Pope couldn't have had anything to do with it.'

They regard one another as if there might be a silver lining here somewhere, albeit neither of them is quite sure what it is. Then, to DS Jones's alarm, Skelgill without warning leaps out into the road to flag down an oncoming vehicle – it is a police patrol.

He rounds to the driver's window. He leans in and engages in a short dialogue, jerking a thumb in the direction of his colleague. He backs away, and the patrolman pulls in as best he can, and sets his blue lights flashing while he waits, engine idling.

Skelgill reverts to DS Jones.

'I've got you a ride back to your car. Get to the station as fast as you can. Intervene with Smart. Don't let him get wind of the gatepost. If push comes to shove, tell the Chief it'll compromise the murder inquiry – that Pope's our witness – and Smart's taken him hostage.'

DS Jones's hazel eyes widen to reveal their milky whites.

'But he's not, is he – our witness?'

Skelgill makes a face that she recognises: it combines, one, that the answer is too complex (if he even knows it) with, two, just do it.

She opts not to demur, though she persists with her point.

'But – you *do* think Kevin Pope has something to do with – well – something?'

Skelgill scowls impatiently.

'Call it gut feel. Pope knows summat.' He winks at her; it is enough to reassure, and she begins to step backwards. He pats his top pocket where he has placed the mortise key for Pike Rigg Cottage. 'I'll collect all the materials – I'll row back to Gatesgarth and follow on.'

He watches as DS Jones climbs into the police car; now he has a second thought. He crosses to tap on the window and signal for her to lower it.

'Leyton's at Whitehaven, reet?'

DS Jones nods.

'Yes – the woman named Jenny, connected to Abel Ketch – I think we might have a lead – an idea of who she is.'

Skelgill makes a face of fleeting disapproval – as if he needs the added line of inquiry like a hole in the head.

'Get a message through to him. Tell him I'll meet him at the Lamplugh Roundabout on the A66 – he'll need to pass that way. I'll hand over the laptop and camera and whatnot. The roadside services café.' He glances at his watch. 'I'll be there by noon.'

'Sure.'

The driver judges this to be the end of the exchange and shifts the engine into gear. But Skelgill suddenly reaches to place a hand on the sill.

'No, wait – tell him the bookshop.'

And with that he darts in front of the car and vaults the wall.

23.
INTERROGATION

Police HQ, Penrith – 11.40 a.m.

HE'S NOT SEEN the female before. Why have they brought her in? An observer? Like a peacekeeper from the United Nations, to make sure they don't torture him? He wouldn't trust that inspector further than he could throw him, smarmy git. And why's he got rid of the surly male sergeant who was sitting by the door before the break?

At least the female's a big improvement on that score. She greeted him respectfully. She's younger than he is – she can't be much past her mid-twenties. And she reminds him in a way of Tina – it's her calm aura, not her physical appearance. *'Female, early thirties, small and slim with long black hair. Does that ring any bells?'*

This woman copper's better looking than Tina, and honey blonde, her complexion bronzed, with strong cheekbones and full lips and pale brown eyes, like she's a model for a Greek sculpture. But Tina was good enough looking – good enough to be well out of his league. That was the thing – he could never quite believe it – he had to pinch himself each time she came back. What did she see in a no-mark like him? Whatever it was, it wasn't to parade him as a boyfriend – she only ever wanted them to stay in – often, just to stay in bed.

And he can't say that didn't suit him – what bloke wouldn't it suit? And that cold winter especially, those quiet weekdays when the hostel was closed to hikers and they had the place to themselves. It wasn't as if they were confined to his quarters. Though he would love to have taken her down to one of the local pubs. He liked the idea of having a girlfriend, of them sitting together, side by side, hand in hand, having a quiet drink by a cosy log fire. But she never would agree to that. Not that she didn't like a drink – he was sure she was merry that first time – he'd thought she must have been drunk to fancy him. And not that she wouldn't smoke. And if he'd only known her for longer maybe she'd have experimented with other stuff. She didn't need any encouragement to experiment in bed. Test Tube Tina, she once called herself. If she were married, it must have been to a monk, or someone impotent. Or perhaps she had an arrangement, an open marriage that allowed her to go off and satisfy her needs.

It was the sort of thing male fantasies are made of.

Sometimes he wonders if he imagined it all.

They say that smoking strong weed can make you delusional.

'HOW DID YOU KILL MARTINA RADU, POPE, YOU FILTHY CREEP?'

The bawled accusation comes like a thunderbolt. Kevin literally reels in his seat, shaken from his reverie.

He feels a sudden rush of tingles in his fingers and toes. The PTSD. He feels like the walls are closing in and he feels an almost overwhelming urge to escape. He shoves his hands into his pockets and balls them into tight fists.

He wasn't ready for the change of tone. The use of his surname. The spiteful insult.

Before the break, the inspector was all pally. He'd even exaggerated his Manchester drawl. Come on, Kevin, we're both Mancs, aren't we, cock? We know the score. We're old hands at this. We're thick as thieves, aren't we Kevin? Best that you come clean. The more you co-operate the better you'll feel. The more leniently you'll be treated by the court. You can speak safely to me. You don't want these local busies fitting you up, trust me, Kevin, old cock.

He was playing the good cop.

Now he's playing the bad cop.

And he's preening, strutting around – when before he just sat casually across the table, smoking – he even gave him a cig, despite the sign on the wall.

Wait a minute – he's showing off in front of the female officer – that's what he's doing. He's acting the hardman to impress the girl. He's even displaying what he's wearing – posing about like a catwalk mannequin.

Kevin can see why you might want to impress her – but the inspector is making a bad job of it – Kevin can tell that she's discomfited.

As he looks at her, her eyes meet his – and it's almost like she sends him a warning.

But before he can make more of her expression, a fist slams down on the table, spilling his water.

The tingling surges in his extremities – and it strikes home with a jolt, what danger he's in.

'Come on Pope – how did you kill her? We know you suffocated her. Did you drug her first? That's how you killed her, isn't it?'

Kevin stares helplessly at the droplets running off the edge. He wishes he could run off an edge – anything to get away. But his feet are going numb – and he wonders if he could even run.

His mouth is dry, his tongue tacky.

'I n-never killed n-no one. I don't even know who you're talking about.'

He glances over at the female. He can't help feeling that her heart's not in it – that she's having to play along because she's the junior officer.

'Was she staying at the hostel? Did you spy on her, Pope – like you did with naked women in your last job?'

'I never spied on no women – that was a case of mistaken identity.'

'Someone drilled the hole in the wall, Pope. Will we find a hole in the women's showers when we search at Buttermere?'

Kevin is shaking his head. The place is in bad repair, but he doesn't think they'll find a hole. But he wouldn't put it past this inspector to send someone to drill one. And they might plant gear – or find his stash. That won't serve him well.

'Why did you kill her, Pope? Did she knock you back?'

'I didn't kill anybody – I've told you.'

The female sergeant is frowning, she looks unconvinced – and he's sure it's not because of him.

'Never mind *any* body, Pope – we've got *a* body. And she didn't tie herself up in polythene and jump in the lake, did she? Did she do the dirty on you – cheat you on the consignment?'

'I don't even know what you mean – consignment.'

Kevin lowers his head and shakes it determinedly. But he feels on thinner ice when it comes to mention of drugs. He steals another glance through his matted hair at the woman – and it looks like she knows this, too.

A second slam on the table.

Kevin is obliged to look up.

The angry weaselly face is right in his own, just inches away. The eyes are bulging. The skin is flushed red.

Kevin turns his head aside.

'Come off it, Pope. We know you're the local dealer. Martina Radu was your regular mule, wasn't she?'

Kevin grimaces. He feels flecks of spittle land on his cheek.

Mint mouthwash almost masks the reek of cigs on the inspector's breath, and there's a waft of aftershave. He didn't smell like that before the break. He must have done it to impress the young woman.

Kevin shakes his head defiantly.

'I don't have nothing to do with drugs – not anymore – not since I were a teenager –'

The man cuts him off.

'Once a pusher, always a pusher, Pope.'

'No.'

'Who's your supplier in Manchester, Pope? Would you like to tell us – or do you want me to have to tell you?'

Kevin glances at the female. She is perplexed. This inspector's not so smart – it's obvious he doesn't know. It's obvious he doesn't know much, really. All they've got on him is a past record that's not so different to most blokes from his background.

And when the inspector doesn't tell him, he guesses they don't even know about his mate Clem in Manchester. Kevin

168

might not be a pusher – he's nothing more than a recreational user, that's a fact – but Clem is definitely a pusher, even though he claims not to be.

'It was Christmas before last you killed her, wasn't it? Why did you do it then – not a very charitable act, Pope. That's not going to go down well with a jury. A young woman who never made it back to her family.'

The other inspector, the local one – the one who actually did scare him – that's what he said. *'It's a possible line of inquiry. Christmas before last."*

Kevin thinks he's got an out.

'I wasn't even here, not this Christmas nor the one before. We close the hostel over the festive period.'

But the detective pounces.

'Where were you, then, Pope? Where were you over that Christmas? Tell us the times and places.'

But it suddenly terrifies Kevin that he might have to own up to visiting Clem. If he wants a proper alibi, that is. And, true, it was to pick up some weed, as well as a little change of scene before he came back.

'Come on, Pope – who did you spend that Christmas Day with? Where were you?'

He could give them false details – but he doubts they'll release him until they verify them. He'd need to warn Clem they'll be onto him. To get their story straight. But could he trust Clem? Why would Clem give him an alibi and put himself in jeopardy? Can he even risk it – Clem might be livid – and you wouldn't want to mess with Clem.

The thing is, he had intended to be at Buttermere – for Christmas Night, when Tina had promised she'd come. He'd supposed when she could get away from her family or her boring bloke or whatever was her situation.

Kevin's mind is racing. The detectives are staring at him, waiting for an answer. The silent treatment.

He decides just to say the van part. It might lack corroboration – but it's mostly true – isn't it?

Is it, though? When he delves back into his memory, it all seems a hazy blur. What was fact and what was fiction? He had a new load of weed, and nothing else to do but smoke it. Time went into a strange warp. Boiling water a cup at a time. Eating cold food from the supermarket. Trying to keep warm. Passing from consciousness to unconsciousness, slipping from daydreams to dreams ... of Tina lying beside him.

'I were in me van.'

The inspector sneers.

'In your van. What's that supposed to mean?'

Kevin tries to compose himself.

'When I finished up at the hostel, and the last staff left – the day before Christmas Eve – I drove down to Manchester.'

'For drugs, eh? To meet Martina Radu?'

Kevin inhales involuntarily. Everything gets twisted like this.

'No – it weren't to pick up anyone. I just thought I'd see if any of me mates were around – doss down at one of theirs.'

Kevin glances at the female sergeant. She is listening encouragingly. He tries to convey conviction in his expression.

'Except I couldn't find anyone – so I tried to come back.'

'You *tried* to come back?'

'Remember – it were all snowed in. I got diverted off the M6 into Penrith. They closed the A66 on Christmas Eve. Then it came on the radio that the likes of Buttermere were completely cut off.'

The inspector scoffs – but Kevin feels like he is on a little bit of a roll.

'I slept in the van. I lived in the van. I always keep sleeping bags and a camping stove in it, in case I break down in the fells. I used the superstore toilets and bought food from there and from an Asian corner shop that were open on Christmas Day. I didn't get back to the hostel until the day after Boxing Day, when they got the snowplough through.'

Even the night at Clem's he slept in the van – when things got a bit out of hand and a pair of heavies from that Moss Side gang turned up.

'So you lived for what – three days – in your van?'

'Yeah. Three nights. In the corner of the car park of the big DIY store.'

The face is back, inches from his own.

'Three nights with the body of Martina Radu. Just as well it were freezing cold, eh, Pope? You killed her in Manchester and brought the body to dump in the lake. That's it, isn't it? What are you Pope? What kind of person would live with a corpse for three days?'

The sudden onslaught unnerves him. His speech becomes disjointed.

'No – it weren't like that. I mean – I were on my own. I don't know any Martina Radu – I've never known any Martina Radu.'

He glances, panicked now, at the woman.

She seems both understanding and sceptical – in the way that she does on the one hand believe him – but almost as if she can read his mind. He might not know Martina Radu – but he did know the woman who called herself Tina. And what if – like he'd wondered – Martina and Tina really were one and the same person? And Tina came to the hostel – but he wasn't there – he was trapped in Penrith. That she got picked up in the blizzard or was given shelter – by a killer. And that's why she's never come back since.

Once again, he takes courage from the female sergeant's demeanour. He searches his memory. He thinks about what he's heard in the news. Then he has a sudden brainwave.

He turns to look at the inspector.

'Who is this Martina Radu? Have you got a photograph of her? A photograph with me in it? Have you got someone who saw me with her? Someone who can swear to it?'

He can't quite believe his own bravery. But he notices straightaway that it disconcerts the man – and Kevin glances at the sergeant to see that she, too, is watching the inspector closely – and does he detect a brief smile of satisfaction at the corners of her mouth?

The man has been lounging theatrically – posing again – against the door of the interview room – interrogation room, more like. Now he takes half a step forward and beckons to the female with a jerk of his head. He turns and reaches for the handle.

'You declined the duty solicitor, Pope. I suggest you might need one. We'll be back shortly with a list of charges. Number one will be murder. Unless you decide there's something you want to tell us.'

They leave him.

Is it a bluff? Should he ask for the solicitor? He's never trusted solicitors, not since that time back in Shrewsbury. She was on the side of the police all along. And now this inspector's contradicting himself. When they first brought him in, he said to Kevin why would he need a solicitor if he's innocent – it would just count against him.

Alone, he feels another surge of panic coming upon him. The tingling intensifies and he folds his arms, crushing his fingers against his ribs, curling his toes in his shoes as he sits.

If only he could find Tina – prove she was alive – get her to tell them.

But – no – even if she did come forward, that wouldn't prove he hadn't killed this other woman. If he could be shown to be having a clandestine relationship with one woman, why couldn't there have been another?

No – it's best just not to mention Tina, not for the time being.

He shudders. What if they have a photo of the dead body they dragged out of the lake? He'd never recognise her. Even now, though he tries hard, he struggles to picture her. Tina was like a woman from a dream, a presence that lingers into wakefulness, but remains elusive.

That first time she came, afterwards when she'd gone, he was sure that he must have imagined her. Was it a drug-induced hallucination? It was only when she returned the following week that he began to let himself believe it was really happening to him.

He remembers that first day – when he was relaxing out the back – he'd only been in the job a fortnight – early October –

and they'd just switched to weekend openings only. Unlike the other staff who have homes to go to, he's always just lived in, doing minor housekeeping chores between weekends. So he was alone.

It was a spell of Indian summer weather. There was the warmth of the afternoon sun. Flies hovering like tiny angels. Melancholy birdsong.

And she appeared round the corner. He hadn't heard her approach. When he'd said they weren't open until the Friday she'd just smiled and sat on the bench next to him. It was obvious she just wanted a drag on his joint.

He couldn't believe his luck when she ended up staying the night.

He was punching above his weight.

She wanted the experience, the drugs, the sex – like she was doing it for devilment, for some thrill it gave her – not for him.

She was like a butterfly. The sun came out and she materialised. She'd disappear sometimes during the day – he assumed off walking – though she never gave him any warning. She went away just as quickly and mysteriously, unannounced. When it's cloudy, it's like butterflies don't exist.

She never would tell him where she came from – if she even had a permanent home. But surely she must have – she was always nicely dressed and well groomed. She always smelt of the same expensive musky perfume.

And she always arrived on foot – she said she travelled by bus. She never brought much in the way of luggage. Just a little shoulder bag.

She wouldn't give him a mobile number or an address. Or let him take a photo. She used to say the less anyone knew the better for them both. The hint was – not to ask questions, if he wanted it to continue.

Then Christmas came, and it didn't continue.

'You're free to leave.'

For a moment Kevin thinks it's Tina's voice – telling him that he's released from their relationship. But he replays the words in his mind and hears the mild Cumbrian accent of the sergeant; it's only the second thing she has said to him.

'Mr Pope?'

He looks up, blinking at the bright light behind her as she stands framed in the open doorway.

'Mr Pope – I have to return to Buttermere. I understand this might not appeal to you – but I'm quite happy to give you a lift. But I can get a constable to take you along to the bus stop by the railway station, if you would prefer.'

Prefer? Who wouldn't prefer her? Who wouldn't it appeal to?

He feels a rush of adrenaline – but then a sudden unwanted but overwhelming wave of PTSD.

It's a trap. A honey trap.

That's why she's being so considerate towards him. Her expressions of concern during the interview – it was all an act. *She's in on it, after all.* And this is part of the ruse. They want him to go with her – to fall for her charms – and, when his guard is down, to confess to something. The police car will be bugged.

They think he's guilty.

They think he's stupid.

24. HANDOVER

Paige Turner's Bookshop, Cockermouth – 12.00 p.m.

IN A SMALL ACT akin to taking coals to Newcastle, Skelgill enters Paige Turner's wielding in a sealed polythene zipper-bag a copy of the hardback billed as *"The definitive field guide to British Birds"*. He veers across to the sales counter near the entrance and introduces himself, brandishing his police ID. The smartly dressed middle-aged woman on duty does not seem fazed. She eyes the tome knowingly, as if she has deduced that the officer has apprehended a shoplifter and is returning the ill-gotten gains.

'Can you tell me if you sold this book?'

She reaches to accept it, but Skelgill retracts it sufficiently to suggest she need not.

She is wily. She smiles.

'I take it you don't have the receipt?'

Skelgill responds with a rueful grin.

The woman peers more closely.

'That appears to be one of our 3-for-2 stickers. It's a promotion we ran for the January sale.'

Skelgill nods.

'I could ask our IT person to check on the system. It's hardly a top seller. It wouldn't prove it was exactly that copy – but it would be a reasonable inference to draw.'

'Okay.'

'Would you mind? I shall need the ISBN.'

'Aye.'

He hands it over. She writes on a notepad.

'I can't leave the till unmanned. I'll phone through to the depository. It might take a few minutes for them to do it.'

Skelgill is sniffing the cloistered air, the aroma of roasted coffee and toasted bread.

'Is Valentina White available?'

'Oh – she just left.' The woman points rather belatedly past Skelgill. 'As we were talking.'

That Skelgill does not flinch seems to prompt the woman to elaborate.

'I think she may be on a half day. She was wearing her jacket and carrying her bag. She stayed on after closing time last night.' Now she indicates again, this time towards a large central display positioned to intercept customers, some fifteen feet inside the store. 'Today is the start of Macabre May. It marks the beginning of the tourist season – a kind of mini book festival. We have local crime and horror authors performing readings and book signings.'

He turns to gaze at the arrangement of showcards, posters and piles of paperbacks. The woman waits patiently. A customer joins the one-man queue that is Skelgill. She edges a quarter pace into his personal space; it is British for "get on with it, will you?" He seems to realise. He raises the bird book.

'I'll come by on my way out.'

He steps away, towards the interior and returns the guide to the crime scene shoulder bag that he intends for DS Leyton to courier to headquarters. It contains Royston Woodcock's laptop, camera and mobile – and the photograph from the bedroom drawer of the young blonde woman.

At the café counter he places a double order, advising the waitress that he will find a table on the mezzanine platform. Once seated, he pulls out his phone. He tuts. His last text to DS Jones has still not been read. He dials, but the call – like his previous effort – diverts immediately to voicemail.

He tries DS Leyton, with more success.

'Alright, Guv?'

'Where are you?'

'Just parking – in the supermarket.'

'What did Jones say?'

'About meeting you?' DS Leyton sounds doubtful. 'Come to the bookshop.'

'Nay – I mean, what's she up to? I've had no signal. Now I can't raise her.'

'She said she's sitting-in on the Pope interview. Riding shotgun to DI Smart. I assumed you knew that, Guv?'

Skelgill is assailed by the opposing forces of alarm and hope. But the average effect is discomfort. There is a silence while he stews.

'Guv?'

'I've ordered you a toastie. I'm in the little upstairs bit, round from the caff.'

'I'll be two ticks. Save some for me.'

To DS Leyton's relief or good fortune, he and the food order arrive simultaneously – and he seems delighted with the concurrence.

'Cor, I ain't half Hank Marvin – it's the smell of the food when you come into these places.'

Skelgill has wasted no time in tucking in. He nods approvingly.

'Bacon and brie.'

DS Leyton regards his superior with a glint of amusement in his eye – as though he suspects there is a hoped-for prospect that the slightly exotic combination might not be to his taste, and there will be leftovers to scavenge. Skelgill inclines his head, inviting his subordinate to sit.

'Ketchup.'

'Give us a chance, Guv – oh – *ketchup*, yeah. Don't mind if I do.'

He chuckles and makes good inroads into the first third of his sliced panini before he deems it appropriate to comment.

'So, that's a bit of a shocker – Royston Woodcock.'

Skelgill nods but has his teeth into his middle portion of sandwich.

'Emma said you reckon he was coshed.'

Skelgill's eyes flash.

'What?'

DS Leyton sways back in his seat and glances furtively about.

'Just between these four walls, Guv. Whacked on the back of the head and the tunnel roof pulled down on him – to make it look like an accident. Neither his gaff burgled nor him robbed of his camera, right?'

Exasperation is hard to convey with a full mouth, and Skelgill has to settle for a theatrical shrug that does little to quell his colleague's enthusiasm.

'No sooner than we'd sussed out that flippin' gatepost. *Wallop!*'

Skelgill shakes his head while he swallows.

'But not Kevin Pope.'

DS Leyton nods in agreement.

'Thing is – any old passer-by could have noticed the broken slate – taken it.'

Skelgill squints, reluctant to concur. Not exactly any passer-by. There would be a certain malice aforethought. But certainly the shard of rock was not difficult to get at.

DS Leyton continues.

'Looks like Woodcock rattled someone's cage. It's surely too much of a coincidence, otherwise?'

Skelgill remains in sceptical mode.

'We'll need to wait on SOCO. It still could be an accident.'

DS Leyton is unconvinced.

'But what was he doing in that tunnel at midnight? Trying to photograph cave bats?'

'Leyton, there's no such thing as cave bats.' Skelgill scowls, and then concedes some ground. 'There's bats that roost in caves. Daubenton's – feed on insects over the water, laying and hatching.'

But Skelgill is troubled by DS Leyton's point. What was Royston Woodcock doing in the tunnel? Passing through, surely – but what was he intending to photograph in the dark without a flashgun? The night sky? Possibly, it was clear. A person inside a lighted room? Perhaps – it was bedtime, after all. They have identified a tendency towards voyeurism, albeit not on private property. But the next lighted room in that direction would be an unprepossessing lambing barn at Gatesgarth; the rest of the farm would have long retired.

Whatever it was, he never made it. There are no new photographs on the camera's memory card beyond those of the previous day that he and DS Jones had scrutinised, pied wagtails and police officers, snapped from behind the wall opposite the entrance of the Hikers' Hostel.

Skelgill's brooding silence provides a cue for DS Leyton. He takes a drink and clears his throat.

'I don't reckon we can rule out Abel Ketch at the moment, Guv.'

Skelgill looks on implacably.

DS Leyton waves a hand airily.

'So – he was in the navy, alright – but what he didn't tell us was he got a dishonourable discharge for an alleged assault on a female cadet. He escaped a court martial by the skin of his teeth.'

He allows the news to sink in.

'That was over ten years ago. Seems he moved back to Cumbria, set up his boat repair business. Shacked up with a local woman, divorcee by the name of Jennifer Mary Eccles. I reckon she's the Jenny on his tattoo. DC Watson found an address for her – that's where I went this morning. A different address from the one Ketch had given me – a flat in the Corkickle area. Couldn't get any answer. Knocked up a couple of neighbours. They didn't seem to know much – they think there's a geezer living there alone, fits the description of Ketch. The woman ain't been seen in ages – possibly a couple of years.' He raises his eyebrows. 'And she matches the description of the Lady of the Lake.'

Skelgill remains pensive.

'Did you ask Abel Ketch?'

DS Leyton shakes his head.

'I thought you'd want to keep our powder dry, Guv. And we'll need to do more digging on this Eccles woman – she ain't coming up on any top-line searches – but she might be married again and living just round the corner.' He allows a long pause. 'Or not.'

Skelgill stares at his colleague.

DS Leyton waits for a few moments longer.

'I've also got the preliminary results from the lab. The rope and the polythene from Hassness Castle match the composition of the materials used to wrap the body. That's not to say the building site at Hassness Castle would be the only possible source, not by a long chalk – but you can't say it wasn't handy.'

Skelgill nods; it was handy, alright.

'But the new samples – from the builder's yard – they don't match. No surprise there, I suppose. I spoke with the merchants – they reckon they buy in bulk from whichever supplier's the cheapest at the time.'

Skelgill contemplates the final portion of his sandwich; he might be trying to decide whether to eke it out over two bites, but why bother when it fits in one. The distraction affords DS Leyton the opportunity to reiterate an earlier pronouncement with added vim.

'So it's another box ticked, Guv. Ketch's mate Tapp would have had access to those materials while he was doing the plumbing job at Hassness Castle. Ketch is a geezer with boats and a trailer – and a record of violence. Knows his fancy knots. Familiar with the depths of the lake. They dived a lake no one bothers with – and can't get their story straight about whose idea it was – that alphabetical nonsense never convinced me. And they found the body.'

An approximate silence ensues. But when Skelgill finishes chewing and still does not comment, DS Leyton rows back a little.

'Although why they'd want to rediscover her does beat me.'

Skelgill grunts, shifting position in his seat, as if he is finding the hard chair uncomfortable.

'I reckon you'd better locate this Jennifer Eccles.'

'I know that, Guv. But – what with the Woodcock death and Pope getting the third degree – and DS Jones getting roped into that – I didn't want to start pulling our resources in the wrong direction. I mean – when you think about it – we probably ought to eliminate the builders, an' all.'

Skelgill does not take up this suggestion.

'You can forget about Pope, Leyton. That's just Smart trying to shove a spanner in our works.'

DS Leyton nods phlegmatically.

'At least we know he couldn't have whacked Woodcock. Why would anyone want to do that? It would surely mean he knew something – but what?'

'The man with the long lens knows a lot of things, Leyton.'

DS Leyton shows the whites of his eyes.

'You sound like Confucius, Guv.'

But Skelgill merely reaches down and hauls up the crime scene shoulder bag. He pulls it open to reveal its contents.

'Jones reckons there's the thick end of 20,000 images on the laptop.' He lifts the framed photograph. 'This might be Woodcock's daughter, lives in New Zealand. Relatives – that's another job.'

DS Leyton runs the fingers of one hand through his hair.

'*Whew.* Speaking of resources. I'd better scoot, then, Guvnor.'

'Aye.'

The sergeant rises and takes the bag, noticing as he leaves that Skelgill is eyeing the untouched cube of walnut fudge that came free with his coffee.

On departure, Skelgill is informed at the sales counter that the store did indeed sell a single copy of the bird guide in the January sale; quite probably it is the same one. That it was purchased together with *The Lost Birds of Middlemarch* and renowned photographer Eric Hosking's *An Eye for a Bird* to complete the 3-for-2 deal seems to convince Skelgill. He avoids further questions, and besides there are customers wishing to pay. He drifts across to the Macabre May display, set up by Valentina White. It is a striking arrangement, moody and dark, artistically executed. He peruses a suitably graphic poster that lists the guest speakers on a tombstone; there are one or two authors' names he vaguely recognises – though L.L. James is conspicuous by her absence, despite that her books are prominent in the stacks for sale.

A front cover of a fell runner traversing a rocky arête against an uneasy sunrise catches his eye. The word 'murder' in the title infers what fate awaits the athlete. He turns it over and squints at the blurb. He scowls, and shakes his head, and replaces it with a disparaging growl. All this fiction, when there are so many facts to know.

He leaves the store, but pauses one final time, to scrutinise the opening hours displayed through the glass of the door; closing time on a Wednesday is six p.m.

25. BOORACH

Catthwaite Cottage – 2.20 p.m.

'IT'S VERY KIND of you to help me, Inspector. Gordon warned me that I wouldn't manage on my own – but I'm a headstrong type, you know?'

'Nowt wrong with that, Mrs McLeish.'

It seems he is familiar with the criticism. Margery grins over the box that between them they are toting down the side path of the holiday let that she and Gordon jointly own; though she seems to do most of the heavy lifting – right now, literally.

'Wasn't it Bertrand Russell who said the reasonable man adapts himself to the circumstances in which he finds himself, therefore all progress depends upon the unreasonable man?'

This brings a glint of catlike intrigue into the officer's greenish eyes – as if it is a quote he ought to file for future use – but then perhaps a greying of the irises, as though he rehearses a little scenario in his mind and runs into some kind of resistance.

'So, what made you come down alone?'

She notes that, instead, he has picked up on her practical point.

They both gasp a little as they manhandle the long flat package, tilting it to pass the awkward pinch point where the sunken path rounds the corner of the building. She is conscious that he is both taking most of the weight and walking backwards. Even dragging the box, she could not have managed it on her own.

'Och, we've had this flatpack furniture cluttering up our vestibule for the last fortnight. We're planning to come down at the end of the month – we've blocked out the Whitsun week when the schools are off. As you just saw, the Defender is full to the roof, with the back seats down – so we couldn't all four of us and the dogs fit in. Besides, I'm hoping to find a local handyman who can have it all made up for when we arrive. If we get some decent weather it will be lovely to have a comfortable patio set at long last.'

The detective regards her evenly; but it seems she has not supplied the answer that most interests him. After all, she had not mentioned the trip when his colleague had called her the previous afternoon.

'But you're lodging at the Fish. Must feel a bit strange – when you own this place?'

She inclines her head towards the building.

'We're pretty well booked solid. Then a case I'm working on was adjourned last thing yesterday – so I thought I'd just take the opportunity of a flying visit. I couldn't get in at the Bridge but the Fish had a single room.'

He shows no surprise. Quite likely they will have vetted her story – they'll know that her booking was made at the last minute – and that she checked in at just before ten p.m. This policeman would not be doing his job if he did not find out why she was in Cumbria. That he claims he just happened to be passing and caught a glimpse of her – well …

'Of course – I didn't expect – well – you know? What happened. I'm hoping you won't need me to stay any later than this evening?'

He has his head turned, craning as best he can to navigate the meandering stepping stones as they weave between the borders towards the garden shed that is their destination.

'I don't see why we would. I'm told your statement is very comprehensive.' He looks back at her, more intently now. 'I just wanted to make sure you were alreet, like?'

She guffaws involuntarily – it feels unbecoming.

'Och, don't worry about me, Inspector – I'm made of stern stuff. You should see some of the cases I prosecute. Stomach churning.'

Then again, he probably does see that kind of thing, though he evidently chooses not to say so.

'All the same – it's not every day you come across a corpse in a cave. You can't help being shocked.'

She lowers her gaze; why not accept such solicitude? She blinks, several times.

'Gordon has offered to come down by train. To drive me home. I said I'd be fine. But it seems he's insisting.'

'You should take him up on it – you'll be tired – especially with all this lifting, on top of the stress – plus you're an early bird.'

The lawyer in her knows a leading remark when it hears one. But she need not reveal that the call from the police had unnerved her to the point of insomnia.

'Och, I rarely sleep very well in a strange bed – and it was such a glorious morning. There was a song thrush right outside my window, going at it hammer and tongs; I felt it was summoning me. I knew I was in for a Cumbrian breakfast, so I thought – lake walk – these days it's so hard to get the children off their screens – we don't often do it when we're here as a family. I had originally planned to have breakfast, make this delivery, and return – and be back in Edinburgh for just after lunchtime. Then grocery shopping at Waitrose before school runs and sports clubs.'

The officer grunts an acknowledgement – but it may simply be that they have reached the shed where she has propped open the door and cleared a space on one side – and now he heaves the box with its heavy hardwood contents as he backs up onto the raised threshold.

'I thought – just behind you, Inspector, on the left.'

'Aye.'

He takes most of the strain as they lower their burden into place; she notices he immediately stretches his back, pressing his fists into the base of his spine.

'I hope I haven't caused you to do yourself an injury?'

'What? Nay – just precautionary.'

She suddenly feels conscious of the close presence of this stranger – not for the first time today, but in considerably different circumstances, despite that it is an equally confined space. They are both panting a little from their exertions. He is not conventionally attractive; but there emanates from his rangy form and rugged countenance a certain unaffected magnetism. She straightens her top, and she senses his gaze as she brushes her palms over her thighs; she still has on the tight riding breeches, though they are smeared with earth from earlier, and now marked by what must be ink from the cardboard packaging. Had she been expecting him, she might have applied a coat of lipstick.

He seems to linger – though it can only be for a second or two – but she finds herself saying the first thing that comes into her head.

'You must think this place is a boorach. It's such a mess that we don't even lock it – I'm sure it would deter any burglar.'

His eyes rove about – aside from the petrol lawnmower and garden tools there are the children's first bikes; long plastic sledges hanging by their ropes, one red, one blue; two paddleboards – not strictly allowed on Buttermere – but he does not dwell upon them; a rigid clamshell paddling pool; and Gordon's old fishing rod, which does arrest his gaze.

Finally, he nods, his features wry.

'You should see my shed. I had to get another.'

She chuckles, and without thinking reaches to touch his arm.

'You don't strike me as a hoarder, Inspector.'

He looks like he would like to know why she says this – but she retracts her hand and fills the little pregnant pause with an audible sigh.

'The kids have outgrown half of it. Although some of the families who stay use it. But I think I shall sort out a few things. No point going home with an empty vehicle.'

The suggestion seems to prompt him into action. She stands in the way of the door, and he takes half a pace towards her.

'We'd better get the rest in, then.'

She backs away, taking care as she steps down onto the path.

'Och – no – I can manage the rest – it was just the picnic bench – it's three times the weight of everything else. It was such fortunate timing of yours. I don't want to detain you – you must be busy with your investigation.'

They are walking side by side, and he is silent for a moment. It must be obvious that she is fishing for information.

'Did you know the Woodcock chap?'

'Just what I told your constable. I realise we're technically neighbours – but these old smallholdings are several acres, and mostly wooded, as you see. I honestly didn't recognise him this morning. I knew of him, of course – and that he was something of a recluse – our cleaner told us that. I've always warned the kids not to stray onto his land – so as not to annoy him.'

The officer is silent for a little longer. She wonders if he is waiting to see what else she might volunteer. She tries a different tack.

'And to boot I spoiled your angling expedition.'

He shrugs, in a manner clearly exaggerated for her benefit.

'It would have been a matter of time. If it weren't you – it would have been the next walker.' He turns to look at her. 'And they might not have handled it so calmly.'

26. MT DIFFICULTY

Hassness Cottage – 3.10 p.m.

H E KNOWS THAT he has been seen. And he has seen her. But for good measure, she waits half a second before stepping back, and gives the bedroom curtain a twitch. She crosses to the long mirror and strips off her sweatshirt. She rotates slowly, pausing to check over her shoulder. She selects an atomiser from the dresser. She sprays it onto her right wrist and transfers it to her left, and then to her neck beneath her ears. She plucks at her hair to emphasise the casual spikes. She smiles with satisfaction.

Kia ora, Inspector Skelgill.

But it is another five minutes before he knocks. Time enough to make a few adjustments and pour herself a glass of wine. He must detect her heavy shoes as she approaches the door; she hears him clear his throat.

'Gidday, Inspector – for what do I deserve the honour?'

He falters immediately. Whatever he had intended to say, her appearance has disarmed him. She can tell he is struggling to hold her gaze; his eyes wish to drift to her naked midriff with its sparkling diamond piercing. And there is the underlying unease; the familiar response of a red-blooded male to a woman like her; the little inner battle between instinct and logic.

All this in a second.

'I – er – I was actually hoping for a word with Ms Longstaff.'

She pouts a mixture of disappointment and dismay – but quickly breaks into a smile.

'Lena? She went away last night.'

In not showing surprise, he conceals a reaction. She noticed this before.

'Is she gone for long?'

'I really don't know.'

He is clearly nonplussed; he shifts a little from one foot to the other.

'Please, come in. You look thirsty. I'm in the conservatory.'

She flashes another smile. She doesn't wait.

He's following her. He fastens the door and moves quickly to catch up.

She knows that she trails allure.

She can smell the subtle grassy fragrance of her perfume as she crosses back through its floating essence.

And her skin-tight white loon pants that show no VPL – after all, how could they!

'You must think I'm stalking you.'

His voice sounds a little hoarse. Is this an overt reference to the sliding doors moment at lunchtime?

She does not look back.

'Stalking sounds intriguing – that would make me your prey, eh?'

But he does not respond – nor press the point – perhaps he didn't see her leaving.

Bright sunlight flooding the little glazed lean-to seems to reset the mood.

'Have a seat.'

He takes the space not quite at the end of the settee. He sits upright, with his forearms crossed over his thighs.

She leans to pick up the glass that denotes her position. She swirls what is left, an illustrative action.

'Mount Difficulty.'

'Story of my life.'

A quip, a trace of humour, of self-deprecation.

He glances about, as if there might be alternatives on display – although that perhaps he might be worried about them, too.

'I'd better just have tap water, thanks.'

'Sweet as.'

But she returns with a Moorish azulejo tray that bears the chilled bottle and an extra wine glass, along with the tumbler of water. She places the tray in front of him and rotates the bottle to display the label.

'See – it's a real place.'

He reaches and drinks thirstily, skirting a reply. Though he squints at the wine bottle, the pinkish-golden liquid to which fine droplets of condensation add appetite appeal.

Curiously, he does not begin to speak – nor immediately pick up their dialogue begun at the front door.

She waits – she settles back languidly, cradling her glass.

'Is there something I can help you with? In Lena's absence?'

What will he tell her?

'You say you don't know when she'll be back?'

So, he procrastinates. Is it just his way? It seems enough like that, each time he has spoken with her. Or is it a device?

Cat and mouse is fine.

She waves a casual hand.

'I really have no idea.'

'Are you thinking tomorrow?'

'I'm not thinking anything, Inspector – though I'm pretty sure I'll be alone tonight.'

She drinks – and gives a little shake of her head to suggest amusement. She senses that the sun will be catching the highlights in her pixie cut.

He is frowning, looking ahead at the landscape beyond the glass.

'You say she went yesterday – last night?'

'Well – yes – certainly she had gone when I arrived home. I worked late – I came home on the night bus – it was getting on for midnight. The cottage was in darkness. Her laptop was gone. Her duffel bag. A few clothes. Her toothbrush. The bed was empty.'

She twists at the waist; he is obliged to make eye contact.

'She's not left you a note?'

He sounds concerned; she chuckles.

'Don't cry for me, Inspector. We don't live in one another's pockets. I'm accustomed to her whims – it's what she does.'

She touches his arm. He stiffens, though it may be the little puzzle.

'What, like a regular thing?'

She takes a contemplative sip of her wine. He retracts his gaze when she stares unblinking over the rim of the glass. The power of her bright blue eyes.

'Perhaps not exactly regular – regular would suggest every month, or something – but whenever the muse strikes her. When she gets her teeth into a story. She's a discovery writer – she doesn't plot – she writes by the seat of her pants.'

'How long does she go off for?'

'It could be a few days, or more. She spent a fortnight in Paris when she was researching *Death in the Catacombs* – and a month away for *The Curse of La Mezquita* – she returned to Andalusia. Cordoba, eh?' Valentina surprises herself by laughing gaily. 'I'll await her next postcard.'

He looks more bewildered.

'What's she writing now, then?'

'She's working on a Holy Grail theme. Dan Brown meets Bram Stoker – her words. She's been talking about visiting ancient churches. Encoded inscriptions. Sarcophagi. Gargoyles. There's Rosslyn Chapel near Edinburgh. The Temple Church in the City of London. And she's bewitched by the mystery of the hilltop church of St Mary Magdalene at Rennes-le-Chateau in the Languedoc.'

'It's a heck of a drive.'

'We don't have a car, Inspector. Another of the trappings of modern life that doesn't cost us a small fortune.'

His hand with its long fingers drifts to interrogate his unshaven fell-like jaw.

'So, how would she get about?'

'Bus, train. I expect she will have hitched to begin with. Perhaps to Penrith or Kendal.'

Instantly, he looks doubtful.

'It's not always advisable – a lone female.'

He casts a hand in the direction of the lake. There is the unspoken suggestion of "look what happened".

She shifts and affects a little frisson – and presses his arm as if for reassurance.

'The perils of a lone female, Inspector. Lena likes living on the edge. Why wouldn't a horror writer admit a little jeopardy into her life? I'm sure it fires her imagination. Don't you quite admire that? Surely that's rather like being a detective. You thrive on obsession, on turning stones, on forbidden fruits ... finally yielding to your instincts.'

Her hand is still upon him, and now she squeezes, feeling the hard strands of muscle that gird his forearm.

He looks tempted by the subtle flattery. There is a slight swaying of his shoulders, the hint of an inner swagger. Then a small grimace of self-doubt.

'You think of writing – and you think of a cautious type, tucked away in an attic, nose to the grindstone. Making stuff up, like.'

She murmurs mild reproof.

'Authors, they are not like most normal people, Inspector. They run hot.'

Now he frowns, the eyes introspective.

After a moment he indicates to the books on the table and then over to the shelves – as if he is casting about for evidence of his theory: that writing is merely risk-taking by proxy.

'L.L. James isn't listed in your May book festival. At Paige Turner's.'

She finds herself sipping her wine meditatively. So he has noticed. And is he dangling a little bait?

She releases her breath slowly.

'Perhaps just as well – we wouldn't want to disappoint her readers.'

She senses he finds her reply incomplete – but she waits for his cue.

'Her books seem to be popular – going by the amount you've got on sale.'

'Do you suspect me of favouritism?' She laughs – and taps him reprimandingly. 'Have you read anything of hers?'

He seems uncomfortable with the question.

'I don't get a lot of spare time for reading.'

She clicks her tongue.

'You should make time. I'd be happy to provide recommendations. It's part of my job to write reviews for the store. How about this, for instance?' She reaches across him, turning in when she could turn out – stretching her tight crop top – to pick up a hardback from which protrudes a branded Paige Turner's bookmark. *The Talented Mr Ripley.* 'A psychological thriller. It might help you with ideas – solving a crime by getting into the mind of your suspect. If it's the mind you want to get into.'

He remains perfectly still, though he compresses his lips, and she hears him inhale and her fragrance makes him blink involuntarily. She can feel her heartbeat. She is revelling in the challenge, the thrill of the chase. The enchantress in full flight.

He takes the book; it falls open where it is marked, at the beginning of chapter twenty-four. She watches his eyes; he stares vacantly at the top line of the opposite page, a sentence carried over: "… really inviting trouble, and he couldn't stop himself".

He closes the book and presses it onto his thighs, palms down on the cover.

He exhales.

'Last night – you say you got back around midnight?'

She contains a smile. End of the round but not the bout.

She shrugs casually, turning a bare shoulder a little towards him.

'I guess so – I couldn't say exactly.'

Now he regards her evenly; he is more composed than a moment ago.

'Before you came indoors, were you aware of any disturbance in the vicinity? Raised voices, noisy vehicles – that kind of thing.'

'Nothing that I recall. An owl, maybe. A fox crossed the road in front of me when I walked from the bus stop. I don't think I saw a single car. Just me and the Milky Way.'

She waits. Let him tell her.

'Are you acquainted with a near neighbour called Royston Woodcock? From Pike Rigg Cottage about half a mile towards the village.'

'No, I can't say we are. We rather keep to ourselves. You know how it is?'

Now she plies him with a brief but bashful smile.

'He was found early this morning, by a walker. The tunnel on the lake path collapsed and killed him.'

'Oh, my.' She reaches a hand to cover her lips. 'I remember there are warning signs.'

She feels sure he is now waiting to see if she will elaborate.

But she is patient; she merely widens her blue eyes, imploring him to be more forthcoming.

'Just one reason I mention it – he has a daughter living in New Zealand. It's the sort of thing you might have discussed. With your accent –'

He is finding this a little awkward.

'There's no hiding it, eh?' She exaggerates the inflexion. And she helps him out further. 'I suppose if we'd crossed paths and made small talk. There aren't so many of us Kiwis – we have to stick together.'

'He was a Londoner, like – but I thought it was worth asking.'

'It can be a small world. But I'm sorry I can't help. And I'm not much use with Lena, am I?'

She picks up her wine and swirls the liquid around the bowl; it looks cool and inviting, and it draws his gaze. He glances at the bottle and the empty glass beside it.

He gives a little cough, as if he has become conscious that his throat is dry.

'Actually, there is one thing I might ask you about.'

She pounces on the chance to trade. She tops up her own glass, and then pours a splash into the second, leaving it on the tray. She unhooks her left leg from its crossed pose over her right and sinks into the settee.

'Be my guest.'

She waits.

He doesn't move – though he turns to make eye contact.

'I missed a call from her. She mentioned she might have some information. She may have discussed it with you – I say that, since she called it a piece of the jigsaw.'

Did she say a piece of the jigsaw? It's a common enough phrase. He has been keeping this back. This time she does not conceal her smile.

'I suspect she is planning ahead.'

He is looking perplexed – more so than she might have imagined.

'She's thinking of writing a book about this case?'

'Close to home, perhaps – and a little ghoulish – but who can blame her? The Lady of the Lake. The Arthurian legend. It is embedded in our collective folk memory. And now a contemporary twist.'

It takes him a moment to respond.

'So – she didn't say owt specific?'

She smiles – she leans closer – and lowers her voice confidingly.

'Inspector, perhaps it was a little ploy – that she was just hoping to chat with you. Probe your feelings. Pick your brains.'

'That wouldn't get her far.'

She laughs – for he means to be funny – and he smiles in return. The first time.

She sips again – and speaks soothingly.

'Do you not have a theory? You mentioned lines of inquiry.'

He seems suddenly relaxed, as if his guard has slipped but he does not mind, indeed is relieved.

'There's a couple of promising leads. My two colleagues are following them up.'

'While you are free to stalk!'

He appears not to object to her audacity.

'Fat lot of good that's done. But I should have called your friend straight back – just in case.'

Another little opening? It's worth a try.

Valentina stretches to place a hand on his knee and rises, using him as leverage. She feels momentarily dizzy – alcohol and sunshine and adrenaline combine – and she totters on her platform soles. He grabs to steady her, but she regains her balance, and he releases her wrist.

'Sharp reflexes, Inspector.'

She purrs throatily and bends to place her glass on the tray with the half bottle and the second glass, as yet untouched. She lingers close to him – and then picks up the tray with its contents.

'Perhaps Lena did leave a note on my pillow. I may have missed it in the dark. Wouldn't you like to help me look?'

27. KATYA

Honister Hause YHA – 3.20 p.m.

DS JONES CONTEMPLATES the pixelated portrait. A rather mournful pale-eyed brunette of Mediterranean appearance. If it had been Skelgill who had stopped to check his mail before they lost the signal she might have considered it a sixth sense. Alone, she certainly feels that intuition is at play right now. Not that she recognises the girl in the newly transmitted image – the passport photograph of Martina Radu – but she does feel she is on the right track. It wasn't so much what Kevin Pope said, but more the way he said it. And the way he had tried to interact with her. If only there were telepathy! The sense that he had an entirely different tale, if only he could tell it. And – this a point of logic – his vehement challenge to DI Alec Smart, to produce evidence that he had been in the company of Martina Radu.

And there *was* Skelgill's gut feel. Didn't he say, Kevin Pope knows something.

So, it was handy that she had stopped near Low Lorton, before the fells closed in.

Now at her destination she waits; it is a pleasant hiatus. The afternoon sun streams down the fellside from its station above Grey Knotts, glinting off the silvered mat-grass and illuminating the vibrant emerald bracken, where occasional Herdwick yowes trail their tiny black bleating issue, foraging for the tastier fescues and wildflowers that must make uniquely flavoured milk, and in turn lamb. She closes her eyes and tilts back her head; the solar rays upon her skin are like a warming balm. She listens to the soft ululation of the sheep – and the continuous sough of a little cascade; it is the source of Gatesgarthdale Beck that feeds Buttermere with its clear slate-green waters.

Buttermere. She wonders what Skelgill is doing. She suspects he is somewhere in the dale; she did not see his car as she passed through; but he has no signal – or his phone is switched off.

He'll be up to something unconventional.

She inhales slowly, but before her mind can wander onto treacherous ground the door of the youth hostel opens with a bang. With a small gasp she rises from the bench and waves the phone in a greeting.

'Pryvit, Katya.'

The girl looks pleased, if a little surprised to see her.

'Yak spravy, Serzhant?'

'Good, thank you. Can you spare two minutes? Come and sit. Then I'll give you a hand with those hampers.'

With one foot, the girl pushes back the bale of laundry she was about to drag out to the old jalopy that stands nearby with its tailgate raised.

Taking a seat, she looks inquisitively at DS Jones.

'I see you this morning – at the Hikers' Hostel. It is the rotten corpse? You think she was hill walker?'

DS Jones grins ruefully. Rumours, like the babbling becks of the fells, find their own course. It was Monday that the media reported in sanitised terms – but Skelgill was right; half the dale knew of the gruesome find within minutes of the divers' agitated gatecrashing of the inn on Sunday.

She hands over the phone.

'Do you recognise this woman?'

Katya dips her head.

'This is her?'

DS Jones murmurs a suggestion to the contrary.

'This woman is alive. We're trying to find her.'

Katya is scrutinising diligently.

'She look – Balkan?'

'Yes, Romanian.'

Katya hands back the phone.

'I have not see her.'

Her response is quite matter of fact.

DS Jones indicates towards Katya's car.

'How long have you been taking the laundry at the Hikers' Hostel?'

'Over two years – since the invasion.'

The girl swallows.

DS Jones gives her a moment. She wants to reach to press her hand. She sees that she wears a woven yellow and blue bracelet. It is frayed but steadfast.

Now Katya says something in Ukrainian that DS Jones does not understand – though the sentiment is as plain as the bright spring day is clear.

She decides that Katya does not need kid gloves.

'I thought you might know if the manager, Kevin Pope, had a girlfriend.'

Katya glances sharply at her – but DS Jones deflects her inquiry with a palm extended towards the blue laundry hampers piled in the back of the car.

'The bedding.'

Katya's expression is one of fleeting apprehension – until she smiles – and laughs – a beautiful sight – that she suddenly forgets her cares – that they are just like two twenty-something girlfriends sharing risqué gossip. Her giggling is infectious.

When their mirth subsides, Katya makes a serious face.

'He has no woman.'

'Ah.'

'But there *was* woman.'

DS Jones feels the fine blonde hairs on the back of her neck begin to rise.

'When?'

'When I first come. The first year.'

'Can you remember exactly?'

But Katya pouts.

'I am not sure.'

'From early in the year?'

'Yes.'

DS Jones is doing the sums. Kevin Pope only began working at Buttermere Hikers' Hostel in the October of the year to which they refer.

'Until when?'

The girl's gaze traverses the rolling skyline above them, searching for memories.

'All year, I think. Yes – even when the cold weather come. It was like Kyiv. Like home.'

There is a mournful note in her voice. Though she smiles with determination.

DS Jones allows a few seconds to pass before she presses for more detail.

'Did you see a girl – a woman – a girlfriend?'

'No – no – I am not there for very long. I do not clean there.' She gestures over her shoulder, to indicate the contrast between her additional role here at Honister Hause. 'At Buttermere, I just take laundry, as quick as I can. I have other pick-ups.'

DS Jones turns to make eye contact.

'But you're sure about this?'

Katya nods eagerly.

'There is laundry from visitors every day. For staff – it is change just once a week. Sometimes – they are busy – I must take sheets from staff quarters.'

'From the beds.'

'Yes.'

'That's how you know? You stripped Kevin Pope's bed.'

Another mischievous smile.

'I am Miss Marble, yes?'

*

'I'm alone.'

'Aye – I see that, love.'

DS Jones responds with a smile; the woman, refreshingly, has no airs and graces. Indeed, Ann Johnson continues to peer past her – perhaps making quite sure that Skelgill is not behind the tinted glass of the yellow car parked a little beyond the front portico of the Buttermere Hikers' Hostel, his unwilling presence conveniently obscured by the reflection of the sky. She fires off a question before DS Jones can elaborate on her purpose.

'Did you find out about Kevin?'

'I'm sorry, madam?'

'This morning – when you didn't know he'd been arrested.'

'Oh – sure. Actually, he was just helping with inquiries. I expect he'll be back soon. We offered him a lift – but he wanted to make his own way.'

'*Hah!*' That'll be him for t' day.' She plies DS Jones with a look suggestive of some habitual truancy which can only be guessed at.

DS Jones has arrived wondering how duplicitous she may need to be – but the woman seems happy to disparage her boss. And she did, after all, earlier describe herself as the general dogsbody. That she is shrewd, there is no doubt; plain speaking would seem the best tactic.

'Have you worked here long, Mrs Johnson?'

'Best part of seven year it is, now, love.' She watches for DS Jones's reaction and qualifies her answer. 'Summer, like. Good Friday till the August Bank Holiday – that's the peak period. Off-season it's open weekends only – and part-time's no good to me. Winter, I work in the council care home at Cleator Moor – there's staff dropping like flies, what with all this Covid and flu still going about.'

DS Jones hurriedly recalculates the chronology. This woman would not have been employed here when Kevin Pope joined in the October two years ago, nor during the three months running up to the fateful Christmas.

She opts to unravel the conundrum inadvertently raised by Katya.

'The previous manager – before Mr Pope – did he have a partner – or girlfriend?'

'It were a woman.'

'I'm sorry?'

'Ivy Smith, Scotch – she were the manageress afore Kevin. Ms Smith, she liked to be known as. Don't know what was wrong with plain Ivy.' There is a hint of disapproval in the woman's tone. 'But – aye – there were talk that she'd have a fella to stay odd times, on the quiet. Either that, or it were one-night stands with walkers that she fancied.'

DS Jones blinks ingenuously.

'You say there was talk. How would anyone know this?'

Ann Johnson gives a backward jerk of her head.

'It were the old cook, Mildred Lawson – she's retired now. She'd come in early to do breakfast and she reckoned she'd hear someone leaving down t' back stairs from the manager's quarters and out by t' fire escape.'

'I suppose that could have been the manager. Going outside for a cigarette?'

The woman grins in a devious fashion.

'Aye, but it don't make such good crack.'

DS Jones smiles obligingly.

'And Mr Pope – he's single, that's correct?'

Now the woman produces a short explosive laugh.

'Are thee surprised, love?'

DS Jones calls to mind the interview – the rather scrawny figure, lank-haired, scruffily dressed. Though he is not bad looking, he has let himself go. Perhaps a certain unaffected pathos would be his most endearing feature; but it is true, he would hardly be regarded as a good prospect.

The woman seems to read her thoughts – to her apparent satisfaction – and indeed evokes a comparison.

'Danny Skelgill – can't say I've seen him up close for a good few year. Might even be twenty-five, us last year at junior – he went away to a different school after that. Snogged him, I did – he went red as a beetroot. In front of all t' folk watching.'

DS Jones is unsure of what to say; the woman continues before she can speak.

'The headmaster, you see – he were from Cornwall. Made us put on a May Day Parade. I were May Queen – Danny were one of t' lads chosen to pull t' cart.'

'I see.'

'You ask him. See if he remembers – tell him Ann Wilson says *"Hoss! Hoss!"* – he'll mind that, even if he's blanked t' kiss from his thoughts. Today must be our anniversary!'

She laughs artlessly, and now clasps her crown with the fingers of both hands splayed, as though the memories are vivid, the weight of the garland, of trying to keep it in place – of the excited approbation of the crowds lining the lanes, the whirling hobby horse, the cheering and dancing and the merry music of May; of how attractive she once felt.

'Hey up – talk of t' devil.'

DS Jones wheels around, expecting to see Skelgill. Her heart skips a beat but just as quickly sinks. Trudging wearily up the driveway is the dishevelled figure of Kevin Pope. An Uber completes a three-point turn in the gateway and speeds off northwards.

She pulls herself together – glad of the distraction.

'Excuse me – I just need a word with him.' She reaches to touch the woman's arm. 'Thanks – I'll pass on your message.' She smiles, like she will enjoy doing so and thus Ann Johnson née Wilson can anticipate the vicarious pleasure.

She strides towards Kevin Pope, to be out of earshot should the woman linger. He helps this by stumbling to a halt upon seeing her.

It is the homecoming of a defeated rebel; he looks suspicious and a little irate, but there is also a glint of defiant vindication in his bleary eyes.

'I knew you were in on it.'

She does not need to ask what he means.

He tries to step around her but she shifts to stop him and presses a palm lightly against his chest. He seems shocked by the action, but it conducts away the last of his resistance.

'Listen, Kevin – *I* know it wasn't you. I know you haven't murdered anyone.'

He narrows his eyes. It's another trick. Why should he trust her?

She reads all this; she sees a cornered animal.

'No comment.'

She produces her mobile phone and passes security, though when she finds her object she lowers the handset to her side. His gaze follows anxiously.

She must get her timing right. Like Skelgill said – one chance, then he will clam up.

'But you did have a girlfriend.'

She thrusts the phone to his face.

Caught off guard, he blurts out a defence.

'That ain't her – she had brown –'

And he stops – his features contorted in anguish.

'She had what, Kevin? She had brown eyes?'

He turns his head aside in determined but unconvincing denial.

DS Jones persists, keeping the phone in position.

'This is Martina Radu. We know as of last week she was teaching English in Bucharest. As you can see, she's a dark brunette – but she has very pale blue eyes.'

He cannot resist a brief glance at the image.

But he remains resolute.

'I don't know what you're going on about.'

DS Jones can see that his hands are shaking – and he notices and shoves them into his pockets. He retracts his neck, hunching his shoulders. He is retreating into his shell.

'I didn't have nowt to do with owt.'

DS Jones can see that he would like to own up. But in her estimation he would *one percent* like to own up and is *ninety-nine percent* terrified of being framed by DI Alec Smart. A good bit of police work by Inspector Smart, a good bit of work, indeed.

'That's okay. I'll come back to you if I need to. In the meantime, Kevin, I would just like to use your office telephone, if I may?'

28. THE DOGHOUSE

Buttermere – 4.30 p.m.

SO ACCUSTOMED TO the singular presence of Skiddaw, a brooding sentinel guarding the northern reaches of Lakeland, Skelgill keeps doing a kind of double take: that it is the roller-coaster ridge culminating in the more diminutive Haystacks which presently overshadows his angling. And though Skiddaw might be his favourite mountain to look at – on a typically rumbustious Cumbrian day its brindled flanks never the same from one minute to the next – Haystacks undoubtedly has it, when it comes to being upon the fell itself. And in this regard he is torn between two great meditative retreats, time on the water and time on the fells. Unravelling time.

He has never really concluded which is most effective; there may be many invisible factors at play. Certainly, as Wainwright put it, "One can forget even a raging toothache on Haystacks". Right now, he could just as easily row to Peggy's Bridge and be atop Haystacks in little over half an hour. He would even get a mobile signal (although that is of dubious benefit). And would it, any more than drifting on the lake, get him off the horns of his dilemma? His double dilemma; or is it even treble? Or more than that? Can there be such a thing as a small herd of dilemmas? Antlered beasts – like the ancient aurochs – that haunt the shadowy forests of one's nightmares.

He stares broodingly across the water to Buttermere's wooded east bank. From Hassness Castle, its faux crenellations visible above the canopy, he scans slowly northwards. There is Hassness with its miners' tunnel; the hidden wooded smallholdings, Hassness Cottage, Pike Rigg Cottage, Catthwaite

Cottage; Ellerbeck B&B; the projecting angled gables of the Hikers' Hostel; and finally, woodsmoke and slate tiles hint at the village beyond.

His old stamping ground. Has he been drawn back like some dwindling old dog, sniffing long-abandoned rabbit holes? A myopic beating of the bounds; a tiny fiefdom he cannot see beyond?

Or is it one great scene of crime? A crime that it is his destiny to solve; even the Arl Lass said that to Aunt Renie. Buttermere expects. England expects. Justice rests on his shoulders.

Yet, for all he knows, justice has already been undone.

Subjected to Smart's thumbscrews, Kevin Pope may have confessed.

Skelgill flicks his line angrily – he apologises to the worm – but the chutzpah of Smart is intolerable.

More, that Smart would know full well he was wrong – but would not care one iota. Smart would not give a hoot that a donnat like Kevin Pope had neither the wits nor the wherewithal to process a corpse and shift it unseen to the lakebed in the middle of the mere – a task close on impossible, even for the best equipped, informed and skilled operators. For Smart only the verdict counts. Power to his elbow that it be obtained by duress and sham.

And that Smart has somehow wangled it such that Skelgill's loyal aide has played a part, tricked into turning coat. Tricked?

'Shurrup!'

He thwacks the heel of his hand against his forehead.

He must cast off these demons, terrors that dance upon his fear of failure. Such conjecture is futile. And it is not him. Not his style. Not his personality.

Except ... things have got to him. He is a victim of sensory overload. All of the above – vague as it is – has compounded what is the greatest yet most ineffable dilemma of them all. It is so indescribable, indefinable, that he only knows it to be real. Indeed, deep down, he surely knows what it is. But his subconscious is protecting his ego. For it knows his ego will not want to admit what he has fallen for.

He might be afloat in calm serenity, on the mirror surface of Buttermere, its meniscus like mercury – but its placid flatness conceals, far below the flimsy craft, a bubbling seething maelstrom that is ripening for eruption. Never mind the aurochs that blunders through the undergrowth, this is a leviathan of the deep, a behemoth of such proportions that should it breach and reveal itself it would toss him and the boat apart and sink them both for good measure.

Skelgill gets a bite and misses it.

He curses.

But it brings him back to earth, to water.

A cloud slides across the sun; its leading edge draws with it some breeze; he shivers uncharacteristically.

He notices the painter has somehow trailed overboard. He pulls it in and – quite abstractedly – loops it round one of the rowlocks and ties a left-handed bowline; the cowboy bowline – a quick-release knot so reliable that it almost might be made in heaven for a cuddy wifter like him, southpaw, as Leyton prefers to say. He stares at his handiwork. Who would tie a cowboy bowline?

Something in this question makes him look up. The zephyr has turned the prow to face the wooded promontory of Hassness; he spies a figure on the grassy isthmus.

The yoga platform.

A young woman.

Beneath the suddenly reduced light and the against the shadows of the trees she is indistinct.

But she appears dark.

His pulse quickens.

As he watches, the woman, extends her arms out wide.

Lena?

Returned, doing yoga?

He stares.

And stares.

Lena?

But – wait – her demeanour is different.
Taller, more elegantly slender.
He has stopped breathing.
But ...
... just as lightning strikes, the sun comes out.

The leviathan, the behemoth, has breached harmlessly – it has revealed its actuality and gone. Returned to the dark depths. His craft is spared. And he glimpsed enough to understand ... almost.

Simultaneously, the partial revelation – no, the partial *admission* – is eclipsed by planet earth's star's mightier force. He willingly lets it be eclipsed.

He looks anew at the young woman on the shore. In the angled afternoon brilliance she is picked out like a pop starlet centre stage; he can see the bronzed highlights glinting in her hair; there is the familiar, elegant grace, even in repose.

'Emma.' His voice is hoarse.

He sets to his oars – and turns the good ship *The Doghouse*.

She waits patiently, still as a statue, as he rows across.

He swings in close.

'I thought I might find you here, Guv.'

'I had some worms to use up.'

DS Jones grins reprovingly.

She boards easily and he pushes off.

They face one another.

He rows out.

He is content to be short of breath, and to be obviously so.

He sees how she is looking at him.

A powerful post-adrenaline low is rapidly kicking in.

If he does not speak soon, he will go under.

She waits.

'Em – I don't quite know how to tell you this, lass.'

It is her face that sinks.

And slowly another revelation dawns upon him.

Before he can form words, she speaks bravely.

'Go on.'

He makes a wild shy.

'The Chief's going to think I'm tapped in t' head.'
'What?'
A glimmer flickers in the defeated eyes.
'She'll think I'm mad, crazy, insane.'
Now she laughs – it sounds to him like a mixture of hysteria and relief.
'That's okay, then.'
But she gives an involuntary gasp, a stifled sob.
'You alreet, lass?'
'Sure – I'm fine.' She is blinking. She composes herself. 'So – *what is it?*'
And now he disappears beneath the surface.
But a drowning man gets three chances.
He comes up.
'If I'm wrong, Smart'll have a field day.'
He sees her reassuring smile.
'When has that ever stopped you?'
She's right; and he's treading water.
'Give us time, lass – I've only just had the penny drop. Half drop.'
Now she regards him intently; she might almost be interrogating his undermind, when he cannot.
'Maybe I can add a piece or two to the jigsaw.'
That phrase again.
But he is relieved; buoyant, even.
'Aye, go on, lass.'
He gives several hard pulls on the oars and allows the boat to drift towards the centre of the mere.
DS Jones looks about; a black-headed gull catches her eye, bobbing on the new breeze, craning inquisitively for scraps, its sooty underwings contrasting with the flashing white scimitar edges of its forewings, black, white, black, white, black, white – what colour is the bird?
She inhales deeply a couple of times.
She feels the onus, the sense of apprehension shift to fall upon her.

In a sudden reversal of roles, already Skelgill is regarding her in the manner she knows she was looking at him a moment earlier.

She clears her throat.

'So – I sat in on DI Smart's interview with Kevin Pope.'

'Aye, Leyton said.'

She feels relief at this first hurdle overcome. Though Skelgill seems to grind his teeth. And he has called her *lass* more times in the last minute than he does in a typical day. And even her name; a rarity on duty.

She will skirt around DI Alec Smart's fawning triumphalism when she had proposed there may be some overlap between their cases, and that perhaps she would recognise something that Kevin Pope might say as mutually valuable. Or that he had unceremoniously booted his own sergeant out of the interview … so as to have her to himself.

'I didn't really need to say anything about where we were up to – the gatepost, and so on.' Skelgill is paying unusually close attention. 'DI Smart just launched into him.'

'Aye.'

Skelgill's tone is guardedly neutral.

'It's exactly as you anticipated. He's read our reports on the system. He's seen that the misper Martina Radu was from Manchester – *and* Kevin Pope – and that Pope has drug possession on his rap sheet. He's painting Martina Radu as the county lines mule and Pope as the local dealer – and threatening to fit up Pope for her murder unless he reveals his contacts.'

Skelgill looks grim but vindicated.

She continues.

'Obviously, he's barking up the wrong tree. But he did flush out what I believe is a genuine alibi – that Kevin Pope was snowbound in his van at Penrith over that Christmas – when the murder likely occurred. We may even be able to verify it with CCTV.'

Skelgill is nodding faintly.

'I observed the interview – I didn't ask any questions. But it was obvious there was something – something that Kevin Pope wanted to say but wouldn't risk it.'

'Understandable.'

DS Jones pulls out her mobile phone. She locates the shot of Martina Radu and hands it to Skelgill.

'This came through when I was on my way. Martina Radu went home to Romania. She's teaching English in Bucharest. There's no there there – as the Americans say. But when I showed it to Kevin Pope he gave the game away. And – and this is something I went back and checked with Katya – he had an occasional girlfriend staying at the Hikers' Hostel during the three months between his taking up the job and the Christmas in question.'

Skelgill's eyes narrow.

'What about after Christmas?'

She shakes her head.

'Not as far as Katya knows. Nor since. And Ann Johnson – Wilson – is surprised he had a girlfriend at all.'

Skelgill stiffens, but he does not comment.

She waits a few moments longer.

'You said he knew something, Guv.'

There is sudden alarm in Skelgill's eyes – the underlying disturbance oscillates by the minute.

But she is undeterred.

'Could he have known the Lady of the Lake?'

Skelgill does not respond.

She doubles down.

'When I showed him the photo, before he could stop himself, he just blurted out: *no – she had brown eyes.*'

Skelgill glances towards Hassness and the grassy spit.

She continues.

'After I'd spoken with Kevin Pope, I rang Dr Herdwick from the hostel landline. He said they can't be absolutely sure, but the DNA profile from the lake body has genetic markers that predict dark eye colour.'

211

Skelgill turns his gaze back upon her – though he could be looking right through her.

She tilts her head from side to side; she might almost be tempted to wave her hands or snap her fingers.

'Is this any help?'

He starts – and looks sheepish.

The boat has drifted; he gives a few pulls on the oars. He seems to want to maintain their central position – ironically it is above where the corpse lay – as if there is some inspiration to be drawn from the essence that remains.

He is still struggling to engage.

'Guv, Kevin Pope couldn't have killed Royston Woodcock. And now he may have an alibi for Christmas. But if I'm right, it does bring him back into the picture. He knows it – and he won't talk while he thinks DI Smart will frame him.'

Skelgill makes a growl in his throat; after a moment, he responds.

'What's Leyton reckon? He's all for the divers being the culprits.' He slaps the gunnel illustratively. 'Since they'd have a boat, an accomplice, knowhow and knots.'

'I haven't managed to speak properly with him.' DS Jones presses her palms together and frowns in self-reproach. 'Did he have any news when you met him at lunchtime?'

Skelgill leans to peer into the clear water; it seems a symbolic act.

'Looks like Jenny Tattoo might have gone missing round about the right time. Plus, the materials from where Tapp was working at Hassness Castle match those on the corpse.'

He looks back, and grins in macabre fashion.

When she does not respond, he adds a rider.

'Funny how the wrong track can bring you out in the right place.'

The remark is cryptic – and he seems to intend it to be so. She wonders if he means this is exactly what she has done. He seems curiously relaxed about such powerful evidence. But that his mood has suddenly lightened gives her an opening.

'How did you get on, Guv?'

He shrugs, and sways from side to side, causing the boat to rock gently.

'I went back for a word with Margery McLeish. I found her unloading flatpack garden furniture into her shed – gave her a hand. She reckoned that's why she'd come down – ahead of Whitsun. Couldn't fit the family and the dogs an' all.'

DS Jones regards him evenly.

'Naturally, I have been thinking that her visit was connected to my phone call yesterday. Especially as she never mentioned it.'

Skelgill grins.

'Think she's a dark horse, coming up on the rails?'

'I don't know. Look, you've actually met her – twice, now. How was her demeanour?'

He thinks a while, searching for the right adjective.

'Professional.' He adds an afterthought. 'Mainly.'

DS Jones laughs, a little indignantly. 'What's that supposed to mean?'

He shakes his head dismissively.

'Nay – nothing to report.' But it is plain that he thinks again. His gaze drifts to the far shore. 'Maybe summat. I don't know yet.'

A silence of sorts ensues, though ripples plonk rhythmically against the soundbox of the hull.

'You said you went there first?'

He has to yield.

'Aye. I called in at Hassness Cottage.' DS Jones waits for him to elaborate. 'To ask Lena Longstaff about the voicemail she left us.'

DS Jones is hesitant.

'What did she say?'

'It was – the other one. Valentina White. She were on a half day. She reckons her mate's done a bunk.'

DS Jones's eyes widen.

'A bunk – you mean – absconded?'

'She reckons it's her thing. Clears off at the drop of a hat to do research for her books.'

213

'For how long?'

'How long's a piece of string – that were her answer. She's saying she might have hitched to France, some Holy Grail thing. Left no note, not yet been in touch.'

While this is quite startling news to DS Jones, by contrast Skelgill's manner is subdued; he relays these facts as if by rote, and that it is an account to which he does not fully subscribe.

DS Jones holds out an open palm.

'That's interesting – what you say about the research.'

'Is it?'

He sounds still unconvinced.

'You know I said I was going to look up her latest novel?' He nods. 'It hasn't been well received. The initial reviews are one whole star down on her average rating.'

Now he shrugs.

'Happen you can't make every book a best-seller. Mustn't be easy to come up with new plots.'

But DS Jones shakes her head.

'Actually, it isn't so much that. Her regular readers are suggesting she has used AI.'

Furrows crease Skelgill's brow.

'Is it set on a farm?'

DS Jones laughs, unconvincingly – she doesn't really get his point.

'No – it's called *Holyrood Knives* – it's set in medieval Edinburgh, at the time of Mary Stuart. Based on the murders of Darnley and Rizzio.'

'Where do the animals come in?'

She makes a face of puzzlement.

'Guv?'

Skelgill's demeanour shifts into mansplaining mode.

'I were only talking to Jud Hope about it the other night. He's thinking of trying it with a portion of the flock for this autumn's tupping time. Trouble is, there's a lower conception rate than if it's the actual live tup.'

DS Jones emits a burst of laughter.

'What?'

She holds up her palms.

'Okay – we're at cross purposes.'

'Are we?'

'Yes. AI. I'm thinking artificial intelligence. You're thinking artificial insemination.'

Skelgill, in making an indeterminate face and shrugging theatrically might now be judged to be covering his tracks. There is, however, perhaps just the suggestion that he has been pulling her leg.

In the avoidance of doubt, he swiftly picks up her point.

'Cheating, like?'

'Well, kind of. Her readers say it's bland and clichéd, and the style robotic. One described it as a literary version of muzak. Perfectly punctuated – but it doesn't sound anything like her normal author's voice.'

When DS Jones might expect Skelgill further to opine, instead it is apparent that this notion has struck some chord – as though it has rekindled the unease that he has been battling all along. She is prompted to shift the discussion back to practical matters.

'When did she leave? Lena Longstaff, I mean.'

It is the detective's question to ask, and Skelgill nods in earnest.

'Valentina White reckoned she didn't arrive home until nearly midnight – she was setting up a display after hours. Lena Longstaff was gone, along with some of her stuff.'

DS Jones turns to gaze across to the wooded shoreline, and the promontory of Hassness.

'So she could have been here when Royston Woodcock died. Do you think Valentina White is covering for her?'

Skelgill makes a pained face.

His colleague presses him.

'You're sure she wasn't there?'

Skelgill rubs the back of his hand across his lips.

'I only went in the conservatory.'

29. SHIP TO SHORE

Buttermere – 5.25 p.m.

SKELGILL HAS FISHED for fifteen minutes to no avail. He has gone about it half-heartedly, and they are in too deep water for the rig he has brought. And now he is distracted by an alert that emanates unexpectedly from DS Jones's backpack.

She is equally surprised – and digs out her mobile phone. She frowns at the screen.

'No signal. But it definitely bleeped.'

Skelgill is craning to see.

'You sometimes get that. It comes in for a minute, then it's gone. A message slips through while it's got the chance.'

DS Jones is nodding; it is what has happened. She interrogates her account.

'It's an email from DC Watson. A comms and forensics update. The attachment hasn't downloaded. But there's a covering note. She says there's no indication that Royston Woodcock used his mobile phone yesterday – but he made a withheld call from his landline at about seven-fifteen p.m. Recipient presently unknown.'

Skelgill's eyes flash at his colleague.

'Are we any further forward on time of death?'

DS Jones is scrolling.

Slowly, she shakes her head – and then proceeds, half quoting.

'At the moment it looks like we're still working on between ten p.m. and two a.m. Scene of Crime are reporting that he had no other items with him, beyond the camera, and there was nothing to indicate what else he might have been doing. He was normally clothed, with suitable outdoor shoes for walking and a jacket fit for the cool night temperature. On the face of it, he had prepared to go out, and was simply in the wrong place at the wrong time. A mining engineer from Honister has made an examination of the pit props – and there are signs of weakness at points where the tunnel roof is close to subsoil and prone to water percolation.'

Skelgill, as has been the pattern of the afternoon, stares at the impenetrable tree-clad shoreline. He saw Royston Woodcock, and the state of the tunnel is no surprise. It is the anonymised phone call that occupies his thoughts. Between seven-fifteen and ten o'clock a person could drive to Buttermere from the likes of Whitehaven or Pooley Bridge – or Manchester or Blackpool – or even Edinburgh, at a push.

And he does not select at random. Boatman Ketch; plumber Tapp; an accomplice of Kevin Pope; the elusive lodger Mr Black; lawyer Margery McLeish; they respectively hail from these places.

He drives the heels of his hands into his temples. He knows he ought to keep an open mind – despite that his mind has crashed in upon him this afternoon – offering an entirely different explanation, an alternative so crazy that his logical filter, the gatekeeper which guards the wormhole that links subconscious to conscious, stands belligerently with arms folded and brow furrowed.

He can just make out the entrance to the Buttermere tunnel, a darker smudge on the landscape, the northern end where DS Jones had presciently reacted to the warning notice.

He recalls the helping hand offered by Margery McLeish to haul him ashore – the dirt beneath her nails; they were scrupulously clean when he returned the compliment later. Then she did say she moved some of the rocks, in case there was the possibility of administering first aid.

He frowns, picturing the scene in the shifting torchlight. There was something not right about it. And now he realises, it was not the shocking sight of the body, half-buried, nor the boulders strewn about – but the camera lying just beyond the dead man's outstretched hand. *Why didn't he have the broad neoprene strap around his neck?*

'What is it, Guv?'

Skelgill starts. His eyes have been following the progress of a merganser, its sleek form low to the surface. Now it has dived, leaving just a widening ring of ripples.

He looks at his colleague and simultaneously feels his shirt pocket. He takes up the oars.

'Strap in – I reckon we need another deek at Woodcock's place.'

Rather than brace herself DS Jones seems to relax – as if the return of the action version of Skelgill is a sizeable relief.

'What are we looking for?'

Skelgill is grimacing, straining his sinews to turn the craft; his sleeves are rolled up and the tendons in his tanned forearms stand proud.

'I'm banking on us knowing it when we see it.' He gasps. 'Keep us on course for Pike Rigg, will you?'

DS Jones grins.

'In that case, I'd say a couple of degrees to starboard.'

Skelgill feathers an oar. He watches DS Jones's expression – she is staring intently past him.

'What's up, lass?'

'I think we might have a reception committee.'

Skelgill stops rowing and cranes over his shoulder. On the bank, beneath the alders, the figure of a man is facing in their direction. He raises an arm in a kind of salute, and then beckons. Skelgill recognises him.

'That's the Hindlewake bloke.'

'The abrasive landlord?'

'Aye.'

'What can he want?'

'Happen we'll find out, soon enough.'

Skelgill perhaps eases up, not wanting to give the impression that the fellow has some call upon them. But as they come alongside, it is Ted Hindlewake who exhibits urgency. He dispenses with formalities, and solely addresses Skelgill.

'That night you were asking about, Christmas Night – Roger Black saw someone. He were out searching for his dog. After eleven it were – a person pulling a sledge along here.' He indicates the shoreline footpath that weaves through the wood. 'I ask you – what was that all about, eh?'

Skelgill and DS Jones allow their eyes to meet briefly. This question begs several others. Skelgill gives a just-perceptible jerk of his head: that she should go first.

'Mr Hindlewake.' The man looks startled – perhaps that she knows his name – and a little indignant that the inspector's young female companion might butt in. 'I'm Detective Sergeant Jones. We've been trying to contact Mr Black, without success – where you have succeeded.'

She seems to strike the right note, somewhere between making him feel important and subtle persuasion.

'Aye, well – he's moved house, that's why. He's gone into sheltered accommodation. Though I don't know what for – there's nowt wrong with him. And he's taken the dog.'

'How come you have spoken with him, sir?'

The man looks like he thinks she ought to know.

'He's just rang us, hasn't he? Not above half hour ago. He's read in the paper about this body in the lake. He wanted to check if his next booking's alright.'

Skelgill has been manoeuvring the boat and now jumps ashore with the painter to fasten a clove hitch around a jutting alder sapling. He leans back in to give DS Jones a helping hand while the man looks on.

Skelgill now addresses him.

'How come you found us, sir?'

Ted Hindlewake averts his gaze, somewhat charily.

'This new business in the tunnel – it's all over the village. I thought you might be there. Or an officer who'd put me onto you. I set out to walk down – recognised you in your boat.'

There is a wistful note in his tone: the suggestion that he would have liked to have pried into whatever goings-on are on view.

Skelgill nods.

'Aye, well – you've done right, sir. Do you have Mr Black's new contact details?'

The man seems a little chagrined by this question – that they may consider he has come ill-prepared.

'Betty's got it written down. But that's all there is. It were a person in the dark. Pulling a plastic sledge – he heard the noise of it, scraping along on the frozen snow.'

DS Jones offers a gentle prompt.

'Did he happen to say if it was an adult or a child, male or female?'

The man scowls.

'He'd have said if it were a bairn – it were getting on for midnight.' He glares at DS Jones; he might be trying to remember, though he might equally be embellishing for his own purposes, to cover the lack of detail he has obtained. 'They were just a figure – a shadow moving through the trees. The dog came back right then, and they were gone.'

DS Jones nods encouragingly, despite that both she and Skelgill are schooled in the vagaries of eyewitness evidence, not least when it is relayed second-hand.

'You say Mr Black rang to ask about his reservation. What brought up the subject of that Christmas Night?'

'I asked him, didn't I? I'd said to Betty – I remembered I'd had to wait up, to lock the back door. He reckoned his dog had run off – climbed over the fence.'

He turns to appeal to Skelgill for affirmation. It is evident that he has done his own bit of sleuthing here – that perhaps, having put two and two together from Skelgill's visit, he had suspected Roger Black of some malign act. For Skelgill's part, he is fairly sure that the telephone call was made not by Roger Black, but by Ted Hindlewake.

The detectives, of course, will need to question Mr Roger Black. But Skelgill can feel adrenaline running once again in his veins.

'You did well, sir. That's much appreciated. Perhaps we can drop round for the details a little later?'

He turns away and clambers back into the boat. He makes as if he is preparing to depart, and hands down DS Jones. He reaches to untie the painter – but pauses to stare up inquisitively at the onlooker.

Ted Hindlewake hems and haws – but he gets the message and departs with a muttered farewell.

As soon as he is out of sight, Skelgill leaps ashore. Swiftly, he makes fast.

'Howay, lass.'

He sets off directly through the trees; DS Jones has to scamper to keep him in sight – though she recognises he has picked up the fine path that will lead them to Pike Rigg Cottage. She calls ahead.

'What do you think, Guv – about what Black saw?'

But Skelgill merely makes a curious unintelligible rotation of his left hand beside his head.

It is an answer of sorts.

30. TIME & MOTION

Police HQ, Penrith – 5.45 p.m.

DS LEYTON CHECKS his watch – and the time on his mobile phone – and leans to peer at the small digits in the top corner of his desktop computer's screen. But the clocks are in synchrony. He sighs. His dilemma – for he has one, too – is entirely practical and patently loaded: in forty-five minutes he must be parked outside the sports centre in Keswick (gymnastics and football training at least coinciding), and thence take home fish suppers to feed five.

On the lesser side of the equation are two reports: one that he is presently mulling over, and a second that he has just noticed at the top of his inbox.

The former concerns the missing partner of Abel Ketch, presumed to be 'Jenny' of the tattoo. Via the Whitehaven police station, a local uniformed officer has responded to a general request for information with an account gleaned from a relative, an erstwhile workmate of Jennifer Eccles on the tills at the Tesco superstore at the harbour. *Jennifer Eccles was having an affair.* How did the woman know? At least twice a week she would "tart herself up" in the ladies' toilets and hurriedly depart during her lunch break, climbing into a "flashy" Mercedes coupe that would have its engine idling in the car park. She left her job abruptly some eighteen months ago – before Christmas – and has not been seen by the informant since.

This proves nothing, of course – but it is another straw in the wind. DS Leyton cannot help thinking that, were there no other complications – Kevin Pope, Royston Woodcock, et al – they would surely be focusing all their resources on the two hobbyist divers, Abel Ketch and Bob Tapp.

But it is wishful thinking when the Guvnor has his mind set on nothing in particular and everything in general. To the logician, it is an unfathomable approach. But Skelgill is like the hawk – or whatever bird it is, eagle, peregrine falcon, kestrel, buzzard (he surprises himself that he can name so many) – that stays up there in the sky, circling interminably, insufferably patient, leaving the observer wondering if it will ever dive and indeed giving up with a stiff neck. Look back a minute later and it is disappearing over the ridge with a woodpigeon or rabbit twitching in its talons.

The Guvnor. He starts. Two more minutes have ticked by.

He checks his screen.

Of course, the second report is still there. It might almost be red and pulsating, standing out now from the list like the proverbial sore thumb. It concerns the matter ordered by Skelgill that DC Watson has dutifully completed by close of play, that of contacting Royston Woodcock's known family in New Zealand. It was not so much an investigative exercise as a courtesy call – though hardly the type of courtesy call that would ordinarily be appreciated. Moreover, Skelgill would expect relevant questions to be asked, in the context of the fate that has befallen their relative, subject to what they might know. Typical enquiries in suspicious circumstances include whether a person owed money, had enemies, and who might benefit from their demise. Diplomacy would be required when simultaneously conveying news of the sudden death of a loved one.

Or perhaps not.

For the intriguing subject line demands some attention: *Royston Woodcock estranged from family*.

DS Leyton cannot suppress a grin. He recalls once Skelgill bemoaning a particular branch of his maternal Graham clan, with a reputation for lawlessness. He had asked his boss if they were estranged. "Estranged? Leyton, they're totally bloody nuts!"

He inhales deeply, as if in preparation for an act of putting himself in jeopardy.

There's no harm having a look. It will take him five minutes to get his motor on the road, and twenty-five to Keswick. That gives him ten minutes to scan the report, acknowledge DC Watson's efforts, and fire off a message to his superior.

Upon opening it, he is relieved to see contents that are short and succinct.

'Loved one' would indeed seem to be an inapt phrase – in that Royston Woodcock was not. Without beating about the bush, DC Watson has reported that ex-wife Sharon Woodcock and married daughter Dr Val White were each reached and informed – and both reacted cooly. Neither has been in contact with Royston Woodcock for a decade. Not surprisingly, little further information about his circumstances was forthcoming; such questions were rendered moot.

DS Leyton sits unmoving. Shame. Poor geezer.

But there is something else, and it take him a moment to realise what it is.

Val White?

The daughter is named Val White?

His first reaction is that DC Watson has made a transposition error.

He resumes his seat and tries her mobile number. But it rings out. On reflection, she had mentioned she was taking rugby practice tonight because the coach is indisposed. They're probably already scrumming down. As it was, she had stayed right to the wire to finish her report.

Hmm, down to the wire.

He peers at his screen; he sways to find a comfortable focal length. There are multiple contact numbers listed for the Woodcock relatives: for the daughter, home, mobile and the hospital in Auckland where she works as an emergency department surgeon.

He plumps for the mobile number.

It is picked up almost immediately.

'Hello?'

A woman's voice – a little croaky and hushed – though the line is clear; she might almost be down the road in Keswick.

DS Leyton is suddenly apprehensive.

'Miss Woodcock?'

'Er, well – yes.'

He detects a faint estuary accent; it is comfortingly familiar and puts him a little more at ease.

'I'm DS Leyton from Cumbria CID. I'm sorry to trouble you at a time like this –'

'*Ye-es.*'

There is an ironic emphasis – an underlying reproach – and DS Leyton realises there is an alternative interpretation.

'Wait – what time is it there, madam?'

'Er ... it's four forty-five a.m. Friday.'

'Aw, jeez – sorry about that – I never thought. What a pillock!'

'No worries. I've been half expecting to be called again, in view of what happened to my father. And I'm on duty this morning at six – I'll be getting up soon.'

DS Leyton decides it is best just to come to the point.

'What it is, madam – there's been a bit of confusion at our end. A report's been passed to me, and we have your name down as Val White.'

'That's correct. My married name is White.'

DS Leyton hesitates.

'And – you're Val – just Val? Not Valerie or anything else?'

'Yes.'

DS Leyton is perplexed – but at least DC Watson was correct. He glances at the framed portrait on his desk, removed by Skelgill from Pike Rigg Cottage.

'We found a photograph in your father's cottage. We believe it's you – it's like a selfie taken close up in front of a car with the Volkswagen badge in the shot. It seems quite recent.'

She answers without hesitation.

'That's from my Facebook page. My initials – VW – my new car a couple of years ago.' Her tone becomes reflective. 'He must have printed it off.'

There is a small silence – that the distanced father was in some way or another keeping sight of his daughter's life. But DS Leyton is conscious of his ticking clock.

'The thing is, madam – and this is probably just a coincidence – there's a young woman – I expect about your age, who lives in the vicinity of your father's cottage. She's from New Zealand and her name's Valentina White.'

It takes her a moment to respond.

'That does seem to be a coincidence. Were they acquainted?'

DS Leyton has limited information. If Skelgill knows this, he has not conveyed it to him.

'Not that I'm actually aware of. It was just that I noticed the similarity of your names – and having New Zealand in common. We don't get many folk from Down Under in our neck of the woods.'

She inhales quietly.

'Well, we're certainly out on a bit of a limb here. But young people, especially, get a version of cabin fever. Kiwis really punch above their weight when it comes to international trav–'

It is plain to DS Leyton that her train of thought is interrupted.

'Is there something, madam?'

'Yes – well, this may be entirely unrelated – but my passport and some other identity documents were stolen from a locker at the Auckland Beach Club. I mean, this is years ago – six, seven years ago. I'd just travelled back from a Trauma Society conference in Melbourne, so unfortunately I had a lot of personal material with me.'

'I take it you didn't get the passport back?'

'No – I didn't. And, I must admit, I don't know what came of it. I reported the theft to the police – but, you know how it is?'

Her tone is diplomatic; perhaps as someone who works in public service.

'Yeah.' DS Leyton answers rather absently; the clock before his eyes is relentless. 'That's helpful to know – and you've cleared up my query.'

'Or started a new one.'

She is perceptive; but he chuckles amiably. He apologises again for the rude awakening and adds further condolences before concluding the call.

He sits and considers his thumbs as he winds them frantically.

If he doesn't leave in five minutes the nippers will be standing outside on the pavement. Course – they'll be fine, it's not like it's raining – but they'll inadvertently shop him to the Missus under subtle interrogation. Besides, while it is a policeman's lot to become inured to horror, there develops also an exaggerated view of the horrors that are available.

Bang goes driving within the speed limit.

Quickly he logs on to Interpol.

A few clicks and more typing – and his eyes widen and his mouth falls slightly open.

He drags his mobile phone close and taps upon Skelgill's number. It diverts instantly to voicemail.

He tries DS Jones, with the same result.

They must be out of cell tower range, likely near Buttermere.

He sends the page on his screen to print and – as a precaution – deletes the record of his access.

With a last despairing look at his watch, he grabs his jacket and briefcase, sprints for the communal printer and does not break stride as he departs the floor, attracting bemused gazes from the scattering of colleagues still present.

If there were a rugby ball tucked under his arm, DC Watson would be proud of him.

31. SMEW

Pike Rigg Cottage – 6.00 p.m.

DS JONES KNOWS not to ask again what is going through Skelgill's mind, when it is plain that it is best left to its own devices. Indeed, upon entering Pike Rigg Cottage through the back door, they have once more split up; this time she has taken the upstairs.

The interjection of Ted Hindlewake – and the witness evidence of Roger Black, albeit yet to be confirmed from the horse's mouth – has clearly buffeted Skelgill, but it has not knocked him off course. Indeed, it has served only to stiffen his grim resolve in making a beeline for Pike Rigg Cottage, and his introspective demeanour in doing so. Further reason to leave him be. As it is, she cannot hear him moving about downstairs.

In the absence of asking Skelgill what they are looking for, she poses the question of herself. Skelgill had reacted – in a delayed fashion – to the information she had relayed from DC Watson's update. The news that Royston Woodcock had made a phone call at seven fifteen p.m. – and the forensic report from the tunnel.

Unless – was it something to do with what happened to him earlier?

The strange, agitated state she encountered when first joining his boat.

The sinking feeling that made her sure he was about to say something terrible.

She has lowered herself down upon a stool in front of a dresser. Her reflection comes into focus. She takes hold of her hair; it is just shoulder length. She pulls it under her chin. She pouts. How does he see her?

He had said – quite ingenuously – that it was to do with the Chief, with Smart – and, actually, as she read his manner, his own self-esteem.

It wasn't about her – or even them.

She gives a rebellious shake of her head.

The dresser is more like one that a woman would own, with its triple mirrors and sunken holes for perfume bottles. Perhaps Royston Woodcock simply brought it with other furniture from what was the marital home. In the same vein, the headboard of the bed has a feminine style. The room itself is otherwise sparsely furnished. It could be a second-rate guesthouse where utilitarian items have been cobbled together to provide the necessary amenities without thought of theme or coordination.

As she recalls, it was in a drawer of the dresser that Skelgill found the photograph of the woman they believe to be Royston Woodcock's daughter. There are three drawers on either side of the kneehole. They contain variously the sort of clothing items that would be expected. She gets the impression that most have lain undisturbed – as if he rotated a couple of outfits around the drying rack she had glimpsed hanging over the bathtub. When she opens the bottom-right drawer, however, there is something about a folded towel that makes her inquisitive.

Sure enough, it is covering a small treasure trove of women's underwear.

She picks out first a sporty pair of briefs – the kind of item she might herself put on for the gym. There are others – again, to her taste, for what might be considered special occasions, sheer and skimpy. And then a widening spectrum, passing into more practical varieties.

She lifts out the whole lot and begins to arrange them on the bed. Not only do they vary by construction but also in size, from small to extra-large. This would seem to represent a cross-section of femininity – women of all shapes, sizes and ages – and lifestyles.

It looks like amassing photographs of wildlife was not Royston Woodcock's only hobby. And she calls to mind the occasional long-lens shots of female hikers.

She ponders. And nods. This could explain what he was up to – out at night with his camera. If he failed to get photographs – at least he could bring home trophies from washing lines around the village.

Certainly, it ought not to be difficult to reunite some of these garments with their owners.

She decides to leave the collection – she can bring Skelgill up to see her handiwork.

On which note, he is still remarkably quiet.

She descends to find him seated at the desk where she previously perused the laptop.

To his left on the wall is the impressively neat display of wildlife photos, printed and trimmed to standard dimensions.

Skelgill, however, is staring out of the window.

It is a good couple of hours to sunset, but the sense of evening comes early to Buttermere, and it will not be long before the sun dips below the ridge to plunge the dale into a premature twilight. A red squirrel seems to glow with its own aura as the slanting rays illuminate its fine bristling fur. It stands alert, atop the feeder halfway between the cottage and the wood. The feeder is empty and not destined to be refilled.

As DS Jones watches, the squirrel suddenly leaps from its post and disappears into the surrounding undergrowth. Simultaneously, Skelgill reacts. He does not try to follow the hidden trajectory of the rodent, but instead leans closer to the windowpane to crane up at the sky – does he suspect a buzzard is the cause of the little mammal's flight?

DS Jones approaches to his shoulder.

In front of him on the desk are two pictures that he has peeled from their tacked position – now she notices the gaps in the wall display.

He taps the one on the right, nearest to where she stands. A black-and-white duck-like bird floats in a small patch of water surrounded by ice.

'Do you remember if this was on the laptop?'

This feels like a tall order; she skimmed rapidly through the great portfolio of photographs. The team back at the station may have had the chance of a better look.

'Oh – I don't know. There were ducks sitting on ice – I remember saying that.'

Skelgill nods – there is the suggestion that her remark complements his thinking.

'This is a male smew. The one you thought sounded like a marsupial.'

'I'll take your word for it.'

Skelgill taps again.

'He took this on the Christmas Day. He were chuffed about spotting it. Rare vagrant hereabouts.'

'Right.'

A longer silence ensues. DS Jones can tell he is building up to something more significant than bird migration. She does not quite appreciate how significant.

'I know how it was done.' His tone is even – flat, even.

She inhales.

'What do you mean?' She knows what he means – but she dare not ask the direct question.

'The body.'

She waits – but he is no more forthcoming – though she can tell he suffers some tumult. His lupine inscrutability conceals a hunter's urge. She has watched him like this, fishing – when he wants to strike but senses it would be untimely.

He switches the pictures to bring the second better into her line of sight.

It is a photograph of a roebuck, bending to feed, not a great shot – grainy, monochrome and shrouded in gloom. The creature's eyes glow like tiny white headlamps.

'How about this?'

'It's a deer.'

Skelgill shakes his head slowly.

'That's taken with infrared – in the dark. It's a motion-activated camera.'

'You mean – not his regular camera?'

Skelgill waves a finger from side to side over the image.

'That's the shore path.'

'How can you tell?'

'The trees – they're alders. They only grow along the bank. They like their roots in water. The rest of the wood's oak and birch.'

DS Jones finds herself taking an involuntary step back, as if a revelation has been thrust upon her, an invisible hand delivering a sharp push to her thorax.

Her voice is hoarse.

'That's what got him killed. He knew something.'

Skelgill is still.

She ventures more.

'He had some incriminatory photos.'

Slowly, Skelgill begins to nod.

'Wow – Guv. He did overhear us. He put two and two together. He must have had evidence of the murder. His phone call – he must have approached whomever he thought it was.'

Skelgill is staring hard at the photograph.

'We can find this.'

'You mean the spot?'

'I mean the camera.'

'But – how?'

'They're weatherproof. You strap them to a tree or conceal them in the undergrowth. Like as not he's got a few dotted about – probably some set up near his feeders.'

As DS Jones inhales to respond, a double sound – a faint creak and a slightly louder click – emanates from behind them. Both turn their heads. DS Jones instinctively pads across and peers both ways around the jamb into the hallway.

She releases the breath.

'The wind must have closed the kitchen door – I'd left it slightly ajar.'

Skelgill regards her with a frown – as if he might question her analysis – but it is plain he is consumed by the second photograph. As she returns to his side he indicates precisely with a long fisherman's finger. The backdrop to the roebuck is a criss-crossing array of slender trunks, gnarled and rough-barked, and growing haphazardly in the way of alders – stripped of sideshoots by the very deer that embellish the woodlands.

'Look at these – the way they cross. That's as good as a fingerprint.'

DS Jones looks – and nods.

He is right. The tilted, overlapping saplings form a perfectly symmetrical letter X. While the pattern may be aped elsewhere along the shore it will surely never be exactly replicated.

She offers a practical caveat.

'It's quite a long stretch of bank.'

Skelgill glances out, his gaze tracking up the fellsides to the skyline; evening is advancing.

'We'd better get us skates on, then, lass.'

As he rises he gives an ironic laugh and mutters under his breath, *skates*.

He hitches his trousers – and DS Jones suddenly remembers her own more modest finding.

'Before we go – I'd like your opinion on some underwear.'

Skelgill emits a strangled exclamation.

32. X MARKS THE SPOT

Ellerbeck Wood – 6.35 p.m.

'WHAT DO YOU SEE?'

DS Jones blinks, her eyes straining to penetrate the shadows of the shed as she leans in. She peers about. Most of the available space on one side is taken by a stack of boxes of flatpack garden furniture, the rest is more of a disorganised jumble.

'Ah.' Her gaze alights on the two long plastic sledges, nested together, hung from their ropes on a wooden peg. 'I did tell you – didn't I? Margery McLeish said their kids were sledging that Christmas. I bet these weren't even kept in here. They were probably left on full view, abandoned at the foot of the slope, after a last run.'

Skelgill does not answer – though he glances briefly down to the gate into Ellerbeck Wood.

He turns towards the holiday cottage. Two small faces gape from the back window. Their parents have informed the detectives that Margery McLeish has repaired to the Fish Inn to await the arrival of her husband.

Having made this short detour, Skelgill and DS Jones regain the shoreline footpath to complete their search of the northerly section of bank. But they reach the end of the trees without success. The telltale crossed saplings must lie south of Pike Rigg.

A twisted band of blue-and-white police tape closes the path to public access from the first alluvial pasture. Skelgill regards it with some scepticism; DS Jones could guess correctly that he is thinking it wouldn't stop him for a minute. "Do not enter" is exactly the invitation that would tempt a spirited Lakeland lad.

And it does not stop the dog that approaches them; a Border collie that seems to know Skelgill. He drops to one knee to cushion its gleeful arrival. He surreptitiously produces a treat from his thigh pocket.

A grizzled head pops up from behind a part-collapsed section of dry stone wall, some thirty yards away. DS Jones recognises the madcap quad-biking farmer – he of the near miss of two mornings ago. She spies the offending machine, parked up at a steep angle on a bank nearby. The farmer is evidently conducting running repairs.

He hails them.

'Still closed, is it, lad?'

Skelgill jerks a thumb over his shoulder and calls back.

'The footpath should be open tomorrow – but the tunnel, not yet awhile.'

The man seems content to pry no further. He gives a bit of a wave, and whistles back his dog, which responds obediently. He returns to his lifting of large rocks that look beyond a fellow of his age and build.

Skelgill turns and sets off at a brisk pace. At first, retracing their steps, they have no need to concentrate just yet.

DS Jones speaks reflectively.

'You said that, Guv – about Black and his dog. That he might have been a witness.'

Skelgill grimaces; he does not appear wishful to take any special credit for his foresight.

'Aye, pity Hindlewake kept it under his hat – if we'd have known Black was out that late and for that long.'

'It would be useful to know where he saw the person with the sledge.'

Skelgill nods – but without enthusiasm.

'Mind, if he were gone for an hour like Hindlewake reckons – he'd be going round in circles in the dark. The snow would have hidden the path. And the dog likely ran amok – chasing rabbits and deer – getting the scent of a fox.'

In good time they reach the end of Pike Rigg, where *The Doghouse* has its temporary mooring, and they resume their dendrological quest.

DS Jones extends a hand towards the irregular line of trees whose roots cling tenaciously to the eroded bank.

'I never knew that – about alders, I mean. That they're so water-loving.'

'Not only that. The felled timber turns rock hard in water. Amsterdam, Venice – they're all built on alder piles.'

'Really?'

Skelgill gives a scoff, that she should not be so surprised by his knowledge.

'Doesn't stop them sinking into the mud, mind.'

She murmurs in contemplation.

'It makes you wonder – that kind of practical knowledge. How many houses were built on piles of oak or birch that collapsed before they got round to alder.'

Skelgill frowns, but she continues before he can object.

'It's the same with poisonous berries and fungi, isn't it? It's curious how so many important facts – matters of survival, life and death – are dependent upon lore.'

Skelgill remains obviously puzzled. As the recipient of 'lore' it strikes him as more a case of common sense; though he has wondered, being such an avid angler, how much trial and error it took the Japanese to learn that to eat the pufferfish without first removing its liver, ovaries, eyes and skin was almost instantly fatal.

He stops to stare at an arrangement of trunks. But it is closer to a Y than an X – though perhaps it offers encouragement.

More diligence is needed now.

DS Jones, too, is scanning intently.

'Do you think it will be this side of the tunnel?'

Skelgill makes a face.

'Let's hope so. The wood pretty much thins out after Hassness – there's more of a beach than a bank.'

The path now takes a few awkward twists and turns, ups and downs over protruding rocks and roots. A plastic sledge dragged over here, even cushioned by snow, would surely have advertised its passage.

In a narrow section DS Jones skips ahead.

As the path straightens out, she exclaims.

'Look!'

But when she turns, she sees that Skelgill has already retreated a few yards into the wood, and is sidestepping, holding in front of him the print taken from his pocket and unfolded, lining up the trajectory from which the photograph with the criss-crossing trunks must have been taken.

He halts.

She approaches, squinting past him into the gloom.

'I don't see –'

But Skelgill spins on his heel and strides towards a mature oak tree. He raises an arm in avoidance of doubt. At some ten or twelve feet a rather dilapidated bird nestbox has been hung. It is the sort with an open window designed for the scarce and delightful pied flycatchers that may be found in some of Lakeland's deciduous woods.

Beneath the shadow of the canopy it is not possible to tell whether anything is inside; there is just a dark aperture.

DS Jones voices concern.

'Do you think it's in there? He must have used a ladder to inspect it.'

Skelgill is grim faced, yet in an appreciative manner.

'It's a neat way of stopping the camera from getting nicked. And hidden in plain sight.'

In the absence of a stepladder or rope, Skelgill still assumes he can climb anything – it is just a question of working out how. But there are no handholds, just the crocodile-skin bark of the broad oak – unforgiving to bare flesh if a slip is made. The trunk's circumference is well beyond any mode of shinning. He scowls at the overhead boughs as if he is working out a route.

But in the end, he turns to DS Jones.

'I'll need to give you a bunk up, lass.'

She laughs – as though he cannot be serious. But adrenaline kicks in. She steps forward.

'How do we do this?'

'You need to get on my shoulders.'

'What – like circus acrobats?'

He parts his lips to speak – but his gaze tracks away past her. There is a flash of concern in his features, and his eyes dart back and forth through the trees towards the shore.

'What is it?'

'I thought I just saw someone.'

She turns. But there is no sign of movement.

'I suppose not everyone wants to obey the signs.'

Skelgill stares for a moment longer – but dusk is pressing.

He turns back and squats on his haunches, facing the oak, bracing with his hands against the trunk.

'Would it be better for you if I were barefoot?'

'Aye – and it might help you keep steady.'

She climbs into position – she has good balance – but she hesitates.

'The hardest thing is there are no handholds.'

Skelgill shifts away a little.

'Just lean your weight against the tree.'

First, she extends her legs, and then he gradually rises.

She perks up.

'Oh – I'll make it easily.'

But she lets out an exasperated hiss.

'The box won't come away. The nail's rusted and it's too big for the hole.'

'Try the lid – it must raise.'

DS Jones strains to reach.

'Help!'

Her sudden appeal is that Skelgill unilaterally grabs hold of her ankles and raises her off his shoulders.

But she sticks to her task. As quick as she can she flips up the top of the nestbox and deftly pulls out its contents – and not a moment too soon – for holding the lift is impossible for any longer – and Skelgill's dropping her sends them both off balance and collapsing with a shriek from her and a groan from him.

Reflexes save the day.

Skelgill topples back in a controlled roll onto the soft leaf litter of the woodland floor, in turn cushioning with a wide embrace his plunging colleague – though not without a gasp as one of her knees digs into his solar plexus. For her part, she holds aloft the camera two-handed, like a precious Ming vase, saving it from any potentially damaging impact.

They lie for a moment, entangled, their faces close.

Skelgill, winded, cannot speak.

DS Jones puckers her lips – but then she grins and rolls away and pulls on her trainers.

'We might be caught on camera.'

They struggle to their knees – their shared sense of urgency returning.

The camera is of the regular motion-activated type, a waterproof plastic casing in camouflage colours, hinged to reveal its battery compartment on one side and a digital screen with control buttons on the other.

With a thumbnail DS Jones moves a slider to the position marked REVIEW.

There is an electronic musical flourish and the screen lights up.

The batteries are still good.

The first shot – that most recently taken – is indeed of them, a close-up, peering into the lens.

In the top corner of the screen a counter reads 2403/2403.

She clicks the REWIND button.

The first seven images, back to 2397, describe their arrival and retrieval of the device. Even a blurred action shot of the fall is recorded.

'There's one for the office noticeboard. Guess what's happening here.'

Skelgill's tone is wry.

DS Jones points to a tiny camera icon with "10s" against it.

'It must be set for a ten-second interval before it takes another shot.'

'What about the date?'

Skelgill leans closer, slipping an arm round her waist. He is still panting from his exertions.

'It's correct – May Day, today. And the time – give or take a minute.'

'Scroll back.'

But she needs no encouragement.

She holds down REWIND, pausing every so often. Like a flip book the seasons change and change again; deer come and go; occasional walkers move along the shore path; Royston Woodcock makes cameo appearances (though he must approach with his ladder from the rear); sporadically a squirrel or a bird investigates, the latter perhaps disappointed to find a cuckoo already in the nest.

'I expect he brought along a portable card-reader each time he checked it.'

But Skelgill is intent upon the receding date, and whether the library will stretch back to The Big Freeze of eighteen months ago.

They watch with bated breath.

'January – slow down, lass.'

But she seems to be able to process the flashing images faster than he.

Snow appears.

'*Whoa!* Go back!'

Now she obliges.

It is their turn to freeze.

After a few moments, slowly, she scrolls to-and-fro, covering four photographs dated 25 December, Christmas-but-one ago.

They are captured in darkness, an eerie snowscape.

A dim figure passes along the path.

A pale snorkel parka reveals little of its wearer. There are ski gloves, snow boots, perhaps.

An anonymous nightwalker.

But, for the detectives, there is a wealth of data.

DS Jones reverts to the first of the four images.

Now she reads off the times.

'22:02.' The person is walking north.

Next shot.

'22:36.' The person is walking south. Pulling a sledge. Leaning into the task.

Again.

'23:17.' The person is walking north. Pulling a sledge. Effortlessly.

And the last.

'23:29.' The person is walking south.

Both detectives exhale, but Skelgill continues to breathe heavily, as if a second windedness has returned; DS Jones turns in alarm, that he might almost be hyperventilating.

His hands visibly shaking, he takes the camera from her and removes the memory card, and pointedly inserts it into the small zip pocket on the upper arm of his hiking shirt. He pats it, indicating its safekeeping.

With a gasp, he manages to declaim.

'This is exactly what we need.'

DS Jones's widened eyes flash their clear white sclerae in the darkening wood.

'But Guv – *who is it?*'

Skelgill takes one further breath, especially deep, as if it will replenish whatever chronic oxygen debt he is battling.

Snap.

There is literally a snap – the onomatopoeic breaking of a twig nearby.

Their heads turn in tandem towards the shoreline path.

Some sixty feet away, like a creature of the forest, between two trunks stands the figure of a woman – little more than a silhouette – though there is a mass of dark hair spilling from a white hoodie – and the dark shadowed eyes are unblinking, penetrating, panther-like.

Despite the distance, and his proximity to his colleague, Skelgill knows that she is staring at him.

It is the gaze of the fiend and the temptress rolled into one.

And then she is gone.

There is a moment's more silence, the detectives unmoving.

DS Jones is first to speak.

'Was that Lena Longstaff?'

Skelgill is staring, dumbstruck.

But rather than reply he staggers to his feet.

'Come on!'

He hauls up his colleague and they set off at a jog.

The pursuit takes them north along the path.

They have no one in their sights nor any way of knowing if their quarry has struck off into the cover of the woods.

But DS Jones does not protest – she trusts to Skelgill's instincts.

And he is right – to a point.

He skids to a halt just as they reach Pike Rigg, where the path runs straight and adjacent to the shore. His double-barrelled expletive is one of astoundment.

DS Jones does not understand at first – until she sees he is glaring across the water. Beneath descending gloom, *The Doghouse* is being proficiently rowed, true as an arrow, diagonally towards the northwest corner of Buttermere.

Skelgill turns to his colleague; he thrusts the camera upon her and begins to back away. When she moves towards him, he raises a halting palm. Then he points directly into the wood.

'Go to Woodcock's place – use the landline. You'll know what to do. I'll head her off.'

And he turns again and begins to jog away – though he stops to call back.

'Make sure those sledges stay in Margery McLeish's shed – she was talking about carting junk to Edinburgh tonight.'

33. SERGEANTS' DILEMMA

Lorton Vale – 7.20 p.m.

'Emma?'

'Yes – where are you?'

DS Leyton splutters with relief.

'I'm driving down to find you and the Guvnor – you pair ain't got no signal between you. We've just come level with Crummock Water.'

'We?'

Now he produces an agonised groan.

'I've got the two older nippers in the back – had to pick 'em up from clubs.'

'Oh – but you shouldn't be –'

'Nah – don't worry – they're getting stuck into fish and chips. Little adventure.' Though he hesitates. 'The Missus probably won't agree when she gets hers stone cold.'

DS Jones's mind is working fast.

'I think you should stop – I need you to make some calls while you have a signal. I'm at Royston Woodcock's cottage – but I can't stay long – I need to –'

Now DS Leyton interjects.

'Listen, girl – there's some news concerning his daughter – that's why I was coming to find you.' He pauses again, this time to swerve into a passing place. 'That's me in a layby.'

'Okay.'

Though she has urgent business, she means him to speak first.

'DC Watson tracked her down in New Zealand. I saw the name – Val White. I thought, that can't be right – so I phoned her. Turns out it's her actual name. To cut a long story short, her passport and other personal documents were stolen, seven years ago. This was from a locker at her beach club in Auckland. The suspect was a young woman who was being questioned in connection with a drowning – of a male employee at the same club, where she worked as a lifeguard. There was a question of negligence on her part – perhaps even more serious than that. The geezer who drowned was the fiancé of a girl the suspect knew – and there was the suggestion of some kind of love triangle.'

'Wow.'

'Yeah – so here's the thing. The suspect's real name is Chaie Hadlee. Pronounced *Shay* but spelled C-H-A-I-E. She's the right age for our Valentina White – described as naturally blonde, blue eyes, five foot three. The stolen passport was used almost immediately to travel one-way to Kuala Lumpur. There are reports that she's been living in Spain and London – but the trail's gone completely cold in the past three years. Interpol have issued a Green Notice – that's the one that warns she's considered a threat to public safety.'

DS Leyton halts for breath. His colleague is silent.

'Sorry, Emma – I've completely butted in on your thing.'

'No – it's okay.' She is processing, catching up. 'It's alarming. I'm trying to see how it fits – I'm sure it does – with exactly where we are right now. We've found photos on a hidden camera – it looks like Royston Woodcock had evidence of the Lady of the Lake murder. He may have been blackmailing someone.'

'That does fit.'

DS Jones continues, the note of urgency in her voice growing.

'We were followed in the woods. I think it was Lena Longstaff – yet she had supposedly left the area.'

DS Leyton begins to anticipate matters.

'So, where's the Guvnor, now?'

'He's given chase on foot. He's trying to block her route to Buttermere village. That's what I need you to do. If she doubles back to the B5289 she could hitch a lift or flag down a bus. But there are only three exit routes – Honister Pass south, Newlands Pass east – and then Lorton Vale north.'

'That's where I am.'

'But we need uniforms to stop traffic.'

'Yeah, right enough, girl. I'd better call the cavalry.'

'And then you'd better get home.'

DS Leyton sighs resignedly, as if he views the prospect with trepidation.

And now he vacillates, unready quite yet to end the call.

'Who's who in this case? It seems to me it's Valentina White – so-called – that we need a word with. Why's this Lena woman on the run?'

'Well, she fled, I suppose – but – you know how it is.'

DS Leyton chuckles drily.

'Yeah – I gave up trying to read the Guvnor's mind years ago.'

DS Jones murmurs in sympathy. But it strikes her that such clairvoyance might in any event be in vain. Though he would never admit it, Skelgill seems driven to the point of obsession, that the Lady of the Lake is a matter of duty and destiny, a race against the clock, a mission compounded by DI Smart's Machiavellian intervention.

DS Leyton adds a rider.

'Maybe it's just as well he's chasing Lena Longstaff. This other bird – she sounds proper chicken oriental.'

'She's what?' The lapse into East End lingo throws DS Jones.

'*Mental* – a right little psycho.'

34. "THE WHITE DOWNFALL"

Red Pike – 7.20 p.m.

AS DS JONES is concluding her call with DS Leyton, Skelgill is pounding across the alluvial plain at the foot of Buttermere. He has kept *The Doghouse* in sight, and now sees its able occupant beach the craft and clamber ashore. The question he has been asking himself is about to be answered. Why make for the northwest corner and not directly for the point nearest to the road? To the north is only Crummock Water, and west the long, undulating ridge that towers over the dale. Is her aim simply to put distance between them, by taking the shortcut across the lake?

The wearer of the distinctive white hoodie – hood still raised – scrambles up the short stretch of pebble beach and vaults the fence at the foot of the fell. He sees that she stops for a second to look back in his direction. His pale khaki hiking shirt stands out in the twilight, and she must see that he is on her tail.

She turns and disappears into the wood.

She is taking the steep path beside Sourmilk Gill.

She is heading cross country.

His question is only half answered, and doubts begin to flood his mind. The tide of confusion, ebbing and flowing since his call at Hassness Cottage, rises once more. But he steps up his pace, as if he can outrun its cold tentacles.

He clatters into the boundary fence some two minutes behind. Thus far, the fugitive has demonstrated both prowess and fitness – is that what yoga does for you? DS Jones is always nagging him to try it. But running uphill is a singular craft.

Though he has never been quite the same since he injured his back, and he is a few inches too tall ever to have ranked among the elite fell runners, his credentials are nonetheless impressive. And he has muscle memory in his column – he has climbed Red Pike this way a hundred times.

Surely the woman will be no match for him on the hillside.

Does she think she can make it to Loweswater, where the maze of lanes would provide means of escape, or even over the ridge into Ennerdale? But these options would each rely on either some further means of getaway, or somewhere to hide out and lie low. Neither is impossible – but this flight seems spontaneous – she stalked them, not knowing where they could have been going; taking the boat was surely opportunistic, a spur-of-the-moment decision. Yet the chase in which he is involved feels calculated; it has the hallmarks of a strategy. She looked back from clearing the fence like she was absolutely making sure he was following her.

And now it might be his imagination – but as he scales the stone-lined flight beside the tumbling beck he detects opposing wafts of fragrance – a scent that is one moment musky and another floral – as if a fox has been scent-marking amongst the bluebells, crushing the foliage – though no sly old tod would unwittingly lay such an easy trail for the hound.

But a hound would follow her scent, so why wouldn't he? An autonomic, primal hunter's instinct. And like him she must surely be perspiring, secreting an aerosol of natural pheromone upon the still woodland air. In the sheltered lee of Red Pike, Skelgill sweats profusely; his hair is plastered to his brow, and already the back of his shirt clings uncomfortably.

His progress up through the lower wooded section of Sourmilk Gill is further hindered by practical uncertainty. What if she simply leaves the path and conceals herself among the trees – and waits for him to pass, in order to creep back down? Thus, she could give him the slip. There are endless side-ways to explore and check – but he has to satisfy himself with continual glances left and right, and trust to the sixth sense that keeps him going.

And – sure enough – when he emerges through the treeline, the first five hundred feet of ascent under his belt, he sees her. There can be no mistaking the white hoodie, even in the fading light. He is shocked – not only has she maintained her distance from him – but perhaps she has even extended it. And she is waiting.

She stands on the false horizon that is the lip of Bleaberry Tarn, where Sourmilk Gill has its outfall.

Immediately, she turns and disappears.

Skelgill redoubles his efforts. At least now they are in open country – he can simply follow his quarry by eye. Though his quarry might indeed be a fell fox, for all her agility and craft.

It is another eleven hundred feet to the tarn – and by the time he reaches the outfall his lungs feel fit to burst. He has painted all manner of scenarios for what he might find – so he is not surprised to see her on the summit of Red Pike, five hundred feet above.

On a different day he would stop to survey the tarn; to appreciate the Lakeland gem, a sapphire set in a ring of burnished bronze, a crystal blue teardrop deep in the echoing comb; to watch for rises of the hungry mountain brownies that eke a living out of the magical pool; to admire the pair of ravens that circle beneath the savage cliffs of Chapel Crags, their barks echoing about the resonant mountain amphitheatre.

That he does not break stride or that the water does not turn his head tells something of his disposition.

He watches hawklike.

That a game of hare and hounds is being played seems more certain by the minute.

She seems to make it clear that she is turning north. Ennerdale is ruled out. She sets off from the summit in clear sight along Lingcomb Edge. He considers trying to cut her off by striking through Ling Comb itself – but it is a rough traverse, boulders under heather, and if she veers west for Starling Dodd he could lose her completely. He girds his loins for one last haul – the conventional walkers' route, from the tarn up onto The

Saddle, the little col between Dodd and Red Pike, and thence to the summit itself.

At the ridge he halts abruptly, momentarily blinded.

The sun, long lost to the dale, lingers above the northwestern horizon; a vista of orange-infused mists, an impressionist's landscape, of hill and sky with little distinction; just hints of Ennerdale with its eponymous water and beyond to the coastal plain and the glinting Solway.

He is soaked.

That he stops makes him a target – midges immediately move in – and he begins to stumble on, scratching with futility at his temples and cursing the near-invisible creatures that possess such power to disorient and disable, winged Lilliputians to his defenceless Gulliver.

He sees now that he could have gambled on Ling Comb – she has eschewed the fork to Starling Dodd and is continuing north. It is the logical exit route, via Scale Force, Lakeland's highest waterfall, the path that descends to the southwestern shore of Crummock Water.

It is all downhill now. And, as far as Scale Force, a comparatively gentle descent, the better part of sixteen hundred feet over the course of a mile of open fellside. The figure in white is halfway there. Skelgill begins to jog – and then to run – the path weaves between a patchwork of mat-grass, heather, rock and lichen; startled meadow pipits rise in occasional alarm, the odd wheatear bobs from boulder to boulder, flashing its warning white rump – but he is not seeing like he normally does.

But his mind finds a small window for logic. Could she have some escape planned from Crummock Water? A second boat that really would leave him stranded.

Skelgill realises he will likely have a mobile signal – but DS Jones, somewhere deep in the dale, will not. He has no way of guiding her to set up an ambush, a pincer movement.

Besides, he is gaining at last.

Below him, the path drops more sharply to pick up Scale Beck, and the comb deepens to become an increasingly steep-sided gill, where eventually the waterfall will pour over its crag.

Now Skelgill loses sight of his quarry – though he is unperturbed; there is only one route hereon.

A short stretch of path levels out – and he rounds a last spur of rock.

Twenty feet ahead, at the crest of the fall, lies a shallow pool.

A muted roar, its source hidden, cautions approach.

He stops short of the water.

Beyond, on the grassy lip, the white hoodie lies crumpled.

His chest heaving, he narrows his eyes.

Dusk hangs heavy in the gill.

And then – an apparition, almost supernatural.

The flat surface of the pool rises into the form of a woman.

An apparition, yes – but one that gasps for breath, her torso heaving.

And of solid form, for she remains as water streams away.

A black outfit glistens, skintight, flimsy, all-revealing.

Long black hair covers the face.

Coal eyes peer through the sodden veil.

Those panther eyes.

It is a creature at bay – and yet, in control.

Silently, the gaze never leaving his, she backs up onto the shelf.

With a sensuous unfolding of one arm, she indicates down to her side.

Skelgill sees the bed of soft, dry turf, embellished with tormentil and wild thyme.

He steps into the pool and begins slowly to wade towards her.

At six feet apart the woman dips her head and parts her hair.

Thus bowed, she plucks at her eyes.

She straightens, and with a sorceress's flourish, fingers splayed, she casts apart her arms and then shapes an entreaty to embrace.

And now she speaks.

'Come, Inspector – your fantasy threesome.'

Electric blue eyes.

Lightning strikes again.

The behemoth rises again.

And now he sees it in all its naked glory.

A kaleidoscopic whirlpool, his subconscious empties into his consciousness like the wild waterfall at the woman's back.

Black clothes. *White clothes.*
Red wine. *White wine.*
Raven brunette. *Pixie blonde.*
Flat pumps. *High platforms.*
Musk. *Floral.*
Painted nails. *Unvarnished nails.*
Right hand. *Left hand.*
London accent. *Kiwi accent.*
Brown eyes. *Blue eyes* ...

Half-drowning, half-elated, he hears her voice again, coaxing, cajoling, seductive.

'Take off your shirt, eh? It's soaked through, anyway.'

He tears, not caring for buttons, and tosses it aside.

She makes a sudden visceral gasp and leans to clutch him.

As he sways into the embrace, as the warm lips beckon and the cold eyes hypnotise, as the cool fingers close around his forearms and nails dig into his flesh, and the judo throw comes, he is ready for it.

He braces his left foot and drops his centre of gravity.

In the instant, she reacts to the unexpected resistance – she pulls to her limit – and her hands slide off his slippery sweat-coated skin and she loses her grip and staggers backwards, overbalances.

Skelgill makes a desperate lunge.

But in the cartoon moment – the split second when she teeters on the brink before she drops like a stone his snatch gets only a handful of tresses.

And she – the azure eyes suddenly knowing – utters one word.

'Sweet.'

And she is gone.

Skelgill stands in shock.

He crumples to his knees and crawls to peer over the edge.

Cascading white water and flying foam obscure his view.

White noise cancels all other sounds.

It is a hundred and seventy feet to the plunge pool; *the white downfall.*

Skelgill must resort to scrambling, putting himself in danger.

He reaches a jutting outcrop, hangs on a rowan – and finds a line of sight.

She lies supine, her feet in the pool, her head on the rocks, her arms splayed. The blue eyes are open and – unblinking, darkening – might just be reflecting the cobalt evening sky.

And Skelgill, for the second time today – and now fully, comprehensively, and irrevocably – has sensations, images and revelations play out in his mind. He might be a survivor, hit from behind by a bus, able to watch his floundering caught on CCTV.

A voice – repeating itself, far off – gradually penetrates his darkness.

A shaft of light.

'*Guv!* Where are you? *Guv!*'

Skelgill is uncertain of how long he has been there.

Dusk is well advanced upon the dale.

He clambers up.

DS Jones stands by the little pool, its waters placid – she holds the discarded garments – the hoodie at arm's length, his shirt pressed to her breast.

She cannot at first find her words.

He approaches silently, takes his shirt.

She watches while he puts it on.

'Where is she?'

Skelgill does not reply.

He rounds to the narrow bed of bruised turf.

He stoops and picks up a long, trailing mass of tangled black strands.

He raises it.

'She didn't make it, lass.' He seems to read disbelief in her eyes. He gives the item a shake. 'A wig. Valentina White's wig.'

DS Jones's lips part – but she holds back to let him speak.

'There is no Lena Longstaff. Not anymore. Not since two Christmases ago.'

And now he sighs – long and low, to the limit of his lungs, as if to expel every last trace of some foul vapour that has possessed him.

She sees in his eyes discomfort, of admission and perhaps humiliation. Dismayed, she steps forward and clasps his upper arm.

'No – actually – you know – strictly speaking, it's Chaie Hadlee's wig.' She smiles as he recoils. 'Don't worry, I'll explain. You got it right.'

Skelgill stares at her for a few moments – and then nods slowly, and he places the item carefully on a rock and kneels at the water's edge. Now he drinks thirstily, and then dunks his head in the pool.

He shifts into a sitting position and drags back his hair with splayed fingers.

Refreshed, bright-eyed even, he regards her earnestly.

'How did you know where I was – and how did you get here so quick?'

DS Jones drops down beside him.

'I hitched a ride on your farmer friend's quad. He knew where you'd gone – then we spotted you running along the ridge. He brought me along the Crummock Water track – I only had to climb the last stretch – he said just five hundred feet and half a mile. A fraction of what you've done.'

Skelgill growls approvingly.

DS Jones has questions of her own.

'Do you think she had a plan?'

Skelgill's left hand moves to the zip pocket on his right sleeve. He feels for its contents.

'She'd been following us – she knew what we'd found. She wanted the memory card.'

DS Jones swallows – she hesitates for a moment.

'How come you took off your shirt?'

Skelgill gives an ironic laugh and casts a hand towards the smooth water that slides over the lip of the fall.

'If I were going with her, I made damned sure the evidence weren't.'

DS Jones inhales sharply – and now there is a longer silence before she speaks again.

'When did you realise?'

For a simple closed question, it provokes in Skelgill's mind a fleeting, flashing return to the crazy kaleidoscope of subconscious revelations. What is the answer? Was it as dangerously late as when he felt her about to throw him? Or seconds before, when deliciously the brown eyes became blue and she revealed herself, drunk on her victory? Or the white hoodie in the woods – surely the same top he had earlier glimpsed in the bedroom window of Hassness Cottage?

Or was it from the very first – all the way back to the distant vision of the woman in the yoga outfit – when he heeded her siren call and dismissed instinctive suspicion as merely the confused scrambling of deeper primeval urges?

'Pass. Ask me again, later.'

35. CORNER PIECES

Hassness Cottage – 8.45 p.m.

BENEATH THE poor light of an underpowered bulb DS Leyton casts a blue-gloved hand at the four images spread on the window sill over which they pore. Skelgill is similarly clad – and they both sport blue plastic overshoes – like poolside parents at the public swimming baths; but the cottage is now officially a crime scene – albeit that the crime was probably committed on Christmas Day some eighteen months ago.

'So, what's going on here, Guv?'

Skelgill rearranges the creased prints into chronological order. Retrieved from a basket beside the hearth, they had been carelessly crumpled ready for destruction by fire.

'She went to get the sledge. Took the piece of gatepost. Dragged it back on the sledge.'

'That fancy knot, Guv. She'd been a lifeguard.' DS Leyton hisses. '*Lifeguard* – there's an irony.'

Skelgill grimaces. The cowboy bowline – it should have come to him. He'd seen just how left-handed she was. Even down to stirring honey into tea, or the opening of a bottle. He gazes ahead – and, though beyond the glass of the conservatory are just shadows, he sees well enough in his mind's eye.

'Dragged the body from here. Tied the shard on by the shore. Took her out across the ice on the sledge – towards the middle where there was a patch of unfrozen water. Probably shoved it the last few yards onto thinner ice, attached to a length of rope. Sank her. No boat needed. Returned the sledge.' He touches the third of the four photographs.

DS Leyton nods pensively.

'And these are what she whacked Woodcock for?'

Skelgill considers.

'Aye. These – and she took his key and went back to his cottage – wiped copies and anything incriminating off his laptop – took his camera and dropped it beside the body. Left no trace of a burglary – as if he'd just popped out, leaving it unlocked like most folk round here. Pulled the loose pit props down so the tunnel roof caved on him. Made the whole thing look like an accident.'

DS Leyton's exclamation of disgust has just a hint of reluctant admiration. He taps the second photograph, the figure pulling the sledge in the direction of Hassness.

'No boat needed, Guv – nor much strength needed. And all that evidence of her MO just melted away. Literally.'

'Aye. Literally – *hah* – very good, Leyton.'

DS Leyton looks momentarily perplexed.

'Oh, yeah. *Literally.* Emma told me she reckons she was using AI to keep producing the books by L.L. James. Killed the goose without cutting off the flow of golden eggs. Just carried on – pretending Lena Longstaff was still alive. Horror from beyond the grave. No wonder she never did a signing at the bookshop. She didn't dare take it that far. Just impersonated her if she needed to.'

Skelgill turns to stare hard at his colleague.

'Or when the fancy took her.'

There is something chilling about Skelgill's delivery.

'Don't get me wrong, Guv – I see why you kept your cards close to your chest. Once you'd told us you'd met Lena Longstaff – we'd have thought you were crackers if you'd started claiming her and Valentina White were one and the same.'

Skelgill stiffens and folds his arms.

'Leyton, I only met her once – got up like that. And I met her first. Why would I think – here's a woman in a wig, coloured lenses, make-up, fake London accent?'

DS Leyton holds up a palm.

'Don't worry, Guv – I'd have been the first to fall for it, me.'

Despite his sergeant's best efforts to assuage his sense of culpability, Skelgill doubles down.

'Next day in the bookshop – the accent's broad Kiwi. The second woman's taller, blonde crew cut, coloured specs, blue eyes, fair skin ... baggy clothes – you know?'

DS Leyton rolls his eyes, suggesting he reads some innuendo into Skelgill's rather desperate resort to an explanation.

'*Ahem.*'

Guilty faces, like schoolboys caught sharing inappropriate phone content, turn to see DS Jones in the kitchen doorway, the flyscreen parted. But she does not embellish her reproach.

'On the subject of disguise ...'

She raises an arm to display a second black wig.

'There's a loft ladder. More or less a secret dressing room and den.'

She sees that Skelgill is plying her with a look tinged with peevishness. He had insisted upon making an urgent room-to-room search of the property – she assumed, to satisfy himself that he was not delusional, and that Lena Longstaff would not be found, sleeping like Goldilocks. She smiles disarmingly.

'I sat on the loo seat – it's not easy to spot the concealed hatch otherwise. It goes up above the bathroom door.'

Skelgill manages to contrive an appreciative grin.

DS Jones continues.

'There's a treasure trove up there. This wig – and packets of coloured contact lenses and the make-up she would use to darken her complexion. In a desk there's personal admin – some relating to Lena Longstaff – recent bank and tax statements – as if her life has been continuing as normal.'

Skelgill inhales to speak, but she steps forwards and hands him a sheaf of documents.

'Look at these – they seem to be excerpts printed from emails – they refer to Royston Woodcock and his daughter. I wonder if she gained access the real-life Dr Val White's account. You know – it could explain why the two women moved here – after all, she's effectively been impersonating her.'

DS Leyton is leaning to squint at the top paper.

'That couldn't be why she ended up doing him in?'

But Skelgill shakes his head.

'More likely he didn't know, Leyton. Stick with a straight case of blackmail. Remember, he were no saint himself.'

DS Leyton nods reflectively.

'I suppose he didn't bargain for a psychopath. Just as well she met her match in you, Guv.'

Skelgill growls.

'Are you saying it takes one to know one?'

Though it is a complaint, there is the suggestion that he would not be entirely offended.

But DS Leyton pivots, all the same.

'It was smart work – tracking down that memory card. Now I see it – the puzzle's starting to take shape. You were miles ahead of me, Guv.'

Skelgill's left hand drifts absently to his sleeve pocket.

'I was just the one on the spot, Leyton. The long-lens camera was planted in the tunnel. That meant she'd been back to his cottage to destroy evidence. But she overlooked the pictures he'd printed and stuck on the wall. That's what led to the hidden camera. And then the smew in the patch of open water surrounded by ice – you could call it two birds with one stone.'

DS Leyton clicks his tongue admiringly.

'The reason she killed Woodcock – and how she disposed of Lena Longstaff's body.'

Skelgill nods pensively; he exhibits no great signs of triumph in his demeanour.

DS Leyton raps his folded knuckles together.

'So, what about Lena Longstaff – why did Valentina White kill her? Was it just for the money?'

Skelgill shoots a sideways glance at DS Jones.

'Like to answer that?'

She balks for a moment, but he gestures casually, as if to say, what's to lose.

'Okay. Well – perhaps there was some truth in what Valentina White said about Lena Longstaff's sudden absences. On some of those occasions she simply went to the Hikers' Hostel. And Valentina White found out about it. If Kevin Pope had tried and failed to return from Manchester – and she slipped out on Christmas Day to meet him, to no avail – she'd have had to come back here. I guess we'll never know what took place between them. Maybe nothing violent or even immediate – but I suspect it was the trigger.'

DS Leyton interjects.

'Maybe she followed her on Christmas Day – and that's when she saw the broken gatepost?'

But Skelgill inhales in the way of dissent.

'I reckon she'd already done a recce – the gatepost – the building materials at Hassness Castle – the sledges in the garden at Catthwaite Cottage.' He taps the documents with the back of his free hand. 'She was a planner, calculated in her actions. When she murdered Lena Longstaff, she was good and ready – and the conditions were perfect.'

He hands the papers to DS Jones and flexes his back and stretches, as though hanging about any longer will be inadvisable for a body that has endured his singular day. He relaxes his rangy frame, as if an invisible weight has been lifted from his shoulders.

'I reckon we've got more than enough to convince the Chief – and I'll put my shirt on Lena Longstaff being the Lady of the Lake.'

His pronouncement draws inaudible sighs of relief. And a smile from DS Jones, who divines a double meaning in his idiom.

Skelgill claps his hands together.

'Let's get this place locked up and turn it over to Forensics.'

Outside in the stillness of Buttermere they can hear the distant throb of a helicopter from further down the dale, the team that will be extracting the body from below Scale Force.

Skelgill sniffs the cool air.

'Nice evening for a spot of night fishing.'

His colleagues know he is not serious – but that he is not one hundred percent not serious.

Perhaps he detects their trepidation.

'You'd want a flask and bacon butties, mind.'

DS Leyton puts a palm to his ample stomach.

'Tell you what – I've been to the flippin' chippy twice tonight and still not had me tea.' He checks his wristwatch. 'Now they'll be closed.'

Skelgill reaches to slap his sergeant between the shoulder blades – perhaps in recognition of his diligence in returning after hours to assist and ferry them about.

'Don't fret, Leyton – I know somewhere we can be eating hotpot in less than five minutes.'

ONE WEEK LATER

36. THE BIG PICTURE

Police HQ – 9.45 a.m.

'SO, THIS SECTION collates information from various sources – Interpol, the New Zealand Police, the Met – along with our own findings and assumptions made where reasonable. We have Chaie Hadlee – later *aka* Valentina White and, in some respects, *aka* Lena Longstaff – first coming to the attention of the New Zealand authorities around eight years ago. A young man named Mitch MacQuoid drowned in the sea at the Auckland Beach Club, despite the claimed best efforts of the lifeguard on duty to save him. That lifeguard was Chaie Hadlee. There were no witnesses to the incident. At the inquest doubt was cast on events by a safety expert. The water was shallow and it was a warm, calm day. Chaie Hadlee was close at hand, well equipped and fully qualified. She came from a sailing family and had been a regional schools swimming and martial arts champion. Following post-inquest publicity, the police received an anonymous tip-off to the effect that the drowning victim had recently become engaged to a young woman with whom Chaie Hadlee had previously been involved. There was the suggestion that she saw Mitch MacQuoid as a love rival. The police began to make discreet inquiries – and it was shortly after that when Dr Val White's locker was broken into and her personal possessions and documents stolen.

'Chaie Hadlee disappeared immediately and was believed to have travelled via Malaysia to Europe. Initially, at least, she would have been able to use two identities to give the authorities the slip: her own New Zealand passport, and Dr Val White's British passport. The New Zealand Police alerted Interpol, who deemed the circumstances sufficiently serious to issue a Green Notice, but in a world of international terrorism, drug-running and people-trafficking, not surprisingly border police had bigger fish to fry. There were, however, possible sightings in Andalusia and the Home Counties – which correspond to what she told you.'

Skelgill continues working his way through his bacon roll; indeed his eyes fall on the side plate and mug of cooling tea across from DS Leyton's regular seat beside the tall grey filing cabinet. The chair is empty, but the side plate still bears his absentee sergeant's breakfast. Skelgill has been impatient to start, both on his food and the less welcome administrative task in hand. DS Jones, for her part, has resisted the temptation of the former, and instead has her end of Skelgill's expansive desk covered in a tiled arrangement of papers: the corner pieces and frame of their jigsaw in place, now they must best position the main features of the bigger picture.

'What can't be true is that she met Lena Longstaff after they both left college in London – although the real Val White attended the Faculty of Medicine at Imperial, and Lena Longstaff studied contemporaneously at Central St Martins College of Art in Covent Garden. However, they did live together in West London for a year, Seville for two years and then briefly back to Hammersmith before moving up to the Lakes three years ago.'

DS Jones looks up to check whether Skelgill is paying attention; this time he is staring at her, though he does not react to her eye contact in the normal way, and it takes her inadvertent movement, brushing at stray strands of hair that have fallen across her cheek, before he seems to register her unspoken entreaty. He starts.

'Aye – go on, lass.'

She turns the page of the stapled document.

'It does appear that Chaie Hadlee was keeping track of Royston Woodcock's whereabouts. When Hassness Cottage became available, she was clearly involved. It's her handwriting on the lease, despite that the property is rented in the name of Lena Longstaff – and rent has been paid through Lena

Longstaff's bank account. The assumption being that her credentials were more suitable and no guarantor was needed. Obviously, Lena Longstaff was alive at this point and must have acquiesced in these arrangements – but it looks like Chaie Hadlee was the driver in eventually following him to the Lakes.'

DS Jones leans to peer at a list of points – some ticked off – on a single page attached to a clipboard.

'We're still waiting to receive information from Royston Woodcock's solicitors, bankers, email providers and other sources – but I think it will be borne out – and that Chaie Hadlee, posing as his daughter, was preparing the ground to step forward as his heir.'

Skelgill makes a kind of hiss.

'Should he have died.'

DS Jones nods pensively.

'You know – since Royston Woodcock was estranged from his daughter and ex-wife, I think it's quite probable that he could indeed have died and had his assets stripped without them knowing anything about it. You said she was a planner, Guv. His demise was in her plan – he just precipitated it sooner than she might have intended. I'm stating that we don't believe he was aware of Chaie Hadlee's true identity – quite likely not even the name similarity.'

Skelgill interjects.

'Plenty of folk in the village didn't know their names.'

'Possibly they were nodding acquaintances. However, we know he stalked women. If he'd taken photos of them – later deleted by Chaie Hadlee – perhaps he realised that latterly he never saw the two together – and suspected there was only one person. Then he learned of the Lady of the Lake and overheard us. In his warped little world it was too good a chance to miss. The call he made on the night of his death has now been traced to Paige Turners. We know he shopped there, you established that. Perhaps he tried to see her first at the bookstore but got cold feet – and instead rang her after hours.

'The bus driver on the route from Cockermouth remembers a woman matching her description alighting at the stop between

Buttermere and Gatesgarth – but not as late as Chaie Hadlee told you – it was the nine o'clock service, which gave her time to prepare to meet him. My guess is that the tunnel was her suggestion for their rendezvous.'

She pauses to give Skelgill the opportunity to comment; he makes a face of agreement, that her assumptions are plausible. If Royston Woodcock had long been in her sights, quite likely Chaie Hadlee had eyed up the dangerous tunnel as a one place among others where he might meet with an accident. As a wildlife photographer, he probably got himself into precarious places, the lake's bank over deep water, a cliff on the fellside, a waterfall.

DS Jones switches documents.

'She'd showed herself capable of playing a long hand. And again with Lena Longstaff. If it weren't for the finding of the body, the person we knew as Valentina White would have been carefully curating her continued existence. Even – with the help of AI – writing her books. And when the divers found the body she had a simple plan ready. If a police officer – the more senior the better – were to meet 'Lena Longstaff' –' (she performs the parentheses) 'then no one would be looking for her. And by logical inference no one would suspect her partner of the murder of someone apparently alive.'

It takes Skelgill a few seconds to respond.

'And I walked right into it.'

DS Jones shakes her head.

'Like you said before – how were you to know? Locals believed two women still lived at Hassness Cottage. Not unreasonably, the couple had a reputation for keeping themselves to themselves. Valentina White travelled by bus to work at Cockermouth. Lena Longstaff fitted the popular image of the reclusive writer. Their appearances were so markedly different that there was never any need to look closer. Even at a cursory glance it was patently obvious there were two women.'

Skelgill remains glum faced.

She bats for him.

'Except you did notice – and that's one of the things that unsettled you.'

He regards her quizzically – that she harbours an insight into his method that he himself does not fully appreciate.

But now she quickly moves on.

'On the murder of Lena Longstaff – we now have a lot more, obviously.'

Skelgill murmurs compliantly.

She indicates to separate documents in turn.

'The positive DNA match to her cousin in the States. The dental records from the surgery in Hammersmith. So there is no doubt about the identity of the Lady of the Lake. And there's Kevin Pope – whom I'll come to in a moment.'

She exchanges the papers she holds for another set from the desk.

'Forensics have positively matched the tiny piece of angel-shaped glitter to samples in a box of decorations from the attic at Hassness Cottage. It looks like they were scattered on the table – and one of them got into Lena Longstaff's meal. It seems probable that she was suffocated whilst asleep under the influence of alcohol. There was likely brandy with the Christmas pudding, rum butter – and various other drinks. I expect Valentina White – Chaie Hadlee – was encouraging her. Besides, if she'd hoped to meet Kevin Pope and had been thwarted by The Big Freeze, perhaps she was drowning her sorrows.' DS Jones hesitates – and picks up a pen to mark the page. 'Sorry – I shan't use that phrase.'

She glances up at Skelgill, but he appears indifferent on this point. She taps her pen against the document.

'I'll attach a pathology report about alcohol and the results of the autopsy. In a nutshell, there is some doubt in this respect, because alcohol can be produced endogenously in a decomposing corpse.'

Skelgill raises an eyebrow, and again desists from any comment.

'Forensics have also found a strand of Lena Longstaff's hair caught in a tiny fracture on one of the sledges from Catthwaite

Cottage. According to Margery McLeish, it's quite probable that they were hung up after that Christmas period and haven't been taken out of the shed since. There was no snow at Christmas last year. We've also managed to get a statement from retired serial killer Roger Black.'

Skelgill grins – that she has not minded his teasing; the occasional bright shaft of black humour that penetrated the dark storm that raged over him for a week. She reciprocates with a smile.

'To be honest, Guv, there's nothing further from him – it seems that Ted Hindlewake managed to pump him for all the relevant facts that he could remember. But his evidence lends weight to our case – he's the nearest we've got to an actual eyewitness.'

Skelgill concurs, and DS Jones moves on to a new chapter.

'Okay, going back to Kevin Pope. He's been in this morning to give a final statement, which this is a copy of. He might still be with DC Watson – she wanted to follow up a couple of points and asked him to wait. As you know, he identified a photograph of Lena Longstaff as the woman he had been dating.' She turns the document illustratively towards Skelgill. 'In here, he explains that she would appear unannounced and stay with him for one or more nights. She told him her name was Tina, but not where she was from, nor would she give him any contact details. He assumed she was married and was sneaking off from her husband when she could, at short notice – he thought maybe from Cockermouth. Going by his description she sounds like she was quite a bohemian character in her own right, and plainly not averse to experimentation.'

'She was a writer.'

Skelgill's tone might as well have added, what else would you expect?

But DS Jones regards him earnestly.

'I'll take it a step further. Kevin Pope has described how she first appeared – she was surprised to find him, smoking out at the back of the Hikers' Hostel, not long after he'd arrived. I think he thought all of his birthdays had come together. But for her part I suspect she wasn't expecting him to be there. I think she made up the name Tina on the spur of the moment – that she wasn't too trusting of him to keep things under his hat. Perhaps it was even a bit of a joke – it might have been her pet name for Valentina.'

'Aye.'

'We've interviewed the previous manager – Ivy Smith, the Scot. She freely admits to a casual affair with Lena Longstaff – although the difference is, she knew who Lena Longstaff was, and where she lived. She says Lena was a free spirit who considered herself to be in an open relationship – but she'd told Ivy Smith that Valentina was a narcissist who couldn't cope with idea of not being the sole idol of her talented and successful partner. Perhaps discovering that Lena was two-timing her with Kevin Pope was the last straw.'

Skelgill narrows his eyes; but the sun has come out and his office is flooded with light, and it might just be a natural reaction. DS Jones's bronzed blonde hair is suddenly illuminated.

'Ivy Smith left at short notice to care for her widower father in Benbecula in the Outer Hebrides. He suffered a serious heart attack. She didn't leave forwarding details – and she knew nothing of events that have transpired since. She confirmed that Lena Longstaff didn't have a mobile phone, so she wasn't surprised that they lost contact.'

Skelgill nods reflectively, though his gaze again is attracted to DS Leyton's unattended bacon roll.

DS Jones resumes her narrative.

'So – it looks like we can believe pretty much all of Kevin Pope's account – about being stranded in the snow. And – as we thought – he just didn't dare mention to us his relationship with the so-called Tina because he was terrified of DI Smart. That Tina would turn out to be the Lady of the Lake – and he would be the prime suspect, having had a clandestine relationship with her, right up to her disappearance – which he subsequently learned coincided with her death. And, of course, it was compounded by DI Smart's accusations of his supposed relationship with Martina Radu. At the time, she was a missing person that fitted the bill – and Kevin assumed that 'Tina' was her own diminutive. He thought his Tina was quite likely the murdered woman.'

Skelgill grimaces.

'Just as well Smart never got hold of the gatepost.'

DS Jones lowers the papers she holds and speaks as if off the record.

'You know – I agree with you – that Chaie Hadlee did plan ahead how she would dispose of Lena Longstaff's body. And also that she was alert to other layers of defence, including alibi. If Lena's body had been found quickly, and identified, then the gatepost was a damning piece of evidence against Kevin Pope. All so-called Valentina White would have needed to say is that she was aware that Lena was secretly seeing him.'

Skelgill holds his peace; he can see that DS Jones has more to add.

'Then – by taking the materials, the polythene and the rope from the little building site at Hassness Castle – she also cast suspicion on the workers there, one of whom was Bob Tapp. Even the sledges – several people could have known about them – and again it would have dragged a much wider cast of possible suspects into play. She was thinking ahead – covering her own tracks and laying false trails.'

Skelgill inhales – and this time she waits for him to speak.

'Don't you reckon she did exactly that with Woodcock?'

It seems she is with him on this point.

'You mean in relation to Lena Longstaff's convenient disappearance? To conduct research. Scotland. London. France. Timbuktu.'

Skelgill leans his elbows on his desk and his chin on intertwined fingers.

'Quite a masterstroke. In case making it look like an accident fails – there's Plan B. Lena Longstaff has obviously killed Woodcock – and she disappears off the face of the planet. Of course we'd think it was her. And then we'd never find her.'

DS Jones leans back in her seat and clasps her hands on top of her head.

She exhales; the sound is almost a rueful whistle.

'You know, it would have tied up all Chaie Hadlee's loose ends in one fell swoop. The authorities looking for fugitive Lena – and never thinking that all the time she is the Lady of the Lake.'

But perhaps DS Jones now detects some doubt in Skelgill's expression.

'Am I missing something?'

Skelgill uncharacteristically shudders.

It is the image of the cold corpse lying just a couple of hundred yards from home, and seventy-five feet down – that she even came out and impersonated her friend doing yoga. And the thought of fishing on Buttermere, of trolling deep for ferox, of snagging his line.

He realises DS Jones is looking at him in alarm – it must be that his reaction has inadvertently revealed the nature of his thoughts.

'She got a buzz out of it. And she might have missed the thrill – the risk of being unmasked. Of living on the edge. Of sailing close to the wind. That was her downfall. She sailed so close that she finally capsized.'

DS Jones puts down the papers and folds her hands onto her lap. Now it is she that seems discomfited, and Skelgill finds it is his turn to inquire of his colleague.

'What's up, lass?'

'Well – I don't know. Three murders on impulse, but each time a plan quickly fell into place. And – supposing things had gone her way at Scale Force – what would have been her story?'

Skelgill rises and rounds his desk to stand beside DS Jones and stare out of the window. The day is bright and breezy, the spring landscape fresh with a recent shower, its greens and blues more Van Gogh than Constable; small parties of grey woodpigeons, like distant RAF trainer squadrons, purposefully surf the invisible airstream to secret destinations.

'You know I'm not big on speculation.'

He places a palm on her shoulder – but remains gazing out. She inhales to speak – but pressure from him silences her. Then he pats her a couple of times and spins on his heel and swoops up DS Leyton's bacon roll and returns to his seat to begin munching it.

After a minute, however, DS Jones approaches the matter from a less acute angle.

'But you did have strong suspicions. Right from the start, when my desk research indicated that most lake corpses originated from outside the area, you weren't having any of it. Nor that it was Kevin Pope – nor the divers who found her. Nor even the builders. Despite that logic was crying out for some combination of a vehicle, a boat, the strength of a man, an accomplice.'

Skelgill swallows in order to speak.

'It just took a lateral thinker. A touch of ingenuity. A sprinkling of local knowledge.'

It is not entirely clear to DS Jones whether he refers to Chaie Hadlee's committing of the crime or his unravelling of it – the description might equally apply; though in the subsequent battle of intuition it was his that prevailed.

He shakes his head.

'When I first heard the circumstances – they didn't compute – they didn't fit what was possible in the dale, the lie of the land and the lake. It was like someone telling me Leyton's free-climbed Nape's Needle. But there were specific things, as well. If we'd known who she really was – Valentina White, I'm talking about – I'd have paid more attention to the knots. Her background – sailing, lifeguarding – the left-handed bowline would have pointed to her. Like I said at the time, the builders had used rough overhand knots to fasten down the polythene. The body wrapping had square knots – a bit tidier, but a novice can happen upon them – it's what you use for your shoes. But a bowline – she was in a rush – attaching the stone weight by the lake shore. She reverted to her training. It's exactly what you'd tie to someone you were rescuing – or to a makeshift anchor.'

He takes another bite of the roll.

DS Jones regards him pensively. There is a lot more she would like to understand.

'When you picked me up in the boat – just before we met Ted Hindlewake – it seemed like you were ... well – distracted. Agitated. Did you know more than you felt you could say? What had happened to bring it on?'

Skelgill raises his eyebrows, and perhaps continues chewing for longer than he might ordinarily do so. He is reluctant – nay, incapable – of admitting to the condition he experienced in his encounters with the woman who was variously portrayed as Lena Longstaff and Valentina White; how she had exploited his vulnerabilities and lured him here and there, confident that she was playing with him like a cat with a mouse (and – at times – she was). And yet his instincts had been – like the apparently spellbound rodent – neither to make a dash for the skirting board nor to career into her claws; albeit he came perilously close to the latter.

As he reflects upon first meeting 'Lena', her bravado was palpable; for her, a kind of aphrodisiac. Had he yielded he would have become compromised, emasculated in his role – a captive only good as an informer on their hamstrung – indeed, futile – striving to identify the Lady of the Lake.

For how would he ever have believed that Lena Longstaff was not of flesh and blood?

That there was a photograph on display of the pair of them must have thrilled her by the second. That it sent him clues which remained tantalisingly out of his conscious reach, even when contradicted before his eyes: the two tipsy women posing in front of La Giralda were close to the same height – a fact DS Jones had inadvertently pointed out; and Lena Longstaff – the *real* Lena Longstaff – took the selfie right-handed; sleight of hand, indeed.

The washing on the line – ever so blatantly flagging the pretence of two quite different wearers – yet distracting through its lurid invitation.

Valentina White claiming the couple to be vegan, in denying any connection to Christmas pudding – when he had been told she ordered bacon-and-lentil soup from the instore café.

And other little alarm bells. Like when she was supposed to be at work, at the book depository – and yet she had called him from the cottage in the guise of Lena Longstaff. Or subsequently at the bookshop when she avoided him – why else but to wrest control of the agenda – unwilling to yield to his ad hoc visits and his questions that came close to the mark. He wonders, did she realise her slip of the tongue, to mention "the little piece of your jigsaw" in her siren-like voicemail as Lena, when he had formerly drawn the image for Valentina? Of course, her excuse would have been that 'they' had discussed it.

There was the ostentatious display of yoga. When he first spotted her. Putting herself on show. Wanting to be seen by police searching the area, or by the divers, perhaps. Inviting attention – as Lena – she wanted to plant that flag, put that peg in the ground, implant that image in the minds of the investigators.

She thought she'd pulled it off.

Truth be told, she almost had.

But she couldn't quite read his inner turmoil – there was something vital lost in translation – some crucial if part-permeable barrier that scrambled the signal – some force for good over evil, a guardian angel.

He looks at DS Jones – and, as she comes into sharp focus, he knows what it is.

She smiles.

'That's one hell of a long answer.'

'Eh?' He blinks furiously. 'What was the question?'

Now she chuckles.

'It's okay – didn't I tell you? I come from a long line of clairvoyants – the maternal Ukrainian branch of the family, generations of seventh daughters and all that.' She regards him solicitously. 'There's no need to elaborate.'

He realises he is still holding the last bite of DS Leyton's bacon roll. He despatches it, and drains the dregs of his own tea, making a face that reflects his displeasure at its tepidity.

He gestures airily.

'Like everyone's been saying – the pieces of the jigsaw just started to fall into place.'

She regards him suspiciously, and he concedes a little ground.

'Happen when I saw you – on that spit where she'd been doing yoga. I don't know why – or what I even thought – but summat clicked.'

'And yet you didn't say. You didn't even say it when we saw her in the wood, and I asked if it were Lena Longstaff.'

He shapes to run the fingers of both hands through his hair but, conscious of a greasy residue, pulls out of the move and instead rubs his palms on his thighs.

'When you've been brainwashed, it takes a while to start believing yourself again.'

DS Jones softens her stance. She stretches her legs with her ankles crossed; she has on skinny jeans and trainers with no-show socks, revealing an inch or two of smooth, tanned skin. She intones casually.

'You said to ask you later – about when you knew for certain.'

Skelgill's gaze drifts past her into the middle distance.

Was it as late as at the waterfall?

He inhales and releases the breath slowly, portentously.

'Whatever you reckon sounds best.'

DS Jones shakes her head; she yields to the incorrigible.

'Do I understand that to be whatever gives DI Smart the least satisfaction?'

Now Skelgill smiles.

'That's exactly why you're our chief report writer.'

'Speaking of reports –'

It is DS Leyton who interjects, arriving half an hour late and sounding a little breathless and bearing a thin sheaf of papers. He pauses in the open doorway and casts about – and quickly his detective skills divine that Skelgill has eaten his breakfast. His features reveal a small flash of dismay before his phlegmatic nature gains the upper hand. Besides, he has news.

'Would you Adam and Eve it? I've just had Bob Tapp drop by, unannounced. You couldn't make this up.'

He settles into his regular seat and reaches for the lone mug of tea; he seems unperturbed that it is cold, and drinks thirstily.

There is the impression of a susurration, that a trespassing zephyr has infiltrated the open office window and rifled the room, probing the neat array of papers spread across Skelgill's desk. DS Leyton looks up to see the collective alarm in his colleagues' eyes.

'Nah – don't worry – it don't change nothing.' He makes a sweeping gesture towards DS Jones's diligent handiwork. 'But I reckon I've got to the bottom of what the pair of 'em were up to.'

Though he claims this small success for his own, it seems proper that he should do so – for he has doggedly pursued this particular line of inquiry – and that he appears now to have resolved it engenders fellow feeling. DS Jones leans forward with interest; Skelgill, more regally, makes a bowing movement that hands DS Leyton the floor.

He knows however, not to try the time and patience of his superior. He proceeds to distribute copies of a single page, licking his thumb to separate the sheets.

'Cut a long story short. As you know, I've been suspicious of Abel Ketch – especially since I discovered the missing Jenny. Tapp's come clean – now that we've made public that the Lady of the Lake is Lena Longstaff, and that Chaie Hadlee was responsible.'

He glances briefly at his copy and gives it a shake, as if to satisfy himself that the handwritten words will not flake off and leave him stranded without a supporting text. He clears his throat.

'He reckons he suspected his mate Ketch of doing away with his girlfriend – and that he might well have disposed of the body in a lake, given his nautical background and his access to boats. Thing was, Ketch had been cagey about her disappearance, and would never talk about it. Tapp's idea to dive all the lakes this year – crazy as it seems – was to see if they would come across the corpse. He even thought that maybe Ketch would want it found – that guilt would be weighing heavily on him. Imagine how shocked he was when they actually did find a body!'

DS Leyton glances about, anticipating some scepticism, but his colleagues are all eyes and ears.

'Tapp's been on tenterhooks this last fortnight – swithering on whether to come forward – realising if he did, it would be the end of his friendship – and a complete disaster if he was wrong, and a terrible thing to mistakenly shop his pal. Against that was his public duty. In the end he's relieved he waited it out – but he wrote and dated this straight after I'd first interviewed him, and got his missus to witness it, just in case he needed to prove his best intentions. He'd figured that we'd identify the body soon enough, and that if Ketch had murdered Jenny, it wasn't as though he posed an imminent threat to the community.'

DS Jones reads the handwritten statement intently; Skelgill makes an indeterminate noise, which may suggest disapproval at Bob Tapp's unilateral take on justice – although, in mitigation, had he come forward, they would have wasted even more resources exploring a blind alley.

DS Leyton lowers his page and continues, now off script.

'Last night they went for a pint – had quite a skinful – and Tapp broached the subject of his suspicion in a jokey way. Seems Ketch managed to take it in good spirits – there *was* something he wanted to get off his chest – Jennifer Eccles had dumped him and run off with a hairdresser, and he'd been too ashamed to admit it. She's living with the new geezer in a flat over his salon in Kendal. I've even got her contact details. Just spoke with her – she's alive and kicking and she reckons the new arrangement's permanent.'

DS Jones gets the joke and chuckles.

Skelgill is looking a little perplexed.

'Tapp could have just let this drop. Why's he spilled the beans?'

DS Leyton shrugs.

'His missus told him to.'

The two men make solemn eye contact; DS Jones might just glean that she is the butt of what is, after all, respectful teasing.

DS Leyton now rises.

'So, that's the long and short of it. If you'll excuse me – I need to nip down to the canteen. Can I get anyone anything?'

Skelgill shows no sign of contrition.

'Nay – we'll catch up with you later, Leyton. Nice job on Ketch.'

DS Leyton, already departing, raises a finger in the air and turns in the doorway.

'By the way – I had to pop out to me motor. It was just as Kevin Pope was leaving. I thought he was looking chipper – and spruced up – and guess who was waiting to give him a lift in that old banger of hers? Only the young Ukrainian girl – Katya, right?'

He looks at DS Jones, who nods in confirmation.

DS Leyton grins.

'All's well that ends well.'

Left to their own devices, Skelgill and DS Jones exchange glances that might just be reflecting upon DS Leyton's cliché.

Skelgill, however, stretches his arms above his head and then prises himself up from his seat.

'I need to shift *The Doghouse* back to Bass Lake – now she's finished her tour of duty. This has been the most times I've been in a boat and never caught a fish.'

To DS Jones's ear there is the suggestion he believes that this is something he can legitimately do during working hours – and that a certain temptation is likely to befall him.

She regards him artlessly, not concealing her suspicions.

'Is that not a two-person job?'

He flexes his spine and groans heroically.

'Needs must, I can manhandle it – rope the trailer to the towbar to lug it up the bank onto the verge.'

But she deftly shuffles her documents into a neat pile and stands over it, poised like a croupier.

'That sounds to me like you need an accomplice. Accidents can happen. Worse still, you might get waylaid.'

'Come again?'

There is a twinkle in her eye.

'I've been meaning to tell you – your old flame asked me to pass on a message.'

She pauses, intentionally allowing Skelgill to stew.

'What kind of message?'

'Coded, I should say.'

She makes him wait a second or two more.

'It was about May Day. She was asking if you remembered the phrase: *Hoss! Hoss!*'

'*Wee-Hoss.*'

Before he knows it, Skelgill has muttered the rejoinder under his breath, almost by reflex. His cheeks colour.

'We were just bairns, in the same class, that's all.'

DS Jones tucks the bundle under her arm.

'Don't worry – I told her your kissing has improved since then.'

She skips away – and turns back in the doorway sporting an impish grin.

'Meet you behind the bike sheds in five minutes?'

***

SCALE FORCE

The Lake District's highest waterfall

"Scale Force, the white downfall of which glimmered through the trees, that hang before it like the bushy hair over a madman's eyes."
Samuel Taylor Coleridge

"A fine chasm, with a lofty, though but slender, fall of water."
William Wordsworth

"It sweeps, as sweeps an army Adown the mountainside, With the voice of many claps of thunder, like a battle's sounding tide."
Letitia Elizabeth Landon

NEXT IN THE SERIES

THE LAST WOMAN TO BE TRANSPORTED FROM CUMBRIA

BARELY OF AGE, eighteen-year-old Flora Mary Graham was found guilty by a jury of twelve good Kendal men and true of the murder in his prime of the Seventh Earl of Fellside, by striking him about the head and sending him to his death in Blind Beck, the town's stream running in violent spate on the stormy night of Halloween, 1852.

Apprehended at the scene bearing a babe in arms, the child swaddled and soaked, three gold sovereigns were found in Flora's possession, half a year's wages for a servant girl such as she. The motive ascribed was thus one of robbery, but Flora had been born a deaf-mute and was unable to proffer a defence.

It was speculated by the Prosecution that Lord Fellside, great benefactor and philanthropist, had come across Flora in the act of drowning her child, and in a vain attempt to thwart her had forfeited his own life, an altruist to the last.

Flora would have been for the gallows, to swing against the bleak wall of Carlisle gaol, but for the recommendation to mercy entered by the jury and acted upon by the judge in the interests of the innocent infant. And thus Flora – with her three-month-old son – became the last woman to be transported by convict ship from Cumbria to Van Diemen's Land.

And yet now a revelation. During the renovation of Kendal's ancient paupers' hospital and almshouses, a document has been discovered concealed behind a lath-and-plaster wall, a simple letter – a scrap of paper folded inside a humble locket engraved with the name *Flora Mary* that might surely have belonged to her.

From Flora, a pitiful entreaty to the Almighty. For Skelgill and his team, a cryptic cold case that boils over into the present day.

'Murder at Blind Beck' by Bruce Beckham will be released in early 2025.

FREE BOOKS, NEW RELEASES, THE BEAUTIFUL LAKES ... AND MOUNTAINS OF CAKES

Sign up for Bruce Beckham's author newsletter

Thank you for getting this far!

If you have enjoyed your encounter with DI Skelgill there's a growing series of whodunits set in England's rugged and beautiful Lake District to get your teeth into.

My newsletter often features one of the back catalogue to download for free, along with details of new releases and special offers.

No Skelgill mystery would be complete without a café stop or two, and each month there's a traditional Cumbrian recipe – tried and tested by yours truly (aka *Bruce Bake 'em*).

To sign up, this is the link:

https://mailchi.mp/acd032704a3f/newsletter-sign-up

Your email address will be safely stored in the USA by Mailchimp and will be used for no other purpose. You can unsubscribe at any time simply by clicking the link at the foot of the newsletter.

Thank you, again – best wishes and happy reading!

Bruce Beckham

Printed in Great Britain
by Amazon